Donald MacDonald

Will o' the Wisp Flashes

A Selection of Stories, Sketches, Poems, etc.

Donald MacDonald

Will o' the Wisp Flashes
A Selection of Stories, Sketches, Poems, etc.

ISBN/EAN: 9783744765565

Printed in Europe, USA, Canada, Australia, Japan

Cover: Foto ©Andreas Hilbeck / pixelio.de

More available books at **www.hansebooks.com**

Will o' the Wisp Flashes

A SELECTION OF

Stories, Sketches, Poems, &c.

INCLUDING

LECTURES BY OLD BLOGG,

AND

FELLOWS I HAVE KNOWN.

BY

DONALD MACDONALD.

———

"A little nonsense now and then,
Is relished by the wisest men."

———

DUNDEE:
PRINTED BY JOHN LENG & CO., BANK STREET.
———
1890.

PREFACE.

HAVING of late had more time at my disposal than I could devise profitable means of employing, I set about killing it by preparing the present volume for the press. The work has afforded me considerable pleasure, and has, doubtless, helped to curtail the amount of that other work which a certain obnoxious personage is said always to find for idle hands to do. If the perusal of the book affords a few pleasant half-hours to its readers I will consider that my labour has not been in vain, and will feel a thousand times repaid.

The contents are of such a varied description that the choosing of a title has been full of difficulty. If I called the book "Hotch-potch," as suggested by a friend, those who fancied they were buying a Cookery Book would consider themselves "sold," and I might get into trouble. The same would happen if I called it "Spirit Movings," and my patrons think they were getting a Religious Work. Then, if I entitled it "The Mixture," it might be taken for a quack doctor's book, and the public expect to be supplied with it *gratis*. I have called it "Will o' the Wisp Flashes," because this title means nothing in particular, and is more modest than "Lightning Flashes."

It being barely three months since I first entertained the idea of publishing this volume, it has been somewhat hurriedly put into the press, and I feel conscious that it possesses many shortcomings. Apologies are, however, in certain circumstances, like comparisons—odious—and as I cannot see that it would serve any purpose, I refrain from making an apology, or from saying anything in regard to the contents of the book, further than to state that the sketches entitled "Fellows I have Known" are reprinted, with alterations and revisals, from the *People's Friend*, and that two of the stories and a few of the poems have also seen the light before.

To those ladies and gentlemen who kindly subscribed for the book I tender my sincere thanks, and trust that, although they have been buying a "pig in a pock," they may consider their bargain not so bad after all.

D. MACDONALD.

41 COWGATE,
DUNDEE, *May* 1890.

CONTENTS.

I.—STORIES.

II.—LECTURES BY OLD BLOGG.

III.—MISCELLANEOUS PAPERS.

IV.—FELLOWS I HAVE KNOWN. By NANCY THISTLE.

V.—POEMS.

WILL O' THE WISP FLASHES.

I.

STORIES.

RORY MUGGS,

AND

THE ADVENTURES OF THE GREAT JONATHAN.

CHAPTER I.

AN hour after noon the report of a cannon was distinctly heard above the din of the city.

"Ha! the bombardment begins. Victory or death! Blood and thunder! Bring me a sword!" shouted Rory Muggs, the young man from the country, who had been a fortnight in Burn & Firebrand's office. At the same time he leapt excitedly from his stool, and in doing so his hand came in contact with the ruler—the ruler came in contact with the inkstand, and a stream of black fluid flowed over an account upon which he had been engaged for an hour past.

Jeremiah Dumps, the head clerk, who was enamoured of Miss Jemima Jenkins, and who had just completed a letter to his *inamorata* containing an offer of marriage, entered Rory's apartment in a state of consternation.

"What do you mean, fellow, by shouting such nonsense, and

making such a mess?" he exclaimed. "Have you never heard the time-gun before?"

Rory looked confused, and made no reply. He commenced to lick the ink from off the account with his tongue, and was upon the point of spitting it back into the bottle, when he encountered the eyes of his superior looking "daggers" at him, and, taking a second thought, he swallowed his spittle.

Mr Dumps's visage gradually relaxed, and for a time he seemed unable to decide whether he should burst into laughter or fly into a passion. He did neither, but simply said—

"Tut, tut; it's no use trying to take the ink off; you must write out a fresh copy. But, in the first place, go to dinner. By the way, I can't get home to-day, and want you to take a note to my landlady; so if you choose, you may have my dinner, which will be waiting, and save you going to the coffee-house."

"I thank you from the inmost recesses of my heart," said Rory.

Mr Dumps greeted Rory with a stare of bewilderment, then smiled and began to write.

"Miss Kirtle, 17 Bonnett Row; you will easily find the house," said he, when he had finished, handing the note to Rory, and adding, "When you're passing the Post Office purchase a stamp and post this," taking a second letter from his pocket and placing it in Rory's hand.

"All right," said the latter. "I'm off, like the Great Jonathan when pursued by the two-headed dwarf."

Mr Dumps gazed after him in blank amazement, ejaculating, "The fellow's mad, I believe."

Rory did not appear to be in the least hurry to reach the Post Office or his dinner either. He lingered to read the advertisements on the walls, and stood to stare rudely at every pretty girl who chanced to be passing. All of a sudden his brow became contracted, a dark scowl overspread his features, and he muttered wildly, "Base villain! False-hearted deceiver! Treacherous rascal! dost thou dare come between me and the realization of the glorious and entrancingly brilliant dreams and visions of my youth? Out upon thee, thou bane of my existence, thou needle in my flesh, thou nail in my sole, thou dastard whelp of a bastard cur!"

He had not fully recovered from his frenzy when he reached the Post Office, and entering, purchased a stamp, and posted a letter. On coming out, the letter in his possession bore the address of Miss Jemima Jenkins, 14 Roundabout Road! Enquiring the way of a policeman, he proceeded thitherward, and again commenced to talk excitedly to himself.

"Then let it be a duel! He is a craven-hearted coward who declines. Let the seconds be chosen, and the weapons agreed upon. Blunderbusses or hatchets? Neither. Rifles or tomahawks? Neither. Cutlasses or bowie knives. Neither. Broadswords are the weapons of my choice—yes, broadswords as used by the warriors of historic fame."

Having arrived at Roundabout Road, he discovered that Number 14 was a self-contained cottage, with a garden plot in front. Stepping up to the door, he rang the bell.

"Do you require an answer?" asked the chubby-cheeked maid who opened the door, and to whom Rory presented the letter.

"No, my pretty damsel, but I require a dinner. You know I've come to dine with you to-day."

"Come to dine!" said the girl in astonishment. "Why, Missus never said nothing about anyone coming to dine."

"Very probable, but she hasn't got the letter yet—*it* will explain."

"Better come in and take a seat while I deliver it," said the girl, showing Rory into a room and retiring with the letter, deeply concerned at the prospect of having to prepare dinner for her visitor.

When Rory was left alone, he commenced to make a minute inspection of everything within the room. First, he surveyed the pictures on the walls, and noted down their subjects in his memorandum book. Then he read the title pages of the books on the table. Opening an album, he looked over the photographs it contained, and one in particular he seemed to admire. It was that of a charming young lady, upon which he gazed intently for some time, and then, without the least qualms of conscience, took out of the album and placed in his pocket. Afterwards he bestowed his attentions upon a scrapbook, and even took the liberty of contributing to its pages by writing in pencil the following lines :—

> " Diddle-dum-dee, the cat drank tea,
>   And the hen swam over the pool ;
> The black cat suckled the white duck's brood,
>   And Great Jonathan once played the fool."

Thereafter he fell into a reverie, and, as before, his thoughts found expression in words, which he uttered quite audibly.

"How about the second plot? Yes, yes, elopement is the thing. Adorable, beautiful, transcendent creature, pining in forced seclusion, and madly—devotedly in love. In the dark night, when the world is buried in slumber, approach silently—stealthily, and give the well-known sign. But, ah, her brother ; if he should offer resistance ! Why, blow his brains out—escape by window, through garden, then off—off with the prize, and the Great Jonathan once more victorious. Ha, a grand plot !"

Presently the chubby-cheeked maid re-entered to inform him that " Young" Missus wished to see him in the parlour. Rory accordingly followed the maid, and was ushered into the presence of the identical young lady whose photograph he had appropriated. She was alone, and seemed a good deal excited—Mr Dumps's letter lying open on the table before her.

" Good afternoon, sweet spirit," said Rory.

" Oh, you're——" she said, then stopped short.

" Yes, gentle lady, I'm the bearer."

" I didn't mean that ; but who—who are you ?"

" I'm the young man from the country, and I've come to eat Mr Dumps's dinner, as he can't come himself."

" What on earth do you mean ?"

" Aint you Mr Dumps's landlady ?"

" You're an impudent fellow !"

" Not a bad remark, Miss, but not original. You should never use it without inverted commas, for it was the Great Jonathan who first uttered those memorable words when quarrelling with the two-headed dwarf."

" Leave my presence, fellow ! and tell Mr Dumps I have committed his proposal to the flames," said Miss Jenkins, excitedly, as she crushed up the letter and flung it into the fire.

" Proposal !" gasped Rory. " Can I believe my senses, or is this some frightful hallucination which has seized upon my benumbed and shattered brain ? Let me see; I believe I've made a mistake—yes, I've posted the wrong letter ! Fair lady, can you forgive me, and say nothing about it to Mr Dumps ? As you value my everlasting esteem, don't tell Mr Dumps. Here is my card, and if you should ever require my assistance, do not hesitate to avail yourself of it; and I pray you—I implore you—say nothing about this incident to Mr Dumps."

Rory delivered this speech in the most hurried and excited manner, and immediately bolted from the room, and out into the street, leaving Miss Jenkins in a state of the utmost bewilderment.

Before she had time to regain her composure, her brother Tom entered, looking darkly towards her.

" Who's that fellow, Jemima ?" he asked.

" I don't know, Tom."

" Very likely you don't know ! I happen to know a little more than you suppose I do, however. I was in the closet while he was alone in the drawing-room, and overheard some of his mutterings about the plot. He made a few remarks regarding me, too, which were rather complimentary I must say. But forewarned is forearmed. You are a nice girl, are you not ?"

" Brother, you speak in riddles. What do you mean ?" she

exclaimed, terror-stricken at the wild expression on his countenance.

"Oh, yes; you're quite an adept at acting injured innocence! I suppose you couldn't explain that fellow's message here?"

"Oh, Tom, it's about a—a foolish matter—which would do you no good to know."

"What's the fellow's name, girl?" asked Tom, fiercely.

"Brother, are you mad? There's his card," said Miss Jenkins, bursting into tears.

Tom clutched the card upon which Rory's address was written, and immediately left the room.

Chapter II.

WHEN Rory emerged into the street, he went hurriedly in search of a pie shop, as he began to feel desperately hungry, and had but ten minutes to spare.

Being successful in his search, he stepped in and ordered four twopenny pies and a bottle of lemonade.

"Excuse my curiosity, sir," said the old, bald-headed waiter, as he executed the order, "but do you find ink a good appetizer?"

"What do you mean, old blunderbuss?" asked Rory, looking puzzled.

"I see by your lips you've been swallowing ink lately, and I see by this pile of pies that you've got a fairish appetite, and am curious to know if the one has any connection with the other," explained the waiter with a grin.

"Ah! I see, I see," said Rory, wiping his mouth with his coat sleeve. "No, old cockalorum, I don't use ink as an appetizer, but I've got a white liver, and the doctor recommends it as a medicine."

The old waiter looked grave, and was silent.

Rory despatched his pies in a wonderfully short time, and then hurried along in the direction of Deathshead Crescent, where Burn & Firebrand's office was situate. On the way, he commenced chuckling and muttering—

"How curious!—the Fates favour me—everything turns out for the best—another link for Great Jonathan's chain—another episode in his adventures—and from real life, too. What an angelic creature! but disdainful—contemptuous—how about that? Ah! I have it—she doesn't know—doesn't recognise—that's the rub—the Great Jonathan in disguise; ha, ha, in disguise—grand idea! But now comes the winter of my discontent, when I meet Dumps, and Dumps asks questions."

He had arrived at the office, and, being five minutes late, he rushed up stairs quite out of breath.

"Well, have you had dinner?" was Mr Dumps's first salutation.

"Yes, sir," replied Rory, faintly.

"And what had Miss Kirtle for dinner to-day?"

"Well—it was—let me see—what was it, again? I think it must have been—I really forget the name of it."

"Why, you can surely remember what you had to eat—didn't you have soup?"

"Oh, yes, of course, I had soup."

"And beans in it?"

"Yes, lots of beans—very large beans."

"I thought so—Miss Kirtle knows I like beans; and then you would have some cabbage, I suppose?"

"Yes, an immense quantity of cabbage."

"I was sure of it. Miss Kirtle now knows exactly what I like. Was it pork or mutton you had?"

"Pork—very fat pork, too—required no chewing, but slid unconsciously from mouth to stomach."

"Ha, I knew it would be pork. Then, I trust you've had a good dinner?"

"Yes, sir, most emphatically."

" And you posted the other letter?"

" Yes, sir, I posted another letter."

" Then you'd better set to and make out a fresh copy of the account you got spoiled—it must go with to-night's post."

Rory became at once engrossed in his work, and felt considerably relieved when Mr Dumps retired to his own apartment.

Having completed the account, Rory took down a Day-book in which he commenced to copy some entries, but very soon left off and began to scribble on a sheet of paper. His constant terror of Mr Dumps's entrance made it evident that he was doing some work on his own account. Several times he took from his pocket Miss Jenkins's photograph, gazed upon it admiringly, and returned it hurriedly when Mr Dumps happened to cough or scrape his foot upon the rail of his desk. Having filled the whole sheet of paper with writing, he was in the act of folding it up with the photograph inside when he heard Mr Dumps's footsteps approaching, and, placing it between the leaves of the book in front of him, became at once absorbed in a calculation.

" I want that book," said Mr Dumps.

" Did you say you wanted this book?" asked Rory in confusion.

" Of course I did; you may lock up the presses now, and go for the night," said Mr Dumps, taking up the Day-book and retiring with it to his own room.

Rory stood for a moment irresolute—then shook his head as if he wanted to shake it off—then struck out with his clenched fists at some imaginary object, and, finally, locked up the presses and decamped.

While Mr Dumps was turning over the leaves of the Day-book in which Rory had been writing, the folded sheet of paper slipped out upon his desk. It would not have attracted his attention but for the fact that a corner of the photograph enclosed was visible. On opening it up and gazing upon the image of his adored one, Mr Dumps first reddened and then turned pale. Taking up the sheet of paper he read as follows :—

"Adorable creature. Light of my eyes and sunbeam of my soul—thou who art the moonshine of my existence and the telephone of my heart—whose smile is more radiant than fifty gas lamps, and whose laugh is like the peal of a thousand silver bells—thou who drawest me towards thee with cables, and who bindest me with thongs of love—thinkest thou for the infinitesimal space of a second that I can ever forsake thee? Away with the monstrous thought, and let it be for ever buried in the dark, sepulchral tomb of nothingness and chaos. The steeple clock may cease to chime, the time-gun cease to fire—yea, the influenza microbe may cease to thirst for human blood—but I shall never cease to love thee. No, my beloved! I shall stick to thee like a limpet to its native rock—like paint to a window shutter. The monster who torments thee with his vile protestations shall feel the strength of my power. I shall scourge him with the scorpions of my wrath, and hold him up to the public ridicule and contempt of mankind. Fear not, loved one, the Fates are not unkind, and true love is an unconquerable, undaunted sentinel, which keeps watch on the apex of the Universe."

It is not enough to say that Mr Dumps was excited while reading this. His eyes literally rolled like fireballs, and his features underwent sundry indescribable contortions.

"Ha, ha! Copy of a letter he has written or intends writing her," he muttered, and then bringing his hand down with a blow upon the desk, expressed an emphatic desire that a serious catastrophe might befall Rory's eyes. "The monster who torments thee with his vile protestations," he read over a second time, and then exclaimed—

"The treacherous scoundrel! this is the way he speaks of me, is it? This is the way he returns my kindnesses. He's certainly wrong in the brain, and not fit to be at large. But how has he got Miss Jenkins's photograph? She never presented her photograph to me even. I must be at the bottom of this at once."

Banging the books into the safe, he locked up the office, and hurried away to his lodgings in a half frantic state.

Miss Kirtle was astonished when she heard the speed at which he came bounding up stairs, and fearing something terrible had happened, met him on the landing.

"Bless ma heart! what's the maitter, Mr Dumps?" she enquired.

"Tell me—tell me—if the young fellow—who came to dinner—"

"Whatna young fellow?"

"With the note—the note from me."

"Oh, Mr Dumps, compose yersel.' I'm really alairmed at yer condition. Dinna mak' me waur. Ma nerves got an awfu' shock whan the postman cam' here at five o'clock the nicht wi' a note frae ye, askin' me tae gi'e him his dinner."

"A postman?"

"Yes, indeed, Mr Dumps, a postman."

"But didn't Muggs come here to dinner at one?"

"Na, na, Mr Dumps, never a Muggs nor Puggs cam' here the day."

"Confusion thrice confounded! but I shall be at the bottom of this, if it cost me—yes, if it cost me every drop of blood in my veins. Miss Kirtle, I wont wait for tea; I have urgent duties to perform, and must be off. But I shall return—yes, I shall return—dead or alive."

So saying, Mr Dumps rushed down stairs, and for several minutes thereafter Miss Kirtle might be heard exclaiming, in plaintive tones—"Oh, Mr Dumps, come back; come back, Mr Dumps."

Chapter III.

" Mangel kept here and also Logers," printed in red letters on a green placard, occupied a conspicuous place in the window of a house in Rumby Street.

Mrs Pimples was regaling herself with a cup of tea, slightly flavoured with rum, after two hours' hard work at her mangle, when a railway van halted at her door, and she was startled with the loud knock of the driver.

" Does ane Rory Muggs bide here ?" he enquired, when Mrs Pimples had opened the door.

" Aye ; but he's no' in the noo."

" 'Cause there twa boxes here for 'im—come frae London wi' the railway."

" Twa boxes ! He never said he wis expectin' twa boxes. But ye can tak' them awa' yont tae his ain room."

" Here's ane," said the carrier, bringing in a small box, " its no' big, but fell heavy."

" Losh keeps !" what can be in't?" said Mrs Pimples, feeling its weight.

" Weel, it cudna be heavier though 'twis lead balls," remarked the carrier.

" Lead balls ! things for shootin' fouk wi', d'ye say ?"

" Toots, 'oman, I dinna ken what's intae't, but it's as heavy's lead."

" Gude preserve's ! I houp it's no' lead balls."

" An' here's anither ane ; it's a sicht bigger, but no' sae heavy," said the carrier, bringing in the other box, and taking his departure.

Immediately Mrs Pimples began to examine the boxes. " I wonder what can be intae them," she soliloquised, turning them over from side to side. Taking a table-knife, she essayed to prize up the lid of one of them, but it was too firmly nailed down, and resisted all her efforts.

"Ech, but I wad lek tae ken what's in them," she again muttered, as she turned the address on the larger box towards the light, and endeavoured to decipher it. Her limited education precluded her from making out the written portion, but some printing at the top of the card attracted her attention. After a considerable time she managed to spell the letters— P I S T O L.

Hereupon she flung, her arms frantically in the air, and seemed as if she were instantly going to swoon.

"Pistols and lead balls? Oh, gude save's," she exclaimed wildly. "I aye thocht the fellow wis up tae some mischief; he's been mutterin' aboot plots, an' duels, an' murderin'. Oh, the vagabon'—the vagabon'!"

All in a tremor, Mrs Pimples went to answer another summons to the door.

"Does a fellow Muggs live here?" asked a hoarse voice.

"What wad ye be wantin' wi' him?"

"I want to see him immediately."

"But he's no' in the noo."

"Confound him! when will he be in?"

"Mebbie in the coorse o' an oor."

"Then, I'll come back," said Tom Jenkins, for it was he.

"Gude hev a care o's; what'll I dae?" exclaimed Mrs Pimples, after shutting the door. "I'm sure there's something awfu' gain tae happen. I'm feird there's gain tae be murder. Oh, gude sakes! what'll I dae?"

Instinctively she went to her cupboard, and, as she was trembling from head to foot, took down a bottle labelled "Jamaica," which she placed to her mouth, and took therefrom a pretty copious draught. The effect was instantaneous. She stood erect, threw her head back, and began to address her old tomcat, who sat on the table in front of her.

"I'll tell him tae leave my hoose this very nicht," she went on, "I will that. My hoose is nae to be the habitation o' any murderin', malefacterin' villain', I'll gi'e my aith. Na, na; he can gang whare he lcks, but he'll nae sleep 'neath my respectable roof the nicht."

Just as she was delivering herself of this speech, Rory entered by means of his check key, and at once stepped into his room, closing the door behind him.

"Ech, but he's shoon in the nicht," muttered Mrs Pimples. "I'll go an' tell him tae gang aboot his business, though—I will that."

So saying, she took another potation from the bottle in the cupboard to fortify her for the trying ordeal, and then stepping lightly towards Rory's door, placed her ear to the keyhole. After listening for a moment or two, her heart failed her. She heard him opening the boxes, and returned to her own apartment in a state of the utmost terror.

" Oh, what'll I dae—what'll I dae?" she exclaimed, wringing her hands. " I'm freichted tae gang in, for he micht shoot me in a moment."

Again she was summoned to the door, and Jeremiah Dumps and Tom Jenkins both entered. They had met on the way, and finding they were both on the same errand had compared notes, and come to the conclusion that Rory Muggs deserved a good castigation.

There was a certain fierceness in the looks of her visitors which Mrs Pimples at once noticed, and which brought her terror to a climax. Falling on her knees before them, she exclaimed—

" Kill me at aince, men, richt straicht aff, an' be deen wi't—it's better than by sma' degrees. I'm a lone widow, an' ha'e nane tae defend me, sae juist tak' oot yer pistols and be deen wi't. I ken fine yer a' leagued thegither, ye an' the villain wha bides under my ain roof. Ye're a' a pack o' murderers—sae juist kill me—kill me whare I am."

" You misjudge us, my good woman," said Mr Dumps, when he had an opportunity of speaking. " Rise up, for we mean you no harm, but have come to punish that miscreant, Muggs, who lives here."

Mrs Pimples stared dubiously upon her visitors.

"You need not be in the least alarmed," said Tom Jenkins.

"Are ye speakin' the truth?" asked Mrs Pimples, looking from the one to the other uneasily. On receiving further assurances that they were, she ventured to rise, and pointing to Rory's door, informed them that he they sought was inside.

"But dinna gang in—dinna gang in," she exclaimed, seeing they were about to enter; "he's got a wheen pistols an' lead balls."

This was rather startling information, and even the stout heart of Mr Dumps quailed.

"Pistols and balls! what's to be done, Tom?"

"Burst in, and take him unawares," replied Tom.

"No, no, it might be dangerous. But I have it. You go and fetch two policemen, while I remain here and watch," said Mr Dumps.

Tom set off at once in search of policemen; while Mr Dumps, having provided himself with Mrs Pimples's heaviest poker, stood sentry in the lobby. Mrs Pimples had in the meantime paid another visit to the cupboard, and sunk down exhausted in her armchair.

After a short time, Tom Jenkins returned, accompanied by two limbs of the law, to whom he had explained on the way the nature of the case. On being shewn the door of Rory's room, they at once walked boldly up to it and knocked.

"Come in!" called a voice from within.

The policemen at once entered, followed by Mr Dumps and Tom Jenkins.

"What's the matter?" asked Rory, in consternation.

"You'll soon know the matter, base scoundrel!" said Mr Dumps, angrily confronting him.

"Now prefer your charges, gentlemen," said one of the policemen.

"I charge this fellow," said Tom Jenkins, "with threatening

to blow my brains out, and also with plotting to elope with my sister."

"And I charge him with wickedly and feloniously slandering me, calling me a monster, and attempting to make me appear odious in the eyes of the lady referred to," said Mr Dumps.

"An' I chairge him wi' havin' pistols an' lead balls in his possession—the murderin', malefacterin' villain!" shouted Mrs Pimples, who had put in appearance when she heard the commotion.

Rory gazed from the one to the other with dilated eyes, and remained speechless. Twice he passed his hand across his forehead, and then fell back in his chair.

One hour thereafter Rory Muggs was—lodged in jail? By no means, but enjoying a tripe supper along with Mrs Pimples, Tom Jenkins, and Mr Dumps, provided at the expense of the latter. After Mrs Pimples and Tom had each sung a comic song, and Mr Dumps delivered his famous recitation, "An Ode to the Moon," Rory was called upon to favour the company by reading a portion of his "Adventures of the Great Jonathan."

"With pleasure," said Rory, who mounted a chair, with a number of foolscap sheets in his hand, and commenced to read that wonderful narrative of which he was the author. The tale opened with the youth of the Great Jonathan, described how he was decoyed from his native land by an ogre, related his thrilling adventures with the two-headed dwarf, and his duel with the flat-nosed monster. His soliloquy before eloping with the Maid of the Silver Mask contained the identical words which Tom Jenkins overheard Rory muttering, and the draft letter which so alarmed Mr Dumps was a copy of the Great Jonathan's epistle to the Princess of the Tower.

"Muggs, you're a genius," exclaimed Mr Dumps when he had finished. "I'm proud of you, sir, and heartily forgive you for the mistakes you committed to-day. Great authors are, as a rule, absent-minded."

"An' I forgi'e ye for the fricht ye gied me wi' yer pistols and lead balls. Losh guide's! wha wad ha'e thocht it wis a printin' press an' teeps frae Mr Pistol o' Lunnon!" said Mrs Pimples.

That evening, while Rory was undressing, he might be heard chuckling to himself—

"How curious—the Fates are still with me—everything turns out for the best. Grand adventure! Sublime plot! Original idea! The last link in the chain—the last round in the ladder —the brilliant finishing stroke in the adventures of the Great Jonathan."

Mr Dumps and Miss Jenkins made it up between them again, and are about to get married, while Rory Muggs is presently canvassing for subscribers to his great work, to be issued shortly from his private printing press.

MY UNCLE'S STORY.

I OFTEN wondered why my uncle had never married. Although well advanced in years at the time I write of, he still bore traces of that manly vigour which, in his youth, he must have possessed. His address, too, was such as could not fail to initiate him into the good graces of the ladies, and when in one of his happiest moods, with his little niece Dolly frolicking on his knee, his usually mild eyes would lighten up with rare brilliance, and his face wear a smile which in youth must have been truly captivating.

One evening, my uncle and I sat together before a cheerful fire, smoking our pipes and conversing in that free and easy manner which long and true friendship engenders. I was soon to be married, and, as a matter of course, this formed one of the chief topics of our conversation, and much sage advice did I receive from my good uncle relative to that event. So earnestly did he impress upon me the duties and responsibilities of a wise and faithful husband, and so eloquently depict the joys of a well-assorted union, that on the spur of the moment I could not refrain from asking in a half ironical, half serious tone—

" Why did you never take a wife yourself, uncle?"

The question appeared either to surprise or pain him, and I at once wished it had been unasked. But his agitation was only momentary, the next instant he looked in my face with his accustomed smile and replied—

" I suppose Providence never considered me worthy of a wife, Bill."

" But were you really never in love?" I was further tempted to ask.

C

A tinge of melancholy seemed to pass over his features as he replied—

"Oh, yes, Bill, I've loved—I suppose everybody has at some period of their lives; but my love affair did not turn out so happily as yours promises to do." Then, after a pause, he asked —"Would you care to hear a bit of my youthful history?"

"Nothing could give me greater pleasure," I assured him.

"Listen, then, and you shall hear a story simple and sad withal—a story which I have never yet repeated to human being."

Having relit our pipes, my uncle stirred up the fire and proceeded as follows :—

"You are aware that E—— was my native town. Here your father and I spent the sunny days of childhood together. Happy days! when as boys we romped among those far off woods and meadows; hope shone so bright and life seemed so beautiful. Here we grew up almost to manhood, till a time came when I was forced to proceed to B—— to fill a situation there. The day of my departure is still fresh in my memory. My feelings were those generally experienced by young lads on leaving home for the first time—a mixture of hope and misgiving, of novelty and home sickness—all simmering up and boiling over the too full heart. But in my case there was something more which weighed heavily on my feelings. It was while sitting in the lonely railway carriage—lonely to me, although crowded with passengers—that I first became conscious that I loved Dora M——. Dora and I had been intimate all our lives, I may say. We had grown up together in almost daily intercourse, her father's cottage having stood opposite ours. She was a fair, delicate girl, a year or so younger than I. She possessed a frank and generous disposition, and had such a winning way about her, that I ever felt it a pleasure to be in her company. But not until we had parted did I become conscious of the full strength of my attachment to her. We had never spoken of love, and I do not suppose that Dora had dreamed of such a thing on my part.

After the lapse of a few years, I was journeying toward my native place on a matter of business, which would occupy my time there for several months. I need not say I was extremely happy in the contemplation of mixing among old friends and visiting old scenes again. My passion for Dora had not abated. I had never heard of her, but throughout those years she was ever uppermost in my thoughts—her image ever luminous in my dreams. Absence had indeed made my heart grow fonder, and I had made up my mind to tell her of my love.

We met—had quite a cordial meeting—talked of bygone days and events, and yet there was something—I could not divine what—which left me ill at ease. One of us seemed to have changed. Was it she, or was it I? I asked myself in vain. She had grown to womanhood—lovely, blooming womanhood. To me she seemed the fairest being on earth. I loved her with all the ardour of first love—fondly, devotedly; within my heart of hearts I adored her.

Soon an opportunity occurred when I divulged to her the state of my feelings, and whispered my pleadings in her ear. She listened in silence, and wore a startled and anxious expression. I waited for an answer—pressed her for an answer —when bursting into tears she said—

"No, no, Bill, it can never, never be! I am very, very sorry, but I have no love to bestow except that of a sister."

"Do you love another, then?" I asked, despairingly.

Her silence betokened it was too true, and all at once I saw the fair vision of my day dreams—the brightest hope of my existence—shattered and crumbled into nothingness. I fell into a sort of dreamy stupor, from which I was aroused by Dora pleading that we might return home.

"Let us talk no more about it to-night," I heard her say. "Another time I should like to tell you all—you who used to be my dear friend and brother—I want your sympathy."

Was she raving, or was I dreaming? What sympathy could she expect from me if she loved another? Perhaps I said something which grated harshly on her ear, for again she began to weep.

"Promise to meet me next evening, and I shall tell you all. Will you ?" she asked, amid her sobs.

I promised, and we parted—she, as I fancied, to dream of happiness and her lover, perhaps to be fondled in his arms—I to rush to my room and throw myself distractedly upon my couch, there to ponder and reflect for some hours in bitter agony. It was my first great sorrow. There seemed to be no more happiness for me in the world ; the future appeared a dreary bleak desert.

Dora's words were still mysterious to me as I went to meet her the following evening. She was to tell me all. All about what and about whom? Her lover? What cared I to hear about *him* who was my rival—who had robbed me of my choicest treasure ? And then she wants my sympathy. What hollow mockery ! Does she expect me to sympathise with her because she has rejected me ? Such was my train of thoughts before we met. I had summoned all my courage to appear calm, but how I succeeded I know not. I was at least morose and silent. She appeared to be calm, and assumed a smile, but beneath there was a tinge of sadness, scarcely perceptible, yet it was there.

"Let us have a walk to the cemetery," she said.

It was all the same to me ; I cared not where we went, and walked mechanically by her side. Our conversation by the way was meagre enough. Neither of us mooted the subject uppermost in our minds, and to speak of anything else seemed impossible.

At length in the dusky twilight, as we stepped within the gate of the old cemetery, the painful silence was broken by Dora.

"You think I love another, Bill ; well, it is true, but he lives in this world no longer—he is dead, and here is his grave," she said, pointing to a neat sandstone monument, and taking me by the arm until we both stood in front of it.

That scene I shall never, never forget. Oh, it was beautiful ! Like an angel she stood over that grave, and it seemed as if an heavenly radiance beamed upon the grey tombstone. She shed no tears, but her eyelids drooped, and she was pale and trembling. She looked in my face as if expecting me to say something, but I stood spellbound and speechless. The transition which she assumed in my mind was sudden and overpowering. I had not dreamed of such devotion.

"You see those flowers?" she continued; "I planted them there, and often come to tend them and think of *him*. I sometimes wish I could get back my heart, but I cannot—it lies buried there. I can never, never love another."

If it were possible that my love for her could be increased, it was at that moment. Never had I seen her in her truest loveliness till then—in such a new character—such a pure and noble character. My thoughts ere I met her that evening rose before me in all their meanness. My own sufferings were forgotten for the moment, and I only felt that her sufferings were far deeper and keener. Clasping her in my arms, I tried to comfort her with what words I was able to utter. I told her she had my sympathy; that although the world might scoff and call her foolish and sentimental, I for one should never think lightly of her present sorrow, and should ever treasure in my heart the confidence she had placed in me.

"And now," said she, in a voice which seemed to be charged with all the earnestness of her soul—"For your own sake and mine, cease to love me except as a sister. I have shown you the state of my heart; no longer does love dwell there—love such as a husband would be entitled to. Seek another more worthy and more capable of loving you than I am. Do promise me this, Bill."

I dared not promise. I could not cease to love her, nor could I believe she would never love again—she who was capable of loving so devotedly. Time, I reasoned, would certainly cure the wound in her heart, and although she might never forget the past, it would cease to mar the joys of the present, and be remembered only with sweet regret.

I reasoned with her somewhat after this fashion, but she was inexorable. I must promise to do all in my power to quench my hopeless passion, and never refer to the subject again, or else our intercourse must come to an end. Before we parted for the night I had chosen the former alternative, and promised.

We met frequently thereafter, but that I was successfully accomplishing the feat I had undertaken who can suppose?

One Sabbath morning shortly thereafter, I was seated in the old church where my father had sat before me, and where as an infant I had been baptized. The respected pastor, Mr H——, had ascended the pulpit for the first time after a protracted illness, which awoke a throb of gratitude throughout the whole assemblage. Happiness was depicted on every countenance, and as the well-loved voice resounded within the old walls, tears of joy moistened many an eye, and many a quivering lip muttered heartfelt thankfulness to the Giver of all good. Such singing I think I never listened to. Not only every voice, but every heart seemed to burst forth in praise, and as the bright sun beamed through the stained glass windows, lending its radiance to the happy faces of the worshippers, the place indeed seemed filled with an heavenly atmosphere.

But ere the last verse of that psalm of praise had been sung, a woman's shrill scream changed all this calm serenity into consternation and dismay. It was Dora who had screamed, and in a few minutes thereafter John M——, her father, was borne by several persons into the vestry, in what seemed to be a fainting fit. The pastor quitted the pulpit, and on his return informed the congregation that John M—— had breathed his last, and improved the occasion with sundry reflections on the uncertainty of life, and the duty of being always prepared for the final summons.

And so Dora was left in the world an orphan. Poor girl, my heart bled for her in her new and terrible affliction. She had few friends, but these few were true—like myself, friends of her childhood—and sorely she needed their sympathy now. I saw her the following day, and tried to say a few comforting words. They said she was bearing up wonderfully, and was quite calm. But, ah ! her face was overcast with a deep melancholy—it was the calmness of despair—the tearless agony of a crushed spirit. In a week she was in the delirium of fever, and for many weeks thereafter lay at the point of death."

Here my uncle paused in his narrative. His voice had begun to falter, and he seemed overcome with emotion.

" Did she die then, uncle ?" I softly enquired.

" Aye, she died—the Dora I had loved died to me then, undoubtedly, but a form bearing the name of and some slight resemblance to the former Dora, moved about this earth for some years thereafter. I now come to the most painful part of my narrative. Would to God it had ended here, but I must let you hear it all.

Dora's cousin, a lawyer in an adjacent town, was trustee on her father's estate under his will. On the old man's death he came to carry out the funeral arrangements, and thereafter continued to reside in the house avowedly winding up affairs. I had several times inquired for Dora, and on one of these occasions the door was opened by him. My first impressions of the man were by no means favourable. It was evening, and his face seen in profile against the light in the lobby impressed me most disagreeably. His voice was husky and unnatural, and his manner imperative and rude. This man's appearance haunted me ever afterwards, fancy investing it with additional repulsiveness.

Meantime, I received a letter from the mercantile firm which I represented, informing me that I had been appointed to take charge of their business in New York, and must proceed there with as little delay as possible. Before leaving I endeavoured to see Dora, but without avail. I was told she was improving, but that no one was allowed to converse with her yet. I made arrangements, however, with an old friend to write me occasionally and give me all the news, and with a sigh of regret I left my native town once more.

Arrived in my new sphere, I set manfully to work for my employers, but thoughts of home and of Dora were ever recurrent. I had a letter from my friend which informed me that she was slowly recovering, and I longed to hear of her complete recovery, for then I purposed to write her offering my hand and heart once more. Perhaps she would accept me now —possibly be glad to quit that home begirt with so many painful associations—I fondly imagined. The image of her cousin, too, would sometimes rise before me like a bodeful sprite to torment me. I one night had a frightful dream, in which he was the chief actor, and played the villain's part. I received letters from my friend at regular intervals, and the latest news of Dora was that she had been on several occasions out for a drive, accompanied by her cousin, the lawyer.

Although pleased to hear of Dora's recovery, the news, as a whole, was gall and wormwood to me. What business had the lawyer to take up his quarters in her house? I asked myself. I hated the fellow, and had a strong presentiment that he was treating my adored one with cruelty. I sat down and penned a long letter to her, repeating all my former protestations of love, and using every argument in my power to induce her to consent to become my wife.

For months I anxiously awaited an answer, but none ever came. My friend who had been sending me news from home seemed likewise to have forgotten me. Upwards of three months had passed since I had written to Dora, when one morning I received a newspaper from my native town. On opening it up, I observed one of the notices of marriage marked with a cross, and, oh, horror, there I read of my Dora's marriage with her cousin, the lawyer!

I cannot now describe my feelings—they were violent and painful enough, and for weeks I moved about in a semi-distracted state. To drown my racking thoughts and fill the aching void in my heart, I rushed into sinful pleasures. I sought satiety in reckless, deluding excitement—in wild, mad excess. Oh, those years of sin and sorrow! How they have embittered my life. I wish I could blot them out. But, no, they ever hang over me, dark and threatening. I associated with men and women of low morals, who dragged me down as deep as themselves in the mire of iniquity. Neither the past nor the future gave me any concern. I lived entirely for the present, and for the time being had effaced the past from my memory.

I had been fully four years in the new country, when one evening, as was my wont, I stepped into one of the music saloons which abound in the city, to spend an hour. A lady came on the stage to sing, with whose appearance I was greatly struck. I must have seen that face before, I thought. She commenced to sing " Ye banks and braes." Good heavens! I knew the voice—I recognized the face—it was Dora!

I sat like one transfixed—the perspiration cold upon my forehead. There must be something very far wrong, I concluded, when Dora, who married her cousin the lawyer, sings in a music saloon for her livelihood. Dora, the beautiful, the good, the pure, the tender-hearted Dora—she whom I had loved when my heart was young and unsullied—who was once an angel on earth—and now—following a calling so very unlike *her*—associating with a class which I felt sure she would at one time have shunned. What should I do? Make myself known to her? Yes, I felt I must speak to her. I went outside and waited until she came out. She would have passed me unrecognized had I not whispered, " Dora." At first she recoiled in terror, but the next instant was clinging to my arm.

" I feared it was *him*, when I heard my name mentioned," she said, shivering all over.

" Who?" I asked.

" The monster whom I married, and from whom I have fled," she replied.

" Where do you reside?" I enquired, intending to have offered to see her home.

" Anywhere—nowhere. Oh, Bill, you loved me once—you

will not cast me off now—you will take me with you," she said, beseechingly.

I could not deny her request, and taking a cab we drove together to my rooms.

She made herself quite at home, and chatted and laughed in a way which astonished me. She appeared to be devoid of that quiet pensiveness which characterised her in former days.

"How did you happen to marry your cousin after—after what you told me?" I asked her.

"Oh, Bill, I couldn't help myself," she said. "I was weak both in body and mind after the fever, and this he took advantage of, and forced me into marrying him. My father left a pretty large sum of money, which the wretch got into his possession by his marriage with me. I could not love him—I detested him. He treated me cruelly—shamefully—until, in desperation, I fled from him and came to this country, where I hope he shall never be able to find me. Have you any brandy, Bill?—I feel faint."

I handed her a decanter of brandy, and was surprised to see her take an immoderate draught. The truth flashed upon me now. This man had indeed been her moral destroyer. He had crushed the soul out of my Dora, and driven her to drink.

"I love you now, Bill," she afterwards exclaimed, rushing towards me in strange ecstasy, and flinging her arms round my neck. "You will not cast me off; I can never leave you more."

To such entreaties I succumbed, regardless of consequences. It was not my first step in wrongdoing—rather the crowning error of those years of folly which have since entailed upon me so much misery.

We lived together for some time, Dora passing as my wife. But I was not happy. The consciousness of guilt hung over my head like a Damocles sword. She was no longer the Dora I had loved—merely the casket without the gem. Oh, how she had changed. Her finer feelings were obliterated, and she could speak lightly and laugh at the tender memories of the past. She had become a mere child of pleasure, incapable of a single serious thought.

On my return home one afternoon, after we had been about six months together, I found she had quitted my roof, and left a note stating that she could not endure such a dull existence any longer, and as she had no doubt I had grown tired of her, she considered it best that we should part. I knew not where she had gone, but doubted not she would be singing in some of the saloons again. It seemed as if she could only live in a perpetual whirl of excitement. Poor Dora! her career was nearing its close. In her mad butterfly dance she was approaching the flame which would annihilate her.

Only a few months had passed since she left me, when I received a short letter from her, dated from a town several hundred miles away, and written in a very trembling hand, informing me that she was ill—feared she was dying—and expressing a wish to see me. I at once hurried to her bedside, and found her unconscious. The doctor informed me that her life was fast ebbing away. I was likewise told that she had been very anxiously expecting me, and that the previous day she had wept long and bitterly.

I watched at her bedside for an hour, when suddenly she opened her eyes and recognised me. She made an effort to raise her hand as if to draw me towards her.

"Oh, Bill," she said, in a faint whisper, as I bent over her, "I'm so glad you've come, I've had such fearful dreams. I thought a cruel monster had forced me to marry him, and that I fled to America from his presence. I'm so glad it's but a dream. It's time I was getting ready for Sunday school, Bill; my class will be waiting. 'The blood of Jesus Christ cleanseth from all sin' is the golden text. It's getting dark, Bill; won't you draw up the blind? That's better—it's getting light again. Oh, what beautiful sunshine!"

She closed her eyes, and said no more. She breathed heavily for a short time, and then her heart ceased to beat.

This, then, was the bitter end. The past few months of her life were chequered and painful enough, and now the thick curtain of night had fallen over her grief, her shame, her awful tragedy.

In death she was beautiful—a look of placid calmness settled down on her features, bringing more vividly to my recollection than when she was alive, the Dora of former years.' I followed her body to its last resting-place, and returned back to business with a heavy heart, pondering over these things. Yes, I returned to shed tears of bitter repentance, and to lead a new life. What grieved me most, and grieves me to this hour, was the thought that I, too, had contributed to the misery of her latter days. Why did death spare her when she was first at his portals? I often ask myself. Had she but died then, what misery and suffering would have been spared her. Then it might have been different with me, too, and I could ever hold the past in fond remembrance ; those early years, with their so cherished memories, would have been the comfort of my declining life. But now they are overshadowed with clouds, dark and portentous, and yet there is a ray of hope which pierces their darkest centres, and a voice from its midst seems to speak in accents sweet and melodious—" I came not to call the righteous, but sinners to repentance." "

Hereupon my uncle ceased speaking, and we both sat in silence for some time.

THE COURTSHIP AND MARRIAGE OF TIMOTHY TOMKINS.

CHAPTER I.

INTRODUCTORY.

IT was a stormy November day, the rain fell in torrents, and as a natural consequence the streets became saturated with rain water. A certain male individual might be seen walking swiftly through a certain street, and strange to say he was dry—so dry that he stepped into a certain tavern and quaffed a pint of stout at a single draught. He would not have been so very dry had he not been provided with a large family umbrella, which completely sheltered him from the falling rain. Reader, the individual in question was Timothy Tomkins!

CHAPTER II.

CUPID, YOU ROGUE!

T. TOMKINS was in love. Madly, devotedly, blindly, did he worship at the shrine of Miss Sofia Sofibus. But once had he seen her when the tender flame kindled within him, and in process of time said flame reached the dimensions of a good-sized bonfire. Timothy, although naturally of a bashful and retiring disposition, was no coward when a thing came to the scratch. Scratching his head, he laid himself figuratively at Sofia's feet, and opened unto her his whole heart. What she saw there she was never known to disclose.

CHAPTER III.

A PECULIAR PECULIARITY.

MISS SOFIA SOFIBUS was a proper girl. She was considered

handsome, beautiful, and pious. As a proof of her beauty, she had won the affections of T. Tomkins. As a proof of her piety, she could repeat Psalm cxix. backwards without a single mistake. Yet, like all proper girls, she had a peculiarity—she was a moustachio-maniac!

Chapter IV.

A LABOUR OF LOVE.

TIMOTHY had likewise a peculiarity. No hair would grow upon his upper lip, and this was fatal to the realisation of his love dream. When he laid himself at Sofia's feet, and implored her to be bone of his bone, the said Sofia, drawing a long sigh, answered—

"I love you, Timothy; I do indeed; but I have a peculiarity which I have inherited from my great-grandmother. To you I will disclose it, and trust to your honour to keep it secret. Listen, Timothy. If I were to be kissed by a man without a moustache, I should instantly fly into hysterics; this is my peculiarity."

"But I will grow a moustache," exclaimed the gallant Timothy, "and then come and claim you for my bride."

"Go, then," said Sofia, with a majestic wave of her lily-white hand. "I'll give you three months." And Timothy disappeared.

Chapter V.

LOVE'S LABOUR ALMOST LOST.

IT is difficult to make hair grow where it won't, as T. Tomkins found out to his cost when he had tried all the advertised specifics for moustache rearing without success. Being naturally of a bashful and retiring disposition as aforesaid, he was indisposed to enter personally into a barber's shop, and request to be put under treatment. But as it was not a matter which could be accomplished by proxy, and love being stronger than most barbers, he at last prevailed upon himself to go. For two months he underwent a course of lathering and razor-scraping four times a-day, and at night slept with a linen rag over his lip, said rag being saturated with hare soup. But it was no go, the hair was obdurate and would not come out. The three months had nearly expired, and Timothy was growing desperate, because he was not growing hair.

CHAPTER VI.

HOPE AT THE ELEVENTH HOUR.

IT was the last day but two of the three months. The aforesaid Timothy Tomkins sat in the barber's back shop gazing wistfully upon sundry empty bottles of Rowland's maccassar, Mrs S. Allan's balsam, &c., &c. So intent was his gaze that he fell into a mesmeric sleep, and in fancy beheld a bright vision of bliss. He imagined his angelic Sofia sitting upon his knee, pouring out coffee (he was a great admirer of coffee), and at the same time rocking with her classic foot a cradle, in which slept a babe, the very image of its father. At that moment a fly lighted upon his upper lip, when he raised his hand to aforesaid place, and immediately the fly and the vision were dispelled. T. Tomkins' visage became contorted, and he looked the picture of despair. The barber gazed upon him compassionately (for he was a man with a family), then scratched his head as if concocting a scheme, and whispered softly into his ear. (N.B.—It was his own head the barber scratched, and Timothy's ear into which he whispered.) The idea was good. T. Tomkins brightened up, slapped the barber on the shoulder, and departed.

CHAPTER VII.

A TRANSFORMATION SCENE.

ON the following day T. Tomkins entered the barber's shop at 1 P.M., with his upper lip bare, and at 1.55 P.M. stepped out wearing an elegant moustache. We venture no opinion as to the means employed for its growth, but allow it to remain "a fact for naturalists."

CHAPTER VIII.

BLIND LOVE.

THE same evening, while Miss Sofia Sofibus reclined gracefully upon two chairs in her snug little back parlour, she heard a gentle tap at the door. Not having a maid, she made for the door herself, and, having opened it, her surprise may be easier imagined than described on seeing T. Tomkins enter.

"I come to claim my prize," he said, in a voice faltering with emotion.

"My eye! what a beautiful moustache!" exclaimed Sofia. "Give me a kiss, Timothy."

T. Tomkins clasped her in his arms, and for the space of three consecutive minutes the world and all its vanities had vanished from the mind's eye of the enraptured lovers.

CHAPTER IX.

MARRIAGE.

IN the limited space of one week, a noble steed might be observed prancing majestically through a certain street. Said steed had his ears decorated with white silk lace. Behind him was a cab, on the outside of which sat the driver, and in the inside T. Tomkins and his newly-married wife. They were returning from the minister's. It is certain that if we attempted to portray the leading features of their honeymoon, the effort would prove a miserable failure. We therefore leave it to the vivid imaginations of our readers.

CHAPTER X.

AND AFTER.

T. TOMKINS, like many more, had made up his mind that his whole married life should be one perpetual honeymoon. But alas for the best laid schemes of mice and men! Coming home one evening, about six weeks after his marriage, he found his wife with a bandage over her left eye. For a moment he stood like one petrified; the next he asked—

"What's up?"

"Mustard," said Sofia.

The gushing husband immediately burst into a flood of tears, and essayed to imprint a kiss upon the suffering orb, but Mrs T. resisted. This occasioned some words, and thus the demon of discord gained an entrance.

CHAPTER XI.

A DISCOVERY AND A DISCOVERY.

SOFIA picked something off the floor, greeted her husband with a look of supreme contempt, and retired to her bedroom. Timothy paced contemplatively for some time around the parlour table. Once, and only once, he glanced into the mirror, uttered a wild shriek, and went into convulsions. He discovered his upper lip was bare! When he came to himself, he began groping all along the floor. What he expected to find is a mystery; but he did find something—a bright bit of glass—in fact, a glass eye. When he joined his wife in bed, he had a napkin tied around his upper lip.

CHAPTER XII.

A STUDY FOR AN ARTIST.

And so T. Tomkins and Sofia his wife lay side by side in bed, he with a bandage over his lip, and she with a bandage over her eye.

CHAPTER XIII.

MATRIMONIAL BLISS.

Sofia being first awake in the morning, and beholding the bandaged face of her husband, uttered a slight scream.

D

"My eye ! what's up with your mouth, Timothy ?" she asked, nudging him in the ribs.

The latter awoke with a start, and requested that the question might be repeated.

"What's up ?" again asked Sofia.

"Mustard," replied T. Tomkins.

"Base deceiver !" exclaimed she, dramatically, clutching the napkin and tearing it from his face, exposing his bare upper lip.

Then putting her hand beneath her pillow, she took from thence a bunch of hair, which she ironically placed upon her upper lip, and grinned at her husband. T. Tomkins recognised his moustache and succumbed. But it was only momentarily, for he was courageous, as aforesaid, when a thing came to the scratch.

".Base deceiver !" shouted he in return, tearing the bandage from his wife's eye and exposing a sightless hole.

Then producing the bit of glass, he held it to the tip of his nose, and put out his tongue in derision. Sofia recognised her lost eye and succumbed. Some few hours thereafter they both separated with mutual recriminations.

CHAPTER XIV.

SOFIBUS v. TOMKINS.

An action was raised in the Court of Uncommon Pleas at the instance of Mrs Sofia Sofibus or Tomkins, against Timothy Tomkins, her husband, to obtain separation and damages on account of the said Timothy Tomkins having married her under false pretences, he having avowed a moustache which he wore upon his upper lip to be genuine, knowing the same to be false.

Evidence having been led, the Court returned a verdict of separation, and one hundred pounds damages.

Immediately on the conclusion of this case, another action was raised by Mr Timothy Tomkins against Sofia Sofibus or Tomkins, his wife, to obtain separation and damages on account of the said Sofia Sofibus or Tomkins having married him under false pretences, she having avowed a glass eye, which she wore in her left eyehole, to be genuine, knowing same to be false. Evidence having been led, the Court returned a verdict of separation, and one hundred pounds damages.

CHAPTER XV.

A STRIKING COINCIDENCE.

The following day T. Tomkins met Sofia Sofibus in the street.

"I was just coming to see you," he said.

"And I was just coming to see you," she replied.

"I have a hundred pounds to pay you."

"And I have a hundred pounds to pay you."

"Well, I have been thinking that the hundred pounds which I have to pay you and the hundred which you have to pay me make two hundred pounds together."

"What a striking coincidence! I have been thinking the very same thing," exclaimed Sofia.

"And my idea is this—that we get married again, and with these two hundred pounds embark in some profitable speculation."

"Exactly my own idea, Timothy. How strange!" exclaimed Sofia, slapping him on the shoulder.

The two walked off arm-in-arm.

CHAPTER XVI.

CONCLUSION.

T. Tomkins and S. Sofibus got married over again, embarked in shipping, and founded a colony. They lived happily ever afterwards.

HOW I "POPPED THE QUESTION."

WHAT a strange mortal I used to be ! I was an enigma to myself and to everybody else. Although descended "from a humble stock undoubtedly," my aspirations ran high—many of them quite beyond the range of realization. One of the first objects I wished to possess was actually the moon, and I have been told I wept bitterly because my father declined to take the "bonnie shiney round thing" down to me. When quite an urchin I had a great desire to be a minister, and thinking that the chief acquirement was to have a bald head like the Reverend Mr Thomas, I one day, when alone, took my mother's scissors and in a very short time had divested my head of its ringlets. I was standing on a chair "spouting" to an imaginary congregation, when my mother came in, and I received such a whipping as put the damper for ever on my ministerial hopes. And strange though it may seem, I did not stand high in my own estimation. People sometimes called me proud, but in this they were deceived. They mistook shyness and reserve for pride. I was excessively shy, and especially so in the company of young ladies. It almost makes me blush yet to recall how I used to redden up when I chanced to meet any girl I knew. No one acquainted with me believed I would ever have the courage to propose to a girl, and I verily believe I never would, had things always gone on in their ordinary course. It was entirely through a misunderstanding that I "popped the question," and I am just going to relate how it happened.

After I had quitted the paternal roof, I resided in the same lodgings and shared the same bed with my old school companion, Bill Smithers, and I can say in all sincerity a better comrade I never had. We put up together like brothers—or rather as brothers ought to put up, for too often they make bad bedfellows—and yet he was of quite a different disposition from me. I think we were two of the most directly opposite temperaments that could possibly be found together. Bill was always lively, full of chat and fun, and one who had the knack of making himself at home in any company. He was full of tricks, too, and was always lucky in escaping detection, whereas if I indulged in anything of this sort I was sure to be caught. I shall never forget the night he almost frightened out of her wits poor old Miss Brown, our landlady. He had been at the seaside, and brought home in his handkerchief a number of live crabs. Fixing small pieces of candle on their backs, which he lit, he gently opened Miss Brown's bedroom door after she was asleep, and allowed the crabs to crawl in, and then, with a most unearthly howl, awoke the poor lady. The joke was too serious, for Miss Brown screamed in the utmost terror, and was hysterical for some considerable time. She never neglected to lock her bedroom door at night thereafter.

Bill was a great favourite with the fair sex. He was intimate with every good-looking girl in the place, and one half of them were in love with him. If I happened to be out with him of an evening, it gave him great delight to get me inveigled into the responsibility of seeing a girl home, for well he knew I would rather walk ten miles than be left alone for ten minutes in a girl's company. It was he who introduced me to Olivia Watson, and well do I remember that eventful evening when first I walked home with her. We had scarcely exchanged a word after our formal introduction, and here we were, Olivia and I, with a mile of lonely road before us. Side by side we walked for a good long time in complete silence. I gazed at the stars and chewed my finger nails, all the time taxing my memory for something to say, but couldn't think of anything. At last, with a desperate effort, I mumbled—

"Isn't it a beautiful evening ?"

Olivia failed to hear what I said, and this increased, if it were possible, my confusion. After an awkward pause she said—

"I beg your pardon."

"I was remarking it's a fine evening," I stammered out in a louder tone, and in a voice which grated so harshly upon my own ear, that it brought the hot blood to my temples, and I felt dazed and dumfoundered.

"Yes, it's a very fine evening," she replied.

Thereafter the silence was unbroken until her home was reached.

"I will now bid you good-night, Mr Luke," she said, extending to me her hand.

"Good-night, Miss Watson," I replied, as we parted for the night. I hurried home in a most uncomfortable frame of mind. I was an ass, a booby, a veritable Simple Simon in my own estimation. I felt I could have parted with anything to possess but one-half of Bill's *sang-froid* and loquacity. Oh, how I wished I could overcome that horrid bashfulness and blushing!

Several times thereafter I met Olivia, and by her aid we were a little more successful in conversation. She would ask my opinion about this or the other thing, and sometimes she would have a little anecdote to relate concerning herself or her acquaintances, and this enabled me to put in a sentence now and again. I soon discovered that I had a secret liking for her, but this only tended to make me more bashful and reserved in her presence than I might otherwise have been.

Bill happened to hear me mention her name one night in my sleep—at least he said so—and afterwards he continually teased me about her, and on the very first opportunity he told Olivia that I raved about her every night in my sleep. On learning this I felt so ashamed that I actually shunned her whenever it was in my power, although daily growing more and more enamoured of her.

Christmas was approaching. November, with its foggy skies and sleepy showers, had passed away, and the last month of the year, ushered silently in, had wrought an entire change upon the face of nature. The streets and housetops were covered with snow, and the bright sunshine which filled the clear, frosty atmosphere, bathed the lower world in dazzling light.

I sat musing before a cheerful fire in our room one evening, when Bill came in for the night

"Well, old fellow, not been seeing Olivia to-night?" was his first salutation.

"I don't know why you always plague me about Olivia," I returned, somewhat piqued. "I'm sure I never go to see her, and only speak when we meet accidentally."

"There you are at your blushing again. You can't hear her name mentioned without blushing, John. Ha, ha! you're fairly booked, old man. You can't deceive me. But I won't say more, in case you should go into an apoplectic fit, and I've something to tell you, John. I've been at Mrs Morgan's to-night, and she's invited you and I to her house on Christmas evening. I've accepted the invitation in name of both, so you must make up your mind and go."

"Who are to be there—a lot of girls, I suppose?"

"Oh no," said Bill. "It's to be quite a private affair—not a girl to be there except the girls of the house."

"You know, Bill, I don't want to have a mile to trudge home with a girl after all is over."

"You need have no fears on that score, for the Morgan girls won't require seeing home. So it's settled, then."

"Well, I suppose so," I said.

The days flew quickly past, and Christmas came. Punctually at 7 P.M. Bill and I were at Mrs Morgan's door. In half-a-minute later we were divesting ourselves of our hats and topcoats in the lobby, and receiving the greetings of the motherly widow.

"Oh, Mr Smithers, I'm so glad to see you. Come away, come in—we were just waiting for you. And this is your friend, Mr Luke," addressing me. "Hope you are quite well, Mr Luke?"

I thanked her, and said I was.

"Come along, then, and get introduced to the young ladies. I fancy Mr Luke will be acquainted with some of them already, and as for Mr Smithers he will require no introduction, for I think he speaks to every young lady in town."

"Ladies!" I gasped, greeting Bill with a look of consternation.

"Come along, old fellow, there is no shirking it now," said Bill, seizing me by the arm and half-dragging me forward.

Mrs Morgan had opened the parlour door, and as I heard the sound of female voices chatting and laughing, my heart began to beat against my ribs, and the usual hot flush mounted to my cheeks. By the time I entered the room I was dizzy and half blind. How I got through that fearful ordeal of hand-shaking I don't know. All I seemed conscious of was that Olivia was there, and about half a dozen other young ladies, whose names, although introduced to them, I had no more recollection of than the man in the moon had. By the time I began to gather my wits about me I found myself seated at table with Miss Morgan on my one side and a girl whom she addressed as Miss Poodle on the other. Olivia sat opposite in lively conversation with Bill. Every one save me seemed to be thoroughly enjoying the occasion. Oh, how I envied those who could talk and joke and make themselves at home in a company.

Mrs Morgan's tongue went like a bell.

"Now, my dears, set to and do good justice to your supper. We'll have the fun afterwards. Mr Smithers, you're eating nothing, and I believe you're also hindering Miss Watson from eating, with all these jokes you're pouring into her ear. Mr Luke, you don't seem to be enjoying yourself. You ladies beside him see if you can't cheer him up a bit; he seems quite disconsolate."

I felt as if my brain were on fire, and almost choked on a morsel of roast beef which I happened to be masticating at the moment.

" Do you feel badly, Mr Luke?" inquired Miss Poodle, with an anxious look.

" No, just a slight—sensation," I stammered.   .

" Mr Smithers tells me you're newly off a sea voyage from London—possibly you haven't got over the effects of it yet?" said Miss Morgan.

"Oh, were you very sea-sick, Mr Luke?" inquired Miss Poodle.

" I'm sure I would have been awfully sick," chimed in Miss Morgan.

" I—I—wasn't at London—nor at sea either," I gasped.

"Oh!" they both exclaimed in astonishment.

" I don't know what Mr Smithers means by perpetrating such abominable jokes," said Miss Morgan peevishly.

I looked fiercely across the table at Bill, whose face beamed with a good-natured smile, and I actually noticed him winking to Olivia, which tended to increase my anger towards him.

By the time supper was over, I had regained some little self-possession. The girls on either side of me kept up a constant volley of "small talk," so that I got in a word now and again in reply to a question or in expression of surprise or approval, as the case might be. Once or twice, too, I exchanged a few words with Olivia across the table, my blood all the time boiling hot against Bill.

On the table being cleared, we engaged in various games, and of course I had to take part, and after a time I was beginning to feel a little at home. Miss Poodle devoted a good deal of her attention to me, and as she had a nice frank manner, I was beginning to get much of my accustomed embarrassment brushed off. I could not resist following Olivia with my eyes throughout the evening as she flitted hither and thither through the room. I thought she was really a lovely creature. Oftener than once I fancied I caught her taking a side glance at me, and how my heart did flutter. "Can it be possible she cares ought about me?" I asked myself. "No," a voice within replied.

"How can you fancy a sprightly girl like her would take up her head with an awkward, bashful simpleton like you."

The evening was passing very pleasantly. Game after game had been engaged in, and still the enjoyment showed no signs of flagging. With joined hands we were all in a circle on the middle of the floor, when suddenly the gas went out, and we were left in total darkness. After the first exclamations of surprise had subsided a general titter and laugh broke forth, and there was a scrambling hither and thither. I was standing with my back towards a sofa wondering what was going to happen next, when a pair of lady's arms encircled my neck, and a soft warm cheek was pressed to mine. As sure as fate some girl had kissed me! A sudden impulse prompted me to seize the fairy form, but I was too late, she eluded my grasp, and the gas was re-lit. The first person upon whom my eyes rested was Olivia sitting on the sofa quite near me. I never felt more dumfoundered in my life. I felt as if I could have jumped out of my skin. She gazed on me with a peculiarly inquisitive, half-smiling, half-bashful sort of look, as much as to say, " I hope you're not angry." Yes, it was she who had kissed me. I divined it in her face. I didn't know what to do in my confusion. Something prompted me to throw my arms around her and pay her back ten times over, but this would only be making ourselves the laughing-stock of the entire company. And it might not be her after all. Oh, cruel thought! But I would ask her, I resolved, so summoning what for me amounted to almost superhuman courage, I sat down beside her and whispered—

"Was it you?"

"Yes," she replied, with a slight blush, and then fixing her lustrous blue eyes upon me till mine quailed beneath their gaze, she asked—

"Did you think it was somebody else?"

"No," I replied; "I was sure it was you." And then she looked so sweetly upon me that I am certain, had the gas gone out again, I would not hesitate to put my arms around her and smother her with kisses. But the gas was burning brightly as ever, and on looking around I observed the eyes of nearly every one in the room turned upon Olivia and myself, and a deal of whispering and smiling going on. I noticed Bill standing alone in a corner of the room holding his handkerchief to his face in quite a paroxysm of laughter.

"What are they all laughing at ?" I inquired of Olivia.

"I have no idea," she responded.

"I'll go and ask Mr Smithers," I said, rising from her side and stepping over to Bill, of whom I inquired the cause of his merriment.

"Oh, nothing—merely the sensation of the gas," he said, amid a burst of laughter.

"Bill, you have treated me badly to-night," I said, angrily, "and I won't stand any more of your jokes."

"Ha, ha, John, I do like to see you angry," said Bill, amid another outburst. "But look," continued he, "Olivia is leaving the room and waving on you."

I looked around, and saw she had indeed quitted the sofa, and was nowhere to be seen.

"Bill," I said severely, "you appear to be anxious to make a fool of me to-night."

"Not a bit of it, John," he replied in a serious tone. "Olivia has gone into the next room, and I am perfectly confident she wants you to follow her."

I felt it might be true—in fact, inwardly desired it to be true.

"Well, I'll go and see, Bill, but if this turns out a joke it's the last you'll ever have the chance of playing upon me," I said, as I left him and went in search of Olivia.

I found her sitting in the window recess of the adjoining room gazing out upon the stars. She seemed unconscious of my approach until I stood at her side. When she turned round it was no doubt in a very tremulous voice I inquired—

"Did you wish to speak with me, Olivia?"

By aid of the faint light from the window I noticed she looked surprised. After a slight pause she said, "No," and then in a voice lowered almost to a whisper, "Do you wish to say anything yourself, John?"

This question reassured me—ay, decided me—and for once in my life I struck the iron when it was hot.

"Yes, Olivia, I've got something to say," I replied. "I love you," and while uttering these words I had seated myself at her side, and unconsciously my arm passed around her waist. I was very glad she could not see how I blushed. But she didn't look in my face at any rate, she merely pressed closer to my side and buried her head in my bosom. I need not trouble my readers with more of this evening's proceedings. Conscious of Olivia's love, I went home that night the happiest being on earth.

Several months had passed since Mrs Morgan's Christmas party. One evening Olivia and I were sitting together talking over our prospects for the future—she had just named the happy day which would join us in the holy bonds of matrimony —and as I clasped her to my bosom and imprinted a warm kiss upon her lips, I gave vent to my feelings in words like these—

"Oh, how happy you have made me, Olivia, and it makes you doubly dear to me when I think that but for one act of yours I might never have experienced my present joy. Had you not kissed me that evening at Mrs Morgan's party I verily believe I would never have summoned sufficient courage to tell you of my love."

"I didn't kiss you, John; 'twas you who kissed me," she replied.

"Not a bit of it," I protested. "You put your arms around my neck and kissed me."

"Oh, oh, what a big fib," she exclaimed. "'Twas you put your arms around my neck."

"Olivia," I said, rather severely, "how can you persist in saying so? Didn't I ask you at the time if it was you who kissed me, and you said 'Yes?'"

"I never did," she replied, emphatically. "You asked, 'Was it you?' and I understood you were asking if it was I whom you kissed. I replied it was, and, if you remember, I asked, 'Did you think it was somebody else?' to which you replied, 'No, I was sure it was you.'"

"And did some one kiss you, then?" I inquired.

"Why ask, when you know perfectly well *you* did?"

"Upon my conscience, Olivia, I didn't. But a light begins to dawn upon the incident now. I can see that a trick has been played upon us. Most certainly I was kissed that night by a lady, and finding you at my side when the gas was re-lit, I naturally concluded it was you who had done it, and hence my question, 'Was it you?'"

"What a farce!" she exclaimed. "Did you really imagine I would have put my arms around your neck and kiss you? Well, well, you must have had a very high opinion of yourself, certainly," and then, in more sober tones, she inquired—"Did you really imagine I would so far outstep the bounds of modesty as to kiss you in the dark?"

I had to confess I did believe she kissed me, but as to the act being in any way immodest, I assured her that such a thought never entered my mind.

I now knew it was a trick, and had not the least doubt that Bill was at the bottom of it, more especially when I recalled the fit of laughter with which he was seized after the gas was re-lit, on the evening of the party. Olivia was of the same opinion, and I parted from her that evening resolved to have the mystery cleared up at the earliest opportunity.

Bill was preparing for bed when I got home. I at once accosted him with—

"You remember Mrs Morgan's Christmas party, Bill?"

"Yes, what about it, my boy?"

"What were you laughing at when I came to speak to you after the gas had gone out and was re-lit ?"

"Ha, ha," he laughed, "have you and Olivia been comparing notes at last ?"

"Come now, Bill, just tell me all about it. I know a joke was played on us, and I am confident from your face that you know about it."

"Right you are, old man. I have often wondered you and your lady-love did not compare notes sooner, and was waiting to see how long it would take you to make the discovery."

"Since we have found it out, tell me now, Bill, who kissed me that evening."

"Promise not to be angry, then."

"I promise."

"Well, it was——." Here Bill became overcome with laughter. "But can't you guess ?"

"No."

"Try."

"Was it Miss Poodle ?"

"No."

"Miss Spinks ?"

"No."

"Miss Fowler ?"

"No."

"Then it must have been one of the Misses Morgan ?"

"No—o."

"Tell me at once then who it was, and don't keep me longer in suspense."

"Well, John, it was—Mrs Morgan !"

"What! the old widow !" I exclaimed in dismay. "And who kissed Olivia ?"

"I did," said Bill.

"You did ?"

"Yes ; but why do you look as if you could jump down my throat ? Didn't you promise not to be angry ?"

"Angry? I'm not a bit angry. Ha, I can see through it now. You and Mrs Morgan concocted the plot."

"Of course we did, and I'll tell you how it happened," said Bill. "I knew perfectly well that you had a secret regard for Olivia, although you tried to hide it from me, and I knew equally well that Olivia entertained a high opinion of you, so I asked Mrs Morgan to invite you both to her Christmas party with the view of bringing you together. This was done, but your excessive shyness was like to render our scheme abortive, for you would scarcely speak to her. During the evening an idea occurred to me which I communicated to Mrs Morgan, and asked her assistance to put into practice. It was to put out the gas, and in the confusion which would naturally follow she was to seize hold of you and kiss you, while I was to do the same to Olivia, and to watch that when the gas was re-lit you would both be in close proximity, so that each of you would imagine the one had kissed the other. You know how successfully we carried out our little plot, and I am very pleased it has had the desired result."

"Give me your hand, Bill," I said. "You've played me many a joke, for which I've felt inclined to do something else than thank you, but this one makes amends for them all. Yes, I can forgive you, Bill, aye, bless you from the bottom of my heart."

TABLE-TURNING WITH A VENGEANCE.

"ARE you a believer in Spiritualism?" my friend Bowers asked me one forenoon as we were enjoying our "constitutional" together.

"If you mean spirit-rapping, table-turning, and the other 'tomfooleries' incidental to what are called spiritualistic *seances*, most emphatically, No," I replied.

"But have you ever tested the thing?"

"Tested the thing! why, it carries so much absurdity on the face of it that I would consider the man half an idiot who essayed to test it."

"Oh, but you're wrong there. I was once as sceptical as you are regarding it."

"What! you don't mean to tell me that you're a believer in spirit-rapping?"

"I am bound to believe in what I have heard with my ears and seen with my eyes."

"And what is that, pray?"

"Why, I've heard the table rapped upon and seen it rise from the floor by means of some invisible agency."

"Ha! sleight-of-hand tricks, I've no doubt."

"Not a bit of it, I assure you. I've seen the table rise fully a foot from the floor, and remain suspended thus for a minute or so, notwithstanding the united efforts of four of us to keep it down. No sleight-of-hand about it, I'll be bound."

"Where did you witness this?"

"In Fitznoble's. But I suppose you don't know him. He has lately returned from Australia, and lives in Clinkerton Place. Splendid fellow, with lots of money. Well, you know he's what they call a 'medium,' and not only do the spirits answer questions to him by raps on the table, but he has the power of becoming possessed with spirits of the dead, who can converse with you through him. I have several times put him into a state of *coma* by simply making a few passes with my hand before his face, after which a spirit would possess him, and answer any questions asked."

I had not the honour of being acquainted with Mr Fitznoble, but inwardly set him down for some impostor or practical joker who had been playing upon my friend's credulity.

" Ah, Bowers," said I, " you must have been deceived in some way. The passing into the state of *coma* you speak of might be feigned, and as for the rapping on and rising up of the table, I would like to have a thorough inspection of the table and everything in the room, before believing it was done by an invisible agency."

" Well, come along with me next Friday evening, and you can see for yourself. I have got an invitation, and can bring a friend with me."

" Anything to pay ? Does your friend make money out of this business ?"

"Oh, dear, no ; he has no occasion, being a man of wealth. He just does it to entertain and gratify his friends."

It was chiefly curiosity to learn something of Bowers' new found friend which induced me to agree to accompany him. At the same time I felt a little curious about the table-turning. I had heard and read a good deal about spiritualistic *seances* of late, and although I could not for a moment believe that the phenomena was the result of supernatural agency, I thought I would just like to see for myself what it all amounted to.

George Bowers was one of my oldest and most valued friends. Although in comfortable circumstances, he might have been better off had he been more wide-awake. He was one of those men who have the doubtful reputation of being too honest for this world. Upon the whole he was an average man of business,

E

but too often carried away with novelties, and sometimes went into speculations which turned out unprofitable.

On the following Friday evening he called upon me as arranged, and we both set out in the direction of Clinkerton Place.

Bowers was exceedingly lavish in his praises of Fitznoble.

"You'll find him a regular kind-hearted, well-bred fellow; couldn't find a more thorough gentleman between here and John o' Groat's. I'm sure you'll be charmed with him when you meet him."

"Very wealthy," you said.

"Immensely."

"How did he make his money ?"

"He was principal shareholder and Managing Director of the Prawnbrook Gold Mining Company, Limited, and sold out half of his shares before he left Australia. He presented me with one of the Company's balance-sheets, upon which his name appears as Managing Director, and it appears to be making immense profits, original £20 shares selling at £70."

"That would have been a good speculation for you, Bowers, if you had gone in at *par*," I said, knowing his speculative tendencies.

"Ay, and I have gone in. Though not at *par*, I've got a few shares at £40, through Fitznoble's influence, for he's all in all with the Directors, you know."

"Have you made inquiries about the concern, and satisfied yourself that your speculation is a safe one ?"

"Safe as the Bank of England, my dear fellow. Fitznoble isn't the man to lead one on the ice."

"Well, I hope not," I replied drily, and allowed the subject to drop.

In a very few minutes we had arrived at Clinkerton Place, and were ushered into the gorgeous apartments of Geoffrey Fitznoble, Esquire, by whom we were most graciously received.

I confess I was rather favourably impressed with Fitznoble's appearance and manners. He seemed every inch a gentleman, and performed the duties of host with a degree of politeness and affability which could not have been surpassed.

We had not been many minutes seated when other two gentlemen were announced. They proved to be Sharp and Marsden, both business men, and known to Bowers and myself. From the familiar way in which Fitznoble greeted them, it appeared they had been previously acquainted with him, too.

"Very glad to see you all, gentlemen, and I trust you'll make yourselves at home. You see I live a sort of hermit life here, and it always affords me pleasure to meet a few friends of an evening," said Fitznoble, with a beaming countenance.

Almost immediately we were asked to sit down to supper, which was served in first-class style by a liveried waiter. Champagne followed, and altogether we were as jolly a little party as could well be imagined. Our host drew us into an animated conversation on American politics. Other topics succeeded, in the discussion of which he displayed remarkable conversational talent. He appeared to be well informed on almost every subject, and spoke with the air of a man who had seen much of the world, and studied the problems of the day. He was gaining greatly in my favour. The more I saw of him, the more was I becoming convinced that any bad impressions I had formed of him, were utterly groundless.

By and by the subject of spiritualism was introduced, and Bowers informed Fitznoble that I was very sceptical on the subject.

"Scepticism," said our host, "is the crowning sin of the age, and is the greatest drawback to the advance of spiritualism. Faith in the unseen is at the very foundation of every system of religious belief. Without such faith Christianity would never have existed, and the greater our faith the further are we enabled to peer into the mysteries of the spirit world. Our Saviour said if our faith is sufficiently strong we can remove mountains, but even He could not do mighty works where unbelief prevailed.   It seems to me exceedingly strange that persons who believe, or at least profess to believe, that they are surrounded by a world of angels and spirits, will not allow the possibility of holding converse with them.   The fact is, that spirit manifestations, instead of being inconsistent, are rather in accordance with the teachings of our religion."

This speech, evidently levelled at me, I listened to with meek attention, and although by no means convinced, I did not feel prepared to argue the question.

"Let us have a *seance*," said Bowers, "and no doubt our friend will be converted before it is over."

"By all means let us have a *seance*," chimed in Sharp and Marsden.

"So be it, friends, since it is your desire," said Fitznoble, as he rung the bell, and ordered his servant, when he put in appearance, to light the gas of an adjoining room.

In a few minutes we were conducted into this room, the furniture of which was of a much plainer description than that of the apartment we had vacated.   A plain oak table occupied the centre of the floor, around which were a number of chairs of the same material.   At Bowers' request I made an examination of the table, and as far as I could see it was quite *bona fidê*, and perfectly innocent of any machinery or other appliance which might cause it to rise from the floor or produce the rappings.

"Take your seats around the table then, gentlemen," said Fitznoble, "and I'll screw down the gas.   The reason for so doing," he explained, after he had seated himself beside me, "is to prevent our thoughts from being distracted with surrounding objects.   Now, gentlemen, lay the palms of both hands lightly but solidly on the table.   Let our thoughts be concentrated upon the fact that we are surrounded with spirits, and our faith be strong that they can communicate with us.   Let us desire as with one heart, *will* as with one soul, that they do communicate with us.   On the strength of our faith and our will depends what manifestations may result."

There were five of us around that table, and for five, ten, fifteen minutes we sat in profound silence, and without any token that spirits were near. Was it going to prove a failure? I wondered. I did not doubt that something unusual would probably take place, but I confess I had little faith that the manifestations, whatever they might be, would be the work of spirits from another world. After other five minutes had passed I began to think that surely my scepticism was counteracting the faith of the others, when my nerves received a shock by hearing a succession of raps upon the table.

Immediately Fitznoble began in a slow monotonous voice to interrogate the supposed unearthly visitant.

"To whom are we indebted for this visit?"

Three raps resounded.

"A spirit of the third sphere," explained Fitznoble.

"How long have you been an inhabitant of the spirit world?"

Six raps followed, signifying six years, we were informed.

"Were you known to any of the present company in your former existence?"

To this question there came no reply, which was taken for a negative answer.

"Then good-night, strange spirit," said Fitznoble.

A loud rapping followed, the table literally rose from the floor, and performed a series of forward and backward movements before it became stationary.

After a short silence the table was again rapped upon. The spirit was interrogated as before, and when asked if he was known to any of the persons present replied with a rap, indicating that he was. It promised to be more exciting this time, and I listened eagerly to the questioning which followed.

"Would you have the goodness to assist me to spell your name?" said Fitznoble, who began slowly to repeat the alphabet until he came to the letter "J," when there was a rap. Noting down this letter, he commenced at the beginning of the alphabet again, stopping and noting down the letter whenever a rap occurred, and repeating the process until the full name was spelt.

A strange sensation akin to terror began to steal over me when I discovered it was my father's name, "James Gibson," that was being spelt out!

"Is your son present?" asked Fitznoble.

A rap.

"How long have you been in the spirit state?"

Raps to the number of fifteen came in reply, and I remembered it was that number of years since my father died.

"Would you like to ask any questions?" Fitznoble inquired of me.

At that very time I was extremely anxious to know what had become of my brother William, who went abroad some years previously, and of whose present whereabouts we could obtain no information. A relative had lately died leaving an estate, a share of which fell to William, and we were at the time advertising all over the world for him, as the estate could not be apportioned until he was found, or satisfactory evidence of his death procured. Whether it were my father's spirit or not, I thought there could be no harm in putting the question; and asked—

"Is my brother William alive?"

A rap.

"Where is he?"

"Oldpeak, Sandyhurst," was spelt out by means of the alphabet.

"What is he doing?"

"Badly off—send him hundred pounds at once," was spelt in reply.

Could it be true? I wondered. How could I test the spirit's veracity?

"What was my mother's maiden name?" I asked, feeling that if this were answered correctly I must believe in the genuineness of spiritualism.

A tremendous rapping followed the question, and the table rose fully a foot from the floor, then descended with such force that it ran the risk of being broken.

"The spirit's time is up, and he has bidden us good-night," said Fitznoble. "Spirits are actively employed in the unseen world, and have little spare time. Then the tedious mode of obtaining answers to questions makes an interview lengthy which otherwise would have been short. Your father's spirit," he continued, addressing me, "gave an unusually long manifestation, but he seemed anxious that you should obtain the fullest information regarding your missing brother."

"I'll write to the address given," I said.

"Yes, and send the money as requested."

"Well, I'll consider about it," I replied.

"You might favour us now with a 'medium' manifestation," said Bowers, addressing our host.

"With pleasure," said the latter, lifting his chair to one end of the room and sitting down. Bowers advanced and made the passes in front of his face he had told me of, and in a minute or two Fitznoble was apparently in a comatose state.

"Now, friends, what we have to do," explained Bowers, "is with one mind to will that a spirit shall possess our host, and thereafter we can converse with the spirit, who is enabled to make use of the medium's faculties of articulation."

"Let us call the spirit of some great man—some philosopher, poet, or statesman," said Sharp.

"Suppose we say Lord Beaconsfield," suggested Marsden.

All being agreeable, we repeated after Bowers as he directed—

"Spirit of Beaconsfield, possess the medium."

But Fitznoble remained immovable, and although the command was thrice repeated he gave no sign that he was spirit-possessed.

"Let us try some one else—Shakespeare, for instance," I suggested.

"It's little use trying Shakespeare," said Bowers. "He has

been often requested, but his spirit has never possessed a medium yet, I understand."

"Let it be Byron, then," said Marsden.

All being willing, the command was repeated by each of us—"Spirit of Byron, possess the medium !"

Success appeared to have at length crowned our efforts, for Fitznoble arose and commenced to recite Byron's Address to the Ocean. On its conclusion, Bowers asked a number of questions, and the spirit in his replies disclosed that he had but lately been released from the fires of Purgatory, and was now inhabiting the first sphere. Asked if he had written any poetry in his spirit existence, he said he had lately begun to finish " Don Juan."

"Let us hear some of it," we asked.

At first he objected, on account of its being yet in an unfinished state, but after some little persuasion complied, on receiving faithful assurances that no notes would be taken. Then the recital commenced. If the verses were Byron's, he certainly had not improved as a poet in the spirit world. But probably his unhappy surroundings, being only a stage beyond the fires of Purgatory, were uncongenial to his poetic fancy. The verses proceeded to tell how Don Juan, after having sown his wild oats, amended his ways, and became a very good sort of man ; how he got married to a loving wife, and had "olive branches" growing up around him. I am able to recall a single stanza, being Juan's soliloquy on the birth of his third son, and I trust the spirit of the poet will forgive me for making it public. Here it is—

" What strange emotions fill the breasts of men
    On finding first they have become papas ?
A secret pride they feel, which ne'er again
    Throughout their lives is reinspired, because
When baby number two appears, alas !
    The novelty is gone, and the event
Recurring oft, a baby's looked on as
    Some trifle periodically sent—
    As much a thing, of course, as Whitsunday or Lent."

When Fitznoble was called to consciousness by Bowers waving his handkerchief in his face, he professed to be unconscious of what had taken place, and asked Bowers to give him an account of it.

"Is there no means of calling up a visible spirit?" asked Marsden.

"I should like to see a veritable spirit," said Sharp.

"I do not think spirits can make themselves visible to our material eyes," replied our host.

"But according to your own reasoning, Mr Fitznoble, there is nothing impossible if you have faith," I rejoined. "And it is quite as consistent with a belief in supernaturalism for a spirit to take a bodily shape and appear before our eyes, as it is for a spirit to rap upon a table. I do not see why a spirit should not be as able to make us see as to make us hear him. He cannot do the one or the other without becoming materialized."

"So far you are right," said Fitznoble, "but I fancy it is much more difficult for a spirit to make himself visible than to make himself audible. No doubt by the exercise of sufficient faith we could call up visible spirits, but I doubt if so much faith exists."

"Let us try," said Bowers. "We have been very successful to-night already."

"By all means let us try," said we all.

Fitznoble did not enter heartily into the project, but all the others being desirous of putting it to the test, he agreed to give it a trial.

"We should call up the spirit of some one whom we knew," said Sharp.

"Suppose we ask the spirit of Old Harley to appear, and get the mystery connected with his death cleared up," suggested Marsden.

I noticed Fitznoble give a slight start, and keenly eye Marsden as he asked—"Who was this Old Harley?"

Marsden explained that Josiah Harley, or Old Harley, as he

was commonly called, was a wealthy city merchant who had been murdered and robbed of a large sum of money some ten years ago, and that although every effort was made to discover the culprit or culprits, all remained shrouded in mystery till this hour.

"I remember Old Harley well," said Bowers.

"And so do I, and think we should make the trial," I said.

"Well, friends," said our host, "although I must confess I do not expect any result, I willingly give your suggestion a trial. Each of you repeat after me—'Spirit of Josiah Harley appear.'"

"Spirit of Josiah Harley appear," echoed a chorus of voices.

A moment of deathless stillness ensued, then a slight rustling outside the door was audible. The next instant the door was opened, and, oh, horror, the well-known form of Josiah Harley stood before us!

The consternation was intense, and all of us started to our feet. Fitznoble turned deadly pale, and staggered towards the wall, while Bowers' legs became so weak under him that he sank down into a chair.

I must confess I was myself a good deal startled. Sharp alone seemed to retain his self-possession, and, addressing the apparition, asked—"Is it the spirit of Josiah Harley which appears before us?"

"It is, and if you have any questions to ask be quick, for my time is short."

That voice, although sepulchral in tone, was Old Harley's, I could have sworn.

"How were you deprived of life?" asked Sharp, coming to the point at once.

"I was murdered."

"And by whom?"

"That villain, Tom Scriven, there," said the apparition, pointing towards Fitznoble.

"It's a lie," exclaimed the latter in a paroxysm of terror. "It was not I who killed you, but Bill Tomlies."

"And I arrest you for being his accomplice," said the apparition, throwing aside his disguise, and revealing the well-known face of Morrison, the detective. Then stepping up to Fitznoble, he placed a pair of handcuffs upon his wrists. To this operation he offered no resistance; he seemed to have completely broken down, and looked the picture of despair. The whole performance was so sudden and overpowering that for a time I doubted if I gazed upon reality, or if it was not all a frightful hallucination.

I noticed Bowers gazing upon Fitznoble with a most perturbed expression.

"In heaven's name what's the meaning of all this?" he asked the detective.

"Simply that you see before you Tom Scriven *alias* Geoffrey Fitznoble, who is arrested for complicity in the murder of Josiah Harley," answered Morrison.

Presently two policemen entered.

"Well, Tom, my prodigal son, once more you return to your father's care," said Morrison to the prisoner, as he handed him over to the policemen.

"Yes, the tables are once more turned," replied Fitznoble, with a look full of meaning.

"This is what I call table-turning with a vengeance," said Morrison, greeting the company with a twinkle of his keen eye as the policemen passed out with their prisoner.

"Some of you gentlemen are no doubt considerably astonished at the strange scene you have just witnessed, and I owe you some explanation," said Morrison, addressing us all. "It is only three weeks since I set eyes upon the so-called Mr Fitznoble. Something in his appearance led me to conclude that I had seen him before, which set me a pondering as to when and under what circumstances we had met. Consulting some private memoranda, I came upon the names of Tom Scriven and Bill Tomlies, two desperadoes who had on several occasions passed through my hands, when all at once the identity of Fitznoble and the former flashed vividly across my mind. Another rather minute inspection of him, which I was fortunate enough to obtain, confirmed my suspicions. Notwithstanding the outward polish he had put on, and the great change in his appearance, I failed not to recognise my old jail bird, Tom Scriven. Now, I had all along believed that he and his 'pal,' Bill Tomlies, were the murderers and robbers of Old Harley, and long and diligently did I search for them after that event. I was aware that they had been prowling in the neighbourhood anterior thereto, but after the murder they both mysteriously disappeared, and no clue to their whereabouts could be obtained.

"After being fully convinced that I had once more set eyes upon my man, the great difficulty which presented itself was how to bring the crime home to him. To openly accuse him of murder and robbery would have been foolishness, as the evidence against him had, with the lapse of years, become very meagre. For the past fortnight I have watched his movements very closely, and became aware that he held spiritualistic *seances*. I also discovered that my friends here, Sharp and Marsden, were intimate with him. To them I divulged my discovery, and between us we concocted the plot which has so successfully been carried out to-night. By 'tipping' the waiter, which was no difficult matter, these apartments having only been hired for a limited time by the prisoner, I gained an entrance into the house. You know the rest, gentlemen, and are witnesses to the confession made by the prisoner. I trust the 'ghost' scene has not seriously affected any one's nerves, but from the consternation depicted upon some faces I flatter myself that I played the part well."

"No Hamlet's ghost ever did better," said Sharp, an opinion in which we all concurred.

Poor Bowers was quite morose and taciturn as we walked home that night.

"What do you think of your gentlemanly friend now?" I asked him.

" Hold your tongue, Gibson. I haven't had time to think yet," he blurted out.

" And your shares in the Prawnbrook Gold Mining Co., what about them ?"

" Gibson, don't vex me further. Shares be blowed ! Confound the fellow !"

Tom Scriven, *alias* Geoffrey Fitznoble, was found guilty, on his own confession, of being an accomplice in the murder of Josiah Harley, and expiated his crime on the scaffold. At the time of his arrest he had a gigantic fraud in train, aided by accomplices in Australia, which was fortunately nipped in the bud, although quite a number of persons, including my friend Bowers, had already been victimised.

My brother William turned up in quite another part of the world to that indicated by the spurious spirit of my father. It was evidently an attempt on Fitznoble's part to swindle me out of a hundred pounds, for, had I been foolish enough to send the money to the address in Australia, I have no doubt it would have fallen into the hands of his accomplices.

THE HAUNTED WOOD.

Chapter I.

The Reverend Timothy Taylor, parish minister of Stony-ground, was seated in his study intently seasoning a favourite meerschaum pipe, when Mary, his aged housekeeper, rapped at the door to inform him that a "crood o' men" wanted to see him.

"A crowd, Mary!" exclaimed the minister in surprise. "Do you know who they are?"

"Weel, sir, there's Rory Macfadyan, the tailor; Johnnie Drybanes, the beadle; an' Sandy Macalister, the smith, an' a wheen mair whase names I dinna ken."

"Dear me, what can be the matter? I suppose, Mary, you'd better ask them to come and speak to me here."

"Yes, sir," said Mary, who in a few minutes ushered some half-dozen visitors into the minister's sanctum.

"It's an awfu' affair this," blurted out Macalister as soon as they had entered.

"Yes, sir," added Drybones. "The wid oot by is fairly hunted. The maist inhuman soonds ha'e been heard for some nichts back that ever mortal soul listened tae."

"Ay, an' sic sichts ha'e been seen, tae, as wad mak' the bluid spurdle in yer veins," said one of the others. "Burds without wings fleein' amang the trees, an' warlocks an' blue lowes a' gaen helter-skelter through ane anither."

" Dear me !" said the minister, raising his spectacles to his forehead, "this is indeed serious—most extraordinary."

. "Yes," said Macalister, " an' we've come here the nicht tae ask ye tae gae alang wi's tae the wid, wi' yer big bible below yer oxter, tae skeer awa' the infernal deemans."

" My friends," replied the minister, " resist the devil and he will flee from you."

" Very true, sir," said Macfadyan, " an' that's just what we want tae dae. Wi' a holy man lek yersel' an' a holy buik below yer airm, we want tae mairch for'ard an' defy the fiery darts o' the evil one."

" I appreciate your sentiments," replied the minister, " but really your request is quite inconsistent with the ordinary routine of ministerial duties. As an abstract invisible personification, we are accustomed to combat the evil one in the pulpit, but to meet him in the wood, howling like a beast of prey, does not enter into our theology. In fact, my friends, were I to go out with you to-night, as you suggest, I would be committing such a breach of professional etiquette as would seriously damage my reputation with my brethren."

" An' what are we ga'en tae dae, then ?" demanded Drybones.

" Do—why, under the circumstances, and seeing that the enemy of mankind has descended to this mode of revealing himself in our midst, I would fight him with his own weapons. Go and get Fairlie and M'Nab with their bagpipes, and Soutar with his drum, and march through the wood playing something spirit-stirring. This, I think, will be far more effectual than any services I can render you."

The minister's advice was considered excellent by the whole company. Their countenances brightened up, and Rory Macfadyan could not help slapping his thigh as he exclaimed, " The verra fiddle ! Losh me, wha wad ha'e thocht o' sic a thing, if the minister hedna put it in oor heids ? Come awa', men, an' get the pipes an' drum tae skeer awa' the deemans— it'll shune be growin' dark."

" Come back to-morrow and let me know the result," said the minister, as he saw his visitors to the door.

Thereafter he returned to his study, relit his pipe, and as he sat watching the smoke curl upwards to the ceiling, an amused smile once or twice overspread his features.

CHAPTER II.

The meeting was a clandestine one.   Adolphus St Clair was a young fellow of prepossessing appearance and aristocratic bearing, but perfectly unknown in the district over which the Reverend Timothy Taylor had the spiritual oversight.   He had been staying for over a fortnight in the " Royal," ostensibly spending his holidays, and devoting most of his time to trout fishing and driving.

Evangeline, the minister's only daughter, was a sprightly girl of eighteen.   She had lost her mother when a baby, and had been brought up under the care of Mary, her father's house-keeper, over whom she had now obtained complete mastery, and as the paternal authority of her father was not of the firmest kind, Evangeline naturally grew up a good deal self-willed, and roamed about pretty much at her own sweet will.

When out walking one afternoon she happened to twist her foot in crossing a stile, and Adolphus, who was driving past at the time, noticing the mishap, offered her a seat beside him. She accepted, and this was their first introduction.   Several times thereafter they met accidentally and chatted together. At length Adolphus asked her to meet him on this occasion in Sornie Wood, which was a favourite resort of hers.   She had some qualms of conscience, but having consented, she kept her promise.

They sauntered through the wood for some distance, Evangeline chatting of the village choir and the village gossips, and bemoaning the monotony of her existence; Adolphus waxing eloquent on the pleasures of travelling and the gay life of the upper circles. Arriving at a rustic seat they sat down.

"The villagers of Stonyground are an ignorant, superstitious lot," remarked Adolphus. "They have got it into their heads that some place hereabout is haunted."

"Haunted by what?" asked Evangeline.

"By the devil and his emissaries," as they put it.

"Oh, wisht—if you speak about *him* he will appear."

"So we were taught in childhood," said Adolphus.

The stillness of the summer evening was at that instant rudely disturbed by a series of unearthly sounds, which reverberated through the woods.

"Oh, dear, what can it be?" gasped Evangeline, as with trembling hands she clutched the quivering frame of Adolphus.

"I—I—don't—know."

"Oh, Mr St Clair, you're trembling—it must be something awful. Come, and let us away; let us fly from this spot."

"I—I—ca—can't rise—oh—oh!" groaned Adolphus, as once more the same frightful sounds pealed forth. Clutching frantically at the shawl which enveloped Evangeline's shoulders, he endeavoured to cover his head in its folds. She tried to draw it from him, but Adolphus, now stretched prostrate upon the seat, held it as in a death grip. Evangeline's blood boiled, and unclasping the shawl from her bosom she started to her feet. She was no longer terrified, and at that particular moment could have faced a whole regiment of hobgoblins.

"Coward!" she shrieked, "you're a brave lord of creation—a champion protector for a lady!"

Adolphus made no reply. He was either dead or in a swoon. She cared not. With heaving bosom and head erect, she walked disdainfully from his side.

F

Chapter III.

It was growing rather dark by the time Evangeline emerged from the wood and reached the road which led to her home. She had still nearly two miles to walk, and bounded along at a good pace. After a time, however, her step became slower.

"What if Mr St Clair should be dead?" she began to ask herself. "I don't care—he's only a coward," her fiery temper prompted her to reply. "But he's got my shawl, and what will people think if they find him and it together? Oh, dear, what *will* they think?" she soliloquised, in much mental perturbation.

"And what a fright I am, with my white dress and nothing to cover my bare arms and neck, and—oh, if anybody should meet me! How shall I ever get home, and what will I say to Mary?" she continued in soliloquy. Her courage seemed to be breaking down, and her footsteps began to falter. Suddenly she came to a dead halt, for she distinctly heard the sound of bagpipes and drum approaching.

She stood riveted to the spot in an agony of terror. Her reasoning faculties were for the time being overclouded. She attempted to return to the wood, but her feet refused to obey the promptings of her inclination.

Staggering to the roadside, she sat down upon a grassy slope thoroughly overpowered. Nearer and nearer the music approached her. At length she heard the tramp of feet, and could distinguish, amid the darkness, what seemed to be a crowd of people marching forward. She knew there was an opening in the hedge on the opposite side of the road, and considered, if she got through there, she might remain unobserved until the people had passed. She made a desperate effort to rise, and, having regained her feet, staggered frantically across the road, throwing out her arms to preserve her equilibrium. Having passed through the hedge, she again sunk down exhausted on the grass. No further sounds of music or footsteps being audible, she concluded it must have been some ploughmen out for a walk, and that they had returned back. Getting somewhat composed, she began to consider what she would do. To go back to the wood or remain where she was would be madness. She must get home at all hazards, she concluded. Summoning once more her resolute courage, she rose to her feet and moved homewards, her footsteps gathering firmness as she saw no danger in her path. Only once did her courage nearly fail her. She imagined she saw a number of crouching figures behind the hedge at one portion of the road. Her heart was in her mouth again, but closing her eyes she darted past, and at length reached the manse in safety.

"Oh, Miss Evangeline, whare ha'e ye been till sic a time o' nicht?" was old Mary's greeting on her entrance.

"Oh, dear Mary, I'm glad I'm home," said Evangeline, sinking down into a chair.

"An' sae am I—but, mercy me, what's adae wi' ye? Whare's yer shawl—yer braw, new, blue shawl? Sic a fricht ye are wi' that white frock, an' yer neck a' bare; ye look like a ghaist."

"I've got a terrible fright, Mary, but I'll tell you about it again. Has papa been enquiring for me?"

"Ay has he, an' he's waitin' on ye for worship."

"Oh, Mary, I've got a bad headache, and wish I could get straight to bed. You might ask papa to excuse me to-night."

"Gae awa' to yer bed than, ma bonnie lassie, an' I'll tell the minister ye ha'e a heidache. Oh, ma bairn, ma bairn, may the Lord tak' care o' ye, an' keep ye in the hollow o' His haun'."

'CHAPTER IV.

Stonyground village was astir very early next morning—in fact a number of the inhabitants had never been to bed. As the morning advanced, the gossips might be seen in groups of three and four at every corner, eagerly discussing the events of the previous night.

When Rory Macfadyan made his appearance outside he was instantly surrounded by a gaping crowd.

"An' hoo did ye get on last night, Rory?" was the question on every lip.

"Och, och," replied Rory, "we didna get on ava. It's nae use fechtin' agin' the deevil. Ye micht as weel be a cat withoot claws climmin' up a gless mountain."

"We've hed an awfu' nicht o't," said Johnnie Drybones, putting in an appearance. "The deemans wis fleein' aboot the wid in a' directions, in the shape o' elephants an' bulls an' crokodiles, in thousan's an' hunners, an' mair."

"An' we saw the emage o' a man wi' his heid in a pock," said another. "It maun ha'e been Auld Nick himsel' tryin' tae hide his horns. Johnnie M'Tavish fired a pistol at him, but the barrel burst, an' Johnnie's thoom was blawn clean aff. Ay, it maun ha'e been the deil himsel'."

"Och, yiss," said Alister M'Fletcher, from the Isle of Skye, "an' her nainsell wis ta shoot him twice as fast as wan, put ta blastit tree av a root wis fixt her feet, an' she'll pe lost her poot."

"Nane o' yer braggin' noo, Alister," said Rory Macfadyan. "Ye wis the first tae rin ahint the hedge whan ye saw the white ghaist on the road."

"Och, ay, an' ferry glad wis more ta ran. She'll plaze awa' at ta hee ghost an' no pe feirt, put she'll no can face ta she ghost. An' ye wis jist as worss as more than wan yersel', Rory Macfadyan, ye wis," replied M'Fletcher, testily.

"She's been murdered, I'se warrant ye," remarked another, "for as she gaed alang ye could see her wringin' her hands an' lookin' sae cauld an' gruesome lek. I'se warrant she's been murdered, an' buried somewhere aboot the wid, an' she'll no rest till her body's fund an' decently buried."

As the morning further advanced a new sensation burst upon the village gossips. It had leaked out that the "braw" young gentleman who had been residing in the hotel for some time had failed to return last night, and no trace of him could be found.

"Lod's a mercy! will last nicht's ongain's ha'e onything tae dae wi't?"

"I doot—I doot," replied one old crone to another, with an ominous shake of the head.

"But he wasna lek ane 'at wad ha'e dealin's wi' the deil."

"Ye dinna ken, 'oman. Sautan can mak' himsel' an' his emissaries appear the brawest gentleman 'at ever stappit in shoe leather."

"Aweel, aweel, gudeness be praised, we've aye been proteckit yet frae the witches an' warlocks, an' the loubrags an' langnebbit creeters 'at gang aboot the shore."

"Ye're richt, Jaunet, an' it's nane o' our business tae inquire intae things 'at dinna concern us, but I wad lek to ken what the minister 'ill dae whan he hears a' aboot it."

"Oo ay, he'll need tae dae something."

CHAPTER V.

Early in the forenoon the Reverend Timothy Taylor was visited by a trio, consisting of Sandy Macalister, Rory Macfadyan, and Johnnie Drybones, who proceeded to inform him of what had occurred the previous evening.

"We mairched oot as ye advised us, sir," proceeded Rory Macfadyan, "wi' the pipes an' drum—a crood about twenty or thirty o's, airmed wi' sticks an stanes an' twa pistols, besides ither weapons o' manslachter, an' fully determined tae mak' short wark o' whatever cam' in our way. We hedna proceeded

mair than hauf roads tae the wid whan a fearfu' spectacle
brocht us tae a stan'still, an' took the breath frae the pipers. A
woman dressed in white stood on the road in front o's, wavin'
her han's like some dementit creeter. No tae frichten her
awa', we slippit ahint the hedge an' waited tae see what she wad
dae, but in a moment she disappeared. We waited an' waited,
confabin' amang oorsel's aboot mairchin' forrad, whan we again
saw her advancin' on the road towards us. We a' skulkit doon,
no' tae frichten her, ye ken, and saw her stappin' past withoot
a steek o' claes 'cept her goon, an' she wis sae thin ye could
'maist see through her."

"Yes," said Johnnie Drybones, "we a' seed her quite
distinkly. She wis dressed in white, wi' bare airms, an' the
bluid was rinnin' doon her shirt sleeves frae a gash in her
throt."

"Most amazing!" exclaimed the minister; "and did you
hear any strange sounds?"

"No," replied Macalister, "but afore that we met Dugald
Morrison comin' hame frae his wark, an' he tell't us that, juist
afore he passed the wid, he heerd an awfu' yellin', lek as if a'
the deemans o' the bottomless pit were soondin' the last day.
It made him doited an' dumfoonded, an' whan he looked up he
saw the taps o' the trees a' movin' lek leevin' creeters."

"Aifter the white ghaist wis past we mairched intae the
wid," continued Macfadyan, "the pipes an' drum playin' a' the
time, an' we hedna gane far whan the deemans, in the shape o'
birds and beasts and reptiles, began whirrin' an' fleein' aboot in
a' directions, an' screechin' an' yellin' lek mad."

"An' we saw the figger o' a man," said Macalister, "aboot
aicht or twal feet high. Johnnie M'Tavish hed his pistol loaded
wi' a bent saxpence an' fired at 'im, but the barrel burst an'
ca'd aff his thoom. Syne the figger disappeared in a blue
lowe."

"An' there wis an awfu' smell o' brimstane," said Drybones.

"Efter this there cam' a beast aboot twice the size o' an

elephant," said Macfadyan, "rushin' through the wid at a tremendous gallop, an' drivin' everything afore him. His e'en glared in the dark lek twa lanterns, an' he roared lek an allegator."

"Ay, there wis mair than a hunner beasts a'thegither," said Drybones, "some shaped lek lions an' teegars, an' some lek bulls an' coos, but four times as big, maist fearsome tae behold."

"We keepit the pipers an' drummer daein' their very utmost, but it wis a' in vain—it only made the deemans mair furious," said Macfadyan, " sae we held a cooncil o' war, an' cam' tae the conclusion that flesh an' bluid cudna cope wi' the prince o' darkness, an' sae we cam' awa' hame."

"Well, my friends," said the minister, after listening to the various statements, "your experiences have certainly been most extraordinary, and quite beyond the range of my comprehension. I consider it my duty to try and solve the mystery, and in half an hour intend to be on my way to Sornie Wood. Rest assured I will leave no stone unturned to get to the bottom of this extraordinary matter."

And thus the interview ended.

Chapter VI.

The Reverend Timothy Taylor was wending his way through Sornie Wood, minutely looking for footprints on the footpaths and elsewhere, or other traces of the strange events said to have occurred there the previous evening. Ere he had proceeded far he discovered footprints in great variety, both of man and of beast. There were prints of "tackety" boots, and there were cloven footprints! It at once occurred to him that the Evil One was represented as being cloven-footed, but he didn't believe in this nonsense, and on examination he discovered that the animals which left these footprints were four-footed, and he was not aware of his Satanic Majesty being ever represented as the possessor of more than two feet. While engaged in this contemplation he was accosted by Mr Jackson, the neighbouring farmer.

"What in the name of wonder is the meaning of these ongoings here last night, Mr Taylor?"

"The very thing I'm desirous of knowing, Mr Jackson."

"Why, if my information be correct, it was by your instructions the band of ruffians came here last night with pipers and drummer, and kicked up such a fearful din that they frightened my cattle out of their enclosure, and sent them chasing all over the wood. Some of the beasts are seriously damaged, and a young bull is yet amissing. I don't know how to characterise such an action on your part, Mr Taylor."

"I'm indeed sorry to hear this," said the minister, greatly perturbed. "The fact is, a number of my people came to me with strange stories about the wood being haunted, and, having no belief in such things, I proposed in a joke that they should go out with pipe and drum to scare away the hobgoblins. They, however, took the advice seriously, and acted upon it. Most certainly, if I had the faintest idea that it would result in inflicting injury or annoyance on any one, I should never have suggested the thing, even in a joke. I'm extremely sorry, Mr Jackson, but trust your loss may not be serious after all."

"Let us hope so," said Mr Jackson, considerably mollified. "By the way," he continued, "I got a lady's blue shawl stuck on the horns of one of my cows this morning. How would you account for this?"

"Lady's blue shawl! very extraordinary. Possibly it might have been left by some one in the wood, and tossed by the cow until it got entangled among her horns."

"That, I think, is a very reasonable explanation. I have kept the shawl, and will be glad to send it along to the manse

—it may lead to some discovery, and can be more readily seen in your possession than in mine."

"Just send it along, Mr Jackson, and I will try and ascertain to whom it belonged. But what about the unusual sounds said to have been heard here at nights? Can you enlighten me on this matter?"

"Captain Clayton's youngster, Bill, can, at all events."

"And what does it amount to, Mr Jackson?"

"Well, the fact is, the youngster discovered somewhere in the house, an old fog-horn which his father used when at sea, and he considered it fine amusement to get it outside of an evening and make it squeal."

"So this explains the unearthly sounds said to have been heard."

"I expect so, and they won't be heard again, I assure you, for I saw Captain Clayton smash the fog-horn this morning."

"And the supposed unearthly visitants seen here last night have been your cattle, I have no doubt, Mr Jackson. Really, the whole thing would be a good joke, were it not for the damage and annoyance you have sustained."

Bidding each other "good afternoon," the farmer went in search of his bull, and the minister retraced his footsteps to the manse.

CHAPTER VII.

Evangeline confided to old Mary her whole relationship with Mr St Clair, and the circumstances under which she left him in the wood. She felt anxious to unburden her heart to her father, but for the time being Mary dissuaded her from doing so.

"Na, na, Miss Evangeline, it wad only vex the minister tae hear o't," said Mary. "An' it striks me the scoondril 'll never be heerd o' mair. I'm a'most sure it's been the deevil in human

form 'at's been tryin' tae tempt ma bairn, an' the Lord be
thankit that ye've been preserved frae his clutches."

Mary had heard most of the gossip about the incidents of
the previous evening, and had formed her own conclusions
thereon. "I'm mista'en," she said, "if it's no' him 'at Johnnie
M'Tavish fired the bent saxpence at, an' it shows him tae ha'e
been the deevil, whan he made the pistol burst an' blaw off
Johnnie's thoom. An' what for did he want ta'e cover his heid
in yer shawl, but tae hide his horns. I'se warrant he kent 'at
the Almichty was proteckin' ye, an' mebbie takin' the glamour
frae yer e'en, sae that ye wad see wha ye wis speakin' tae. Na,
na ; dinna say a word aboot it tae the minister."

Poor Evangeline's mind was ill at ease. She could not
entertain Mary's theory, yet she halted in what her inner
consciousness told her was her duty—namely, to make a clean
breast to her father, and, for the time being, she acted on Mary's
advice. But when a parcel arrived from Mr Jackson containing
her blue shawl, all soiled and torn, she felt that a crisis had
arrived, and that she must divulge everything.

"You sometimes wore a blue shawl?" said her father.

"Yes, and that's it, papa," she answered, tremblingly.

The minister gazed at her with an anxious, troubled expression while she related all the circumstances with which we are
already acquainted. It is needless to say that Mr Taylor was
greatly pained at his daughter's disclosure, and gave her a
severe reprimand   But the matter did not end here. A public,
or rather police, enquiry was instituted regarding Mr St Clair's
disappearance. The proprietor of the "Royal" had a little bill
against him, and was anxious to ascertain his present address.
So was Mr Sloann, the banker, who had obliged him by cashing
a cheque on London, which was returned dishonoured.
Evangeline was cross-questioned by sundry police officials, and
the scandalmongers of the village for a time made great capital
of the incident, as it was retailed from the one to the other
with the usual head-shakings and additions of " legs and arms."

Evangeline was paying dearly for her first false step. The mental anguish she endured was known only to herself. She certainly had no personal regard for Mr St Clair, but she had the misfortune to be last in his company on that eventful evening when he disappeared, and she left him under circumstances so peculiar that the uncertainty of his fate preyed severely on her mind.

It was a salutary if severe lesson to her, which in after life she never forgot.

Chapter VIII.

Months had passed, and one morning while Mr Taylor was reading his Edinburgh paper, he came upon a paragraph which appeared to agitate him greatly. Having read it, he rang the bell for Evangeline, who entered, looking much paler than she did months ago.

"Eva, my girl, the mystery of St Clair is at last solved; listen," said he, as he read the following :—

"Smart Capture of a Notorious Swindler.—On Wednesday last, detectives B—— and D—— succeeded in capturing the notorious Rosa Mayflower, who more than a year ago swindled numerous shopkeepers in C——. She disappeared so suddenly at the time, that it was generally supposed she had succeeded in escaping out of the country. It now appears, however, that in the interval she has been doing a much larger stroke of business in a new *rôle*. When arrested she was dressed as a stylish young gentleman, and from cards found in her possession had evidently been passing under the name of Mr Adolphus St Clair. The *modus operandi* of the *quasi* young gentleman was to take up his residence at the principal hotel of the place he happened to visit, representing himself to be a scion of some aristocratic family, who had come to enjoy a few weeks' holidays. He usually made a small cash deposit with the hotel-keeper to disarm suspicion, and then, in the course of a week or so, managed to introduce himself to the aristocracy of the district; and, possessed of quite a winning manner and wonderful conversational powers, he managed to get on such terms of intimacy with a number, as to ask and receive cash advances. All of a sudden he would disappear, leaving everyone unpaid of course. It is said he made love to a number of young ladies of good position, and that many of them are at this moment pining in secret for news of him. It may not be agreeable to them, but it is as well they should know that their quondam lover is a woman."

"I'm so glad, papa," exclaimed Evangeline, when her father had concluded.

"Yes, it lifts a load from off your heart, I have no doubt, Evangeline. And it will help to stop the tongues of scandal which have of late been so busily endeavouring to blacken your fair fame. It has been a good and timely lesson to you, girl, and I am sure you will profit by it in the future."

"And the blue shawl—may I have it now, papa?"

"I think you should burn it."

"Just what I would like to do, papa. I'll take it to the kitchen, and I'm sure it will delight the eyes of Mary and myself to see it disappear in smoke."

"Do as you propose, girl," said her father, handing her the shawl, which lay wrapped in paper on his table.

There was joy in the kitchen when Mary learned the news, and as they both gazed upon the shawl consuming away in the blazing fire.

"And that's the last of the blue shawl," said Evangeline, as she stirred its black embers among the glowing coals."

"An' may the scandals an' heartburnin's it hes occasioned sae be burnt up," said Mary.

"Amen!" echoed Evangeline.

OLD BLOGG.

CHAPTER I.

JIM STUBBS lived with his aunt, Miss Matilda Stubbs, a fresh-looking lady, although much past the meridian of life. Bob Snooks, the milkman, declared he had seen a thousand worse-looking married women; and John Harrows, her next-door neighbour, whispered confidentially to one of his bosom friends that if ever he should happen to become a *widow man*, he would offer Miss Stubbs the vacancy.

Her nephew, Jim, was left an orphan at an early age, and she, in obedience to his father's dying request, took him under her charge, and reared him up with all a mother's tender care. Jim was a delicate and somewhat impulsive youth. He once mistook a clothes' pole for a ghost, and some one told him he was endowed with a very vivid imagination, and ought to be a poet. Acting on the suggestion, he began to write verses, and in process of time verse writing became quite a mania with him. He passed through all its various developments—first, the consumptive weeping and wailing stage, when he wrote poems commencing, " Oh, well may grief my heart invade," " Oh, death bring back the one I loved," and such like; then the incipient-romantic stage, when he wrote of love and moonshine, and dedicated poems to imaginary Janes and Marys; then the mystical-nonsensical stage, when he wrote pieces which neither himself nor anyone else could understand. These he considered his masterpieces, and frequently enclosed them to editors of monthly and other magazines. Although they never appeared in print, Jim consoled himself with the reflection that he was probably a poet of too high an order to be appreciated in his own generation, and continued writing. He had a great ambition to be connected with the press, and after being two years in the grocery trade, he gave it up, and went to serve his apprenticeship as compositor, in the office of the *Blownfield Chronicle.*

Jim's sweetheart was Miss Fanny Fairgirl. He met her at a grocer's festival, fell in love with her at first sight, and had the satisfaction to find that his passion was reciprocated. He knew nothing about the girl or her family relations, and never enquired—simply asked her to meet him at a certain hour at a certain place on the following evening, which she did, and they walked out together.

"My love is not like that of the common herd of humanity," he said to her; "the flame which illumines my breast is seven-fold intenser than the half-choked flickering thing which the world calls love. My love is deeper than the sea, stronger than an elephant, and swifter than the Scotch express. It is a poet's love—the intense burnings of an inspired soul."

Fanny, unfortunately, was not endowed with much poetic fancy. Her education likewise had been somewhat neglected, and she listened to Jim's flow of rhetoric more in wonder than appreciation. His language was often beyond her comprehension, from which she concluded that he must be very learned.

When he said to her, "You are my adored one, Fanny—my guardian angel—the consolation and pride of my life," she blushingly replied—

"You're a fine *cracker*."

And his pictures of the future acted on her like a spell.

"I see the time approaching," he said, "when my name shall be famous in the world. Like a second Shakespeare, I shall waft the pinions of poesy amid the breezes of time. Then you and I shall live together in one of the fairest palaces of creation. Kings, courtiers, poets, and philosophers shall be our daily visitors—they shall court our society and do us homage. All the glory and fame which the world can shower upon us will be ours. I feel the power within me, which I have but to exert, to accomplish all this, and for your sake, Fanny, I will press onward and upward, and throw down every barrier."

Fanny began to have dreams of future greatness, too, and when her lover told her he was connected with the press, she regarded him with additional awe.

After completing their walk, Jim of course insisted upon seeing his loved one to her father's door, and this occasioned a small piece of deception being practised upon him by Fanny. The truth was, her parents were poor working people, who lived in a small house in Sooty Lane, and she could not brook the idea of permitting her new found, gentlemanly lover to see the mean-looking place. She therefore adopted the expedient of stopping at a rather nice-looking house in a fashionable street, and informed her lover that she was *landed*. Bidding him " Good-night," she said she would enter by the back door and not disturb " Pa." Then waiting in the lane, which separated her pretended house from that adjoining, until she heard her lover's footsteps die away in the distance, she slipped home to her abode in Sooty Lane.

One false step leads to another, and as night after night Jim escorted his lady love to No. 9 Rosebud Street, the house with which she had deceived him, he upon one occasion insisted on seeing the back premises, and in pain and trepidation she was forced to point to a window as being that of her bedroom.

" I must write a poem on that window," said Jim—" that dear entrancing window, from which my Fanny looks out like a cherub as each morning she rises from her sweet and refreshing sleep."

One morning not long thereafter found Jim in ecstacies of delight. The editor of the *Blownfield Chronicle* had accepted and published one of his poems. Yes, his eyes lighted upon his own verses " To Fanny," with his initials J. S. actually in print. He felt as if all his bright dreams of the future were now within his grasp. Spreading out the newspaper, he gazed proudly upon the verses, and read them over three or four times. That poem, he considered, would be read by twenty thousand individuals, and soon he would be famous.

His day's work being over, he hurried home to tea, and then away, newspaper in pocket, to acquaint Fanny of his success, and let her see in print those verses he had so oft repeated to her before. But she was not at the accustomed meeting-place, and his heart sank within him. He waited anxiously for a considerable time, but she came not. "I must see her to-night," he muttered determinedly, " even though I should call at her father's house—and why should I not? Am I not now an acknowledged poet? I will go and place my credentials within her father's hand," and, having thus determined, he walked away towards No. 9 Rosebud Street.

CHAPTER II.

No. 9 Rosebud Street was the residence of Mr Tobias Blogg, a retired shipmaster, a teacher of navigation, and a crusty old bachelor. His antipathy to the fair sex was of long standing—indeed, some asserted that he was a born woman hater. But this is scarcely credible—more likely he had been jilted by some coquettish fair one, and had taken it so deeply to heart that ever afterwards he swore enmity to the sex at large.

"Old Blogg," as he was called, was well known in the neighbourhood in which he resided, and was one of those individuals whom once seen is always remembered. He was a man of great force of character, possessed of a big, bullet-shaped head devoid of hair, except a slight fringe behind extending from ear to ear. He evidently had an antipathy to hair, for he was close shaved on cheek, lip, and chin. But what rendered his identity all the more unmistakable was his wooden leg. How or when he lost his leg nobody ever thought of enquiring. Old Blogg's timber stump had become such a familiar object to the eyes of the neighbourhood, as he hopped out and in, that it came to be regarded as quite a natural appendage—as much a part of himself as his head or arms were.

For a long period his housekeeper and cook was an old man who had been cook on board ship, but he having died, Blogg was very reluctantly compelled to take a female into his house. His new housekeeper was a woman of uncertain age, and to say that she had ever been beautiful would be the sheerest flattery, but after accidentally losing her left eye, and having to wear a black patch over it, her personal appearance was completely marred.

On Blogg's first interview with her he enquired—

" What's your name ?"

" Betsy Jane, sir," she answered.

" Humph, never let me hear you say it again," said he, angrily ; " abominable name ; I'll call you John—recollect—John ! And now, John, if you're to remain in my employment you must never let me hear you speak. If you have anything to say, convey it by signs or write it on a slate. Can you write ?"

" No, sir."

" Humph, don't ' sir' me, and never say ' no.' When you require to say ' no,' shake your head and keep your mouth shut. As you can't write, whatever you have to say must be said in a whisper. D'you understand me, John ?"

" Uphim."

" Uphim be jiggered ! Never say ' uphim.' When you require to say ' yes,' nod your head."

Betsy Jane nodded her head and descended to the kitchen, this being the longest interview they ever had together. She displayed considerable aptitude to suit herself to his eccentrici-

G

ties, and as she had no followers the two got on fairly well together.

For a couple of hours daily old Blogg gave lessons in navigation to young men who contemplated a seafaring life, and notwithstanding his idiosyncracics, he was highly spoken of as a teacher. But probably what pleased these youths better than their navigation lessons, were the short lectures on every conceivable subject, to which Blogg frequently treated them. His terse language and peculiar ideas lent a charm to his lectures, which were always appreciated, if his sentiments were not always endorsed.

" Early to bed and early to rise" was a maxim which old Blogg always put into practice. He had just fallen over into his first comfortable sleep, when he was awakened by some noise at his window. After listening for several minutes he heard three distinct taps upon the window pane, and a slight shuffling of feet upon the gravel path.

He was no coward, but as he lay in bed with only a leg and a half, he felt that, in that condition, he could offer but poor resistance to an attack by a burglar. Hence he decided to buckle on his stump and get partially dressed before interrogating his unknown visitor. While busy with these operations other three taps, louder than before, sounded upon the pane, followed by a voice which pronounced in a loudish whisper—

" Fanny."

Blogg, who detested female names as he did females themselves, was upon the point of seizing his double-barrelled gun and rushing out upon the intruder.

" Is that you, Fanny dear ?" asked the voice outside.

Suddenly an idea seemed to strike old Blogg. With an inaudible chuckle he approached the window and whispered—

" Yes."

" I have something particular to show you," said Jim Stubbs, for it was he.

" What is it ?" whispered Blogg.

"Can't you come to the door for a moment, darling ?"

" No; I've got a bad cold."

" I was sure something had prevented you from meeting me to-night, and you do speak a little hoarse."

" Yes, I'm very hoarse to-night," replied Blogg in his softest tones, and all the time grinding his teeth with rage. " But I'll allow you in at the window," he added.

" Is your father in bed ?"

" Yes."

" Lift up the window then, like a darling."

" Just wait a minute," said Blogg, as he stepped lightly towards a press, and possessed himself of a thick thonged whip. Returning to the window he undid the catch, and, stepping to one side, raised the under half full up.

Then the head of Jim Stubbs appeared, followed by his arms and shoulders.

" Darling Fanny, this is indeed kind of you. I feel as if I were entering Elysium. Oh ! oh ! murder !"

The window had fallen on him with all its weight, catching him about the middle of the back.

Whack ! whack ! went the whip across his shoulders, which made him roar and wriggle with pain, until at length Blogg mercifully released him from the trap in which he had been caught. Once free, he disappeared from the premises in an alarmingly short time. Not once did he look back, but ran as if a pack of bloodhounds were at his heels.

" He won't be in a hurry coming here again," muttered Blogg, drying the perspiration from his face, and preparing to go to bed again.

Jim Stubbs continued running until he arrived home. He felt that if he slackened his pace for an instant he should burst into tears. There was a bladder-full of pent-up grief pressing to his throat and almost choking him. He entered his room without speaking to his aunt, and having locked himself in, lay down on his bed and sobbed for half an hour. His former visions of fame and happiness were all dispelled, and darkness possessed his soul. Wounded pride and wounded bones drove him to the verge of despair. He contemplated suicide, and might have committed it if a razor had been within his grasp. But, luckily for him, he had not yet commenced to shave, and no other deadly implement found a place in his room. To be so treated by Fanny—she on whom he had doated—stung him to the quick. He could never have dreamed of such ingratitude, nor believed that such a depth of duplicity existed in human nature. His love was changed to hate—he felt that if he had the deceitful creature in his power at that moment, he could have strangled her. A thirst for revenge took possession of him, and drying his tears, he rose from the bed muttering—"I'll be revenged."

"Yes, I have it," at length he muttered. "Ha, ha, she'll be sorry for her conduct to-morrow."

Thereupon he sat down and commenced to write on a sheet of paper, which, when finished, he folded and put into his pocket, then taking up his hat, walked deliberately to the front door.

"Ye're surely no gain oot at this time o' nicht, laddie?" his aunt called to him.

"Oh, auntie, I thought you were asleep, and didn't want to disturb you. I have to go and assist on the night shift for a couple of hours," said Jim.

"Better tak' a bite o' supper afore ye go, then."

"No, auntie, I'm not hungry."

"Losh me, what's the maitter wi' ye, Jim? Ye're lookin' skeered like."

"Nothing, auntie," he replied, shutting the door behind him.

"Ech, but I'm feared there's something wrang wi' the lad," muttered Miss Stubbs, as she retired to her bedroom.

Chapter III.

When Blogg awoke next morning he was sadly out of sorts. He had had a frightful dream. A crowd of women and children besieged his bedside, shaking their fists at him and scowling in a very threatening manner. "Miserable man, prepare for your doom," shrieked one of them, seizing him by the throat. Another sprang into the bed and seated herself upon his chest, a third upon his head, while the others held him down on both sides. Then a fierce-looking virago appeared with a long saw and commenced to amputate his other leg. In an agony of desperation he attempted to shout, and awoke, covered with perspiration, to find it was a nightmare.

Sleep having forsaken him, he rose earlier than usual, and strolled about his garden till breakfast time. After breakfast he was conning some share lists received by the post, when he heard a knock at the door. It was such an unusual thing for him to have visitors at that hour, that he rose from his chair and listened until Betsy Jane opened the door, upon which he heard a masculine voice demanding to see the "guv'nor."

"Who is he, and what does he want, John?" shouted Blogg.

"Begging yer parding, guv'nor," said a shabbily dressed individual, thrusting in his head at the door of Blogg's room, much to the consternation of Betsy Jane, who seized him by the coat-tails and endeavoured to drag him back.

"Humph, what d'ye want, fellow?" asked Blogg, angrily.

"You needn't be so saucy, guv'nor—my name is Fiskin M'Fadyan, the proprietor of the world-renowned menagerie of living and dead curiosities."

"You and your curiosities be jiggered! Get out of here at once," roared Blogg, fiercely.

"Take it easy, guv'nor, don't get in a passion—gentlemen never do."

"Gentlemen be jiggered! what d'ye want?" shouted Blogg at the pitch of his voice.

"I'm just a-comin' to that, guv'nor. Ye see, as I said before, I'm the proprietor of the world-renowned menagerie of living and dead curiosities, and I've come to make you an offer for your wonderful baby."

"You villainous scoundrel!" shouted Blogg, seizing a boot-jack, "out of here at once, or I'll crack your skull for you!"

The menagerie proprietor was so taken aback that he could not utter a syllable, and, before he was able to collect his scattered senses, found himself hustled into the street, and the door shut against him. He came to the conclusion that Blogg was a madman, felt thankful that he had escaped without a bruise, and went away to inform the authorities that a lunatic was at large.

Old Blogg returned to his room in a state of fury; several times he ran the risk of thrusting his iron-shod stump through the floor, so fiercely did he bring it down.

"The scoundrel! what could he mean? Spoke about a baby. He must be mad, and it isn't safe to allow such characters to roam about at large. I'd better inform the police of the occurrence," he soliloquised, as he hopped excitedly round the room for several minutes.

His ruffled temper was just commencing to get smoothed down, when another knock at the door set him on edge again.

This time he overheard female voices in conversation with Betsy Jane.

"Women! blow them! what can they want? I wish the whole pack were sent to Botany Bay," he ejaculated.

Betsy Jane entered, and by means of signs and whispers gave him to understand that two females wanted to speak with him.

"Send them about their business, John; tell them I never give charity, and if it's for building a church they want subscriptions, tell them I'm an open-air worshipper."

Betsy Jane nodded her head, and returned to her visitors,

but she found it no easy matter to dispose of them. They insisted upon being admitted, while she was determined they should not, and the shrill wordy war which resulted, set Blogg's teeth on edge. When he could endure it no longer, he hopped to the lobby and shouted—

" What's the meaning of this infernal din ?"

" We've come to see the wonderful child, sir, and this unmannerly woman here has been refusing us admittance," said one of the ladies.

" You've come to see the devil !" hissed Blogg, in a paroxysm of rage.

" Yes, and I think we've seen him," remarked the other, fixing her eyes upon Blogg.

" Be off with you, you impertinent hussies ! ye pests of humanity ! Were it not that you're a pair of poor silly creatures I'd bang your heads together," shouted Blogg, fiercely.

" Monster !" shrieked the one.

" What a villainous-looking reptile," chimed in the other, as they took their departure, greeting him with looks of supreme contempt.

" Two of the fiends I saw in my dreams last night," he muttered as he returned to his room. " I'm surely not dreaming yet. What does it all mean ? asking to see the baby ! Babies be jiggered !"

But little time did he get for reflection, for almost immediately another loud knock resounded on the door.

" Lock the door, John, and don't let them in," he shouted, at the same time advancing to the lobby ; but before Betsy Jane could comply with his instructions the door was burst open, and quite a crowd of people had pressed inside. Betsy Jane swooned instantaneously, and no one being gallant enough to catch her in his arms, she measured her length upon the floor. Old Blogg seized the bootjack once more, and stood in an attitude of defiance.

" Anything to pay, old man ?" " Bring forth the baby," "Ugly old buffer," " He'll be the father," were some of the remarks which greeted his ear.

"I'd like to know what in all the world you want here?" asked Blogg, testily.

"The baby, of course." "We want to see the child wi' the twa faces," said the intruders.

Blogg stood petrified, and stared vacantly at the crowd. He felt that matters were becoming serious, and that either he or they were labouring under some hideous hallucination. In a tone devoid of his accustomed imperiousness he replied—

"My friends, I know not what you want; you must be labouring under some mistake."

"Ha, ha, that's a good un. 'Spose you haven't seen this morning's *Chronicle?*" said one of them, which tended to increase the perplexity depicted upon Blogg's countenance.

"You're a nice old buffer t'invite people to your house to see the twa-faced child, an' then say ye ken naething aboot it," said another.

"Read that, old man," said a third, presenting him with a copy of that morning's *Blownfield Chronicle*, and pointing to a paragraph, which, after putting on his spectacles, Blogg read as follows :—

"WONDERFUL NATURAL CURIOSITY.—Now on view at No. 9 Rosebud Street, a female baby with two faces. This strange specimen of humanity, although in mind a child, is of considerable bodily dimensions, being five feet two inches high, and fairly well developed. The muscles of her neck are supplied with universal joints, so that she can turn her head right round and exhibit her two faces alternately. The faces are greatly dissimilar, that which she usually exposes being fresh and plump-looking, while the other has a somewhat repulsive look. This wonderful prodigy is on exhibition at present at the above address."

When Blogg had finished reading, he took off his spectacles

and carefully wiped his eyes with his handkerchief, to ascertain if perchance some glamour had come over them. But no, his visitors were still there, and anxiously awaited his explanation.

"My friends," he said, in a husky voice, "this is all a pure fabrication ; no baby was, is, or ever shall be in this house as long's I'm alive. What this newspaper paragraph means I don't know, but will before I'm an hour older. I'll at once to the editor of this beastly rag, and if I don't have satisfaction my name's not Tobias Blogg !"

The crowd hereupon gave three cheers for old Blogg's pluck, and departed amid shouts of merriment and sallies of wit at his expense. Having shut the door, he went to his front window, and there the spectacle which met his gaze almost drove him frantic. A crowd of a hundred or more stood laughing and chattering, and pointing towards his house. He was determined to visit the editor of the *Chronicle*, but hesitated to go out in presence of these people.

"John !" he shouted, but there came no reply.

Proceeding to the lobby, he found Betsy Jane just recovering from her swoon.

"Oh, maister, I'm clean kilt," she groaned.

"Humph, don't talk so loud. Away and drink a cup of strong tea, 'twill strengthen your nerves ; then go and order a cab here."

Betsy Jane nodded her head, and, with tottering footsteps, wended her way to the kitchen.

Half an hour later, a cab drove hurriedly up to the office of the *Blownfield Chronicle*.

"Is the editor in ?' asked old Blogg, stepping into the office.

"Yes, sir ; card, sir ?' said one of the officials.

"Card be jiggered ! I must see the editor, and that instantly."

"Some important news, sir ? Railway accident, perhaps ?'

"Very important."

"This way, sir," said the official, leading him to the editor's sanctum, and ushering him into the presence of that august individual.

"Well, sir," said the editor, looking up in amazement at the peculiar figure before him, flushed, excited, and brimful of wrath.

"Don't 'well sir' me !" shouted Blogg ; " explain the meaning of that," pointing to the obnoxious paragraph, and holding the paper in a threatening manner before the editor's face.

"I am extremely sorry that this has occurred, and am willing to make every reparation in my power," said the editor, apologetically.

"Reparation be jiggered !" thundered Blogg. "I want satisfaction ! Show me the dastardly coward who wrote it."

"I am sorry I cannot do that, for I have sent him about his business. He was a compositor here, and stealthily inserted the type of that paragraph after the paper had gone to press," explained the editor.

"And what means it ? What have I done to be so insulted ?"

"As far as I could understand from the young fool, there was some misunderstanding between your daughter and him."

"My daughter ! Would you heap insult on injury ? Take that, you scoundrel !" roared Blogg, aiming a blow at the editor's ear, which the latter evaded by ducking.

"Please don't do it again—it might be dangerous for both parties," said the editor in a voice of forced calmness, at the same time ringing a bell, in answer to which a reporter entered.

"And now, sir," continued he, fixing his eyes upon Blogg, who had considerably calmed down, "I have told you all I know about the matter. I have discharged the young man who inserted the paragraph, and in to-morrow's paper I shall tender you an ample apology."

"Humph, that's no satisfaction to me ; apology be jiggered ! I want to see the young scoundrel who wrote it."

"I can give you his address," said the editor; "his name is James Stubbs, and he resides with his aunt, Miss Matilda Stubbs, 10 Union Crescent."

"Eh? Matilda Stubbs!"

"Do you know her, then?"

"No, and don't want to. I never knew any person called Stubbs, and if any one says I did, I'll knock him down. Stubbs be jiggered!"

And having thus delivered himself, Blogg hopped out of the office as abruptly as he had entered.

"I hope to goodness we have seen the last of that madman," ejaculated the editor, with a sigh of relief.

CHAPTER IV.

Miss Matilda Stubbs was seated in her armchair knitting a stocking. Her household duties left her abundant time for work of this kind, and she was not a woman who cared to be idle. Her mind was ill at case this afternoon, for her nephew Jim had failed to come home to dinner, which had now stood waiting him for nearly two hours.

"I canna understan' what's wrang wi' the laddie; he never did the like o' this before," she muttered to herself. "I'm sure there's something the maitter w'im. He's got some weicht on his mind, for his mainner was unco strange last nicht whan he gaed oot, an' this mornin' he wad hardly speak a word. Puir lad, for his faither's sake I wad like to dae weel t'him, an' it wad brak my heart if he's been daein' anything wrang."

Her cogitations were interrupted by a rattling of wheels, which came to a halt before her window.

"Oh, dear, I houp nae ill has befaun him," she muttered in terror, the idea having flashed across her mind that he had met with an accident, and was being brought home in a cab. Immediately she heard strange footsteps advancing up the passage, and then a knock came to her door, but so overcome was she with fear that when she essayed to rise she was unable, and sunk back in her chair again.

"Come in," she called, in a faint voice.

Immediately her door was opened, and old Blogg stood before her. She turned ghastly pale, staggered to her feet, and steadfastly gazed in the face of her visitor for several seconds, then exclaimed in a shrill voice—

"Tobias!"

"Matilda!" gasped Blogg, in deep consternation, at the same moment catching her in his arms to prevent her from falling. Having led her to her chair and gently seated her therein, the two gazed upon each other in speechless bewilderment. The meeting was evidently an embarrassing one for both. At length the silence was broken by Blogg, who said, in a husky voice—

"There *was* pepper in the soup, Matilda."

"Na, there *wasna*, Tobias."

"But I maintain there was."

"Ye're juist as positive as ever, but ye needna, for I gaed neist day and speered at the cook wha made the soup, and she assured me there wasna a pick o' pepper intil't."

"Do you tell me so?"

"It's a fac', Tobias."

"Well—er—er—I suppose—I will have to—to—apologise, but I daresay you can't—er—er—forgive me now?"

"I've forgi'en ye lang syne, Tobias, an' I've aften thocht what a sma' maitter it wis tae ha'e a pley aboot."

"I've thought so too, and after I went to sea I wrote you from Liverpool, but you were too—too—too high-minded to answer me."

"Dinna say that, Tobias; I never got yer letter."

"Never got my letter! Then have I been misjudging you all those years?"

" If ye thocht any ill o' me, ye ha'e."

" I set you down for a most—er—er—opinionative, intolerant woman."

" Weel, weel, Tobias, I never thocht nae ill o' ye, mair than that ye wir ower positive aboot that affair, an' I cudna gi'e in whan I kent I wis richt."

" How long is it since then, Matilda ?"

" It's many a lang year. Ye mind it wis whan first I cam' tae Blownfield tae service, an' before I gaed hame tae my place ye treated me tae denner in the Restaurant. Ay, I'se warrant it's mair than thirty years ago."

" And we've had a thirty years' dispute on the subject of pepper or no pepper in that soup."

" An' whase blame was it, Tobias ?"

" Humph, never mind whose blame it was. I've been thinking—thinking, Matilda, if it's not too late——"

" Too late, Tobias—too late."

" I mean—to settle—to be friends again, and if it were possible—to—to——."

" Wisht ! Tobias ; here comes Jim at last, an' I'm sae gled, for I was feired something had befa'an the lad. What's come ower ye the day, Jim ?' she asked when he had entered.

" I've left the *Chronicle*, auntie."

" Left the *Chronicle !* Gudesakes, what's the maitter ?"

" I'll tell ye again," replied Jim, as his eyes met those of old Blogg intently fixed upon him."

" I happen to know something about the matter," said Blogg. " This young shaver has got a sweetheart, and last night he went to tap on her bedroom window, but somehow he went to the wrong window, and has thereby got himself and others into trouble."

" Losh keeps, is this true, Jim ?' asked his aunt, greatly perplexed.

Jim made no reply, but hung his head sheepishly.

" My message here to-day was to see this young man,"

continued Blogg, "and in other circumstances it would have fared badly with him. Yes, my fine fellow, I intended to have punished you for your stupid and foolhardy conduct in putting that abominable paragraph in to-day's *Chronicle*, but for your aunt's sake, in whom I have discovered an old and valued friend —I—I forgive you. And, after all, you have not escaped unpunished, for you have lost your employment, lost your sweetheart, and—and—have already got a good whipping."

So saying, Blogg departed. But he returned again soon, and for a time became a frequent visitor at No. 10 Union Crescent. Strange to relate, Miss Stubbs and he not only became good friends again, but, after much persuasion, he induced her to change her name to Mrs Blogg. They got married in their old age, and were happy in each other's society ; but it was a standing regret that they had not done so thirty years sooner, and all through a paltry dispute about pepper or no pepper in a plate of soup.

Jim Stubbs never became reconciled to Fanny again, but, fortunately, neither of them were broken-hearted on that account. At old Blogg's special request, the editor of the *Blownfield Chronicle* reinstated Jim in his old position, and after a few years he rose to be one of the principal reporters on the staff of that important paper.

II.

LECTURES BY OLD BLOGG.

POLITICS.

POLITICS is a term now-a-days synonymous with "fiddle-sticks." It is likewise known as "bunkum" and "gammon." It is a subject very fertile of talk and—and—fruitful of surprises. It is often surprising where you land, and you never know exactly where you are in politics; in fact, as like us not you—you—you—never are there at all. I could talk politics for—yes for days on end, and no one be a bit the wiser. This is owing to the vastness of the subject, and the—er—er—ramifications, underground passages, and mysterious windings with which it is replete. It would take a demagogue—a demigod I mean—to make us thoroughly understand the subject, and, after all, we would disagree with him, and consider our own opinions—if we have any—the best.

The "study of politics" is a misleading phrase. All true political opinions are—are—intuitive and hereditary, and consequently do not require study. In the good old times, when the laird and the parish minister were the conservators of politics, who ever heard of studying them? Those designed by—by—heaven to be our political guides did not require to study "principles" which they knew to be right, and in which they believed as firmly as they did in their own existence. There were no schoolboy nor ploughboy politicians in those days, and the wheels of society ran smoothly. We have to thank the newspaper press, the lawyers—who have no innate ideas—and that—er—er—abominable Free Education Act, which compels a man to pay for the education of another man's children, for making politics a chaos—a perfect quagmire —a—a—a labyrinth of mystification, which it is impossible to plod through. Political economy and political prodigality— jobbery and robbery—social morality, whisky drinking, and Contagious Diseases Acts—laws of emigration, population, education, taxation, and—and—vexation, with a hundred other laws and flaws, are included in that one word—fiddle—that one word " politics." These are a few of the heads of the subject which our present-day politicians profess to study. But this is a delusion and a fraud. They simply study the list of voters, and how best to further the ends of the newspaper or political coterie which "runs" them. Principles be jiggered ! They have no more principles than—than—sucking turkeys—no more stead-fastness than weathercocks.

I would not recommend any one to attempt the *study* of politics, for it serves no purpose, and is consequently not worth the trouble. You require to study mathematics, astronomy, chemistry, navigation, and other useful and important subjects. Even the functions of the—er—brain and the origin of ideas require study, although I do not recommend it as being profitable either. In fact, I have known persons who have studied the functions of their brains until they had no brain functions left to study anything whatever. Yes, mathematics require study ; navigation requires study. There are not two, far less two hundred, ways of doing your calculations here. But in politics it matters not a penny piece what your—your— opinions are. One set of opinions are as good as another, and those which pay best are the correct opinions to have. Politics be jiggered ! It matters not how outrageous your opinions are,

you will get some people to endorse them. Suppose you told
an agricultural audience, that you would introduce a Bill in
Parliament, to have the land set on edge and farmed on both
sides, it would not be more outrageous than many an outrageous
theory which outrageous people are found to swallow. No,
no! don't try to study politics—the game's not worth the
candle. As a means of practising oratory, however, politics
occupy the first place. Where talk, and nothing but talk, is
wanted, the subject is extremely inviting. It is the happy
hunting-ground of—er—er—aspiring orators and village Glad-
stones. The scope for oratorical display is unlimited. Here
you can indulge in the most stinging irony—rearing up your
man of straw and knocking him down. Here, too, there is
ample room for invective—you can throw your arms about and
swear at large to your heart's content. Then if you desire to
be sentimental or statistical, humorous or historical, pious or
profane, here is the arena for rhetorical display. Here is the
field for glorious, gushing oratory, sublime perorations, and—
and—nothing more!

We are being deluged with politics, to which Noah's deluge
bears no comparison, because—because Noah's came from the
windows of heaven; while the deluge political comes from the
gates of—of—Whitehall. Questions and commissions, griev-
ances and agitations, are showered remorselessly upon our heads,
and where—where is the ark of safety? I don't suppose it's
built yet. Never mind. We can go up in balloons and
remain at a respectable distance till the political—er—er—
deluge-mongers are swallowed up and choked in their own—
their own—flood, and serve them right!

CALF-LOVE.

CALF-LOVE is almost as universal as the—er—measles. It is called "calf" love to distinguish it from—er—er—natural love, and because it degrades the—the—intellectual faculties of the imbeciles who are afflicted with it, to the level of the intellectual faculties of calves. It is an affection of the brain and eyes, and, while it lasts, works sad havoc with the faculties of—er—er—perception and reflection. We all know what love is—the pure and unadulterated article—that—er—healthy—natural instinct implanted in the human breast. Look at the school-boy. He loves with all the intensity of a fly-blister. He loves to play—loves to shout and make a noise in the world—loves to torment old men who lean on their staffs, and young men who —er—er—can't leave their shops to give him chase. Oh, how he loves to play "peeries" and "bools" and football. How he disagrees with his companions, and fights and forgives—and love at the bottom of it all. In the very exuberance of love he quarrels. Bursting with love, he fights to bruise out the purulent matter, and then makes up friendship again—is a peaceable, loving friend until the boil fills up afresh. To see a spider catch a fly—to see a dog worry a cat—to see a butcher fell a stot, how extremely lovable to the schoolboy whose head and heart are sound. When we grow up we still love, although the—the—the objects of our affections change. We love money —love to make a good bargain—love applause—love to build houses and sit under our vines and fig-trees, none daring to make us afraid—love to be Bailies or County Councillors, or even School Board members, besides a hundred other things. It is right to love our parents, our brothers, and our sisters, but when we begin to love some other fellow's sister, then is the time that our—er—er—intellectual faculties are apt to get out of order. When a young fellow becomes seized with this enervating, effeminate Calf-love he becomes incapable of any rational enjoyment. The malady is almost confined to early life—between the age of thirteen and twenty, as a rule, and there is no definite period to its duration. Sometimes it is cured in a week, sometimes it continues for a year or more, and in a few cases it proves fatal. Calf-love is easily distinguishable by its symptoms. It makes a young fellow cringe to a girl, blush when he meets her—even blush when her name is mentioned. His manliness leaves him, and he becomes girlish in his ideas and pursuits. He no longer delights in the company of his former companions, but begins to wander abroad in solitude; and the amount of attention he bestows upon his dress and personal appearance keeps him in a state of perpetual uneasiness. The malady not infrequently commences in school-days. I can fancy some young simpleton sitting at his desk, his heart all in a flutter of excitement. He imagines he feels the breath upon his back hair of the—the—silly creature with whom he is—is—infatuated; imagines she is looking over his shoulder reading the exercise he is pretending to write. Oh, the ecstacy of the moment! the—the—the divine afflatus in which he seems to be suspended. Yes, suspended, for in imagination he neither sits nor stands, but floats or swims in an atmosphere of immortal bliss—poor stupid donkey! caring not for the world nor the things of the world, which are poor and paltry and vile and sensual to the eye of his entranced mind. And what an awful abyss of—of—of bottomless reality opens before his disenchanted vision when, after he has braced up sufficient courage to look round, he discovers it is not her—oh, cruel fate! but some one he abhors and detests, who has been playing upon his—his—his full-tensioned heart-strings till they have almost broken, and he wakes up as from a trance, pale and desperate, bloodthirsty at heart, but in body and limb powerless as a worm.

Such is Calf-love—a pure hallucination and unreality. Its ideal is not there in actual existence. The afflicted youth in imagination clothes his adored one with a—er—halo of brightness which finds no place in the sober annals of existence. Never mind though your inner consciousness accuses you of having been once madly in love with some carroty-haired, squint-eyed, bandy-legged anatomy of a girl, in whom at the time you saw nothing but grace and beauty. Thank your stars that you have passed through the ordeal without making a complete ass of yourself, and that your eyes have been opened.

The poor victim of Calf-love is worse than if he were actually blind. The disease which has mixed up his brain, so distorts his vision that he almost sees black white—he takes slovenliness for grace, plainness for beauty, tawdry tresses for ringlets, a clothes' pole with a frock on it for form, peevishness for intellect, and impudence for soul. His friends can see nothing special in the girl with whom he has become infatuated. It is generally a puzzle to them, and always is to the girl's companions of her own sex, what he can see to admire in her. But it's easily explained. There's a glamour over his eyes which gradually wears off as the disease abates, and after a time, when he begins to see with his right eyes, he can't help saying to himself—" What an idiot I have been !"

Calf-love be jiggered ! Like the measles it is not deadly in itself, but its after consequences may be serious. If the haughty, slatternly—er—er—toffy eater, whom the disease invests with angelic charms in the eyes of the afflicted youth, spurns him and treats him with contempt, the malady will pass off without danger. Or if the object of the—er—er—young blockhead's Calf-love be, as is often the case, a woman who might be his—his—mother-in-law, the chances are against dangerous results. But should the girl happen to be affected with the same disease, and the booby be the light of *her* eyes, as she is of his, the consequences may be serious enough. They may actually go and commit—er—er—matrimony under the influence of the disease, and then when the eyes of both are opened, and they look upon each other as they are—what's the result? Gall and wormwood—execration—ruination—poker and pandemonium! The miserable simpletons have bound themselves with galling fetters which they cannot burst, except by making bad worse, and appealing to that—that—superlative abomination—the divorce court. Even should the result not be so serious as marriage, the booby may have committed himself so far, before the glamour is removed from his eyes, that he is liable in an action for breach of promise of marriage, and has to "stump up" the hard cash by begging, borrowing, or stealing, and have his maniacal love letters published to the world, as a solatium to the wounded feelings—wounded feelings be jiggered!—of the designing hussy.

Although I don't believe in matrimony, it seems, like women and babies, to be among the necessary evils of this world; and, therefore, my advice to those who *will* marry is—is—set about it in a business and common-sense manner. Look upon matrimony as a matter o' money—as a mercantile transaction. Examine your woman all over as you would a piece of furniture, to see that there are no cracks nor flaws about her, and that you are making a good bargain. Trot her out as you would a filly you are purchasing, to see that she is sound in limb and wind, and free from vice. The three chief points to look to are health, wealth, and good temper. If you find a girl possessed of these, and willing to have you, why—marry her and be—be jiggered!

TROUT FISHING.

Fishing for trout is a pastime which in—er—time past I greatly enjoyed. It is a highly—er—catching and gratifying exercise, for if you don't catch trouts you are almost sure to catch—yes, to catch something, were it only a cold. And although your expectations of a good basket may not always be —er—gratified, the trouts are no doubt grateful for the—the—interest you take in their habits and movements.

There are various modes of catching trouts. One of the simplest is called—er—er—"guddling," and requires neither rod nor line. You take off your—your coat and roll up your shirt sleeves, if you have a shirt on. Then lying flat on your—your—breast, lean over the bank of the stream, taking care not to fall in, and grope with your hands in the hollows underneath the banks until you come upon your rat—your trout I mean. Grasp him firmly with both hands, and toss him over your head. He is then caught. By the way, you must be careful not to seize a water rat, as this would be—er—er—dangerous.

There is another mode, which has got no particular name that I know of. The requisites are a dam, with mill lade and sluices. You take off the grating from the—the sluice at the dam, and allow a good flow of water down the lade for half an hour, taking care that no trouts get through the sluice on the lade. Then put the—the—dam sluice—I mean the sluice of the dam—hard down. In a very short time the lade will run dry, and your trouts are caught.

For boys and youths of all ages, who have a taste for sport, these are—are—exceedingly healthful and salubrious pastimes, and from the—er—er—prevention of cruelty to animals standpoint, are preferable to fishing with rod and line, inasmuch as the trouts are spared the pain caused by the hook being fixed in their jaws, and the—er—poor worms the pain of having the hook passed through their—their entrails.

In fishing with rod and line, bait or fly may be used, or both combined. The "fliest" fishers use a bait called "marmalade," "stuffy," or "putty." Some—er—er—ignorant people believe it to be salmon roe, but this is sheer nonsense. It is simply hard-boiled egg yolks beaten up with—er—sour buttermilk into a paste. It is then seasoned with *aqua-fortis* and croton-oil, and after being pressed into an old jelly jar, is ready for use. It is simply—er—delicious to sit on the bank of some favourite pool, for six or eight hours on a stretch, fishing with this bait, and intently watching for a nibble. To old "fogies" whose joints have got stiff with rheumatism, this mode of fishing is specially adapted, as the exercise is not over violent, and it does not entail a great deal of trouble, suppose they provide themselves with the—er—er—luxury of a camp stool, or even erect a tent at their favourite spot on the water side.

Fishing with worm is a very taking and invigorating exercise, if the trouts happen to be—er—taking. It is best adapted for young men who have got a lot of—er—er—physical energy about them, as to fish worm properly you have to trudge up and down the stream, and never lay up and down your rod.

Even salmon may be caught with a big bunch of worms. You provide yourself with a strong tackle and pretty large hook, capable of holding about a dozen worms. Insert the hook in the middle of their bodies, leaving their heads and tails free, for in this case it is the—er—worms who take the fish, and they require freedom of limb to "go" for him. At certain seasons and certain—er—states of the water salmon lie in a half-dormant condition in deep pools, and when you throw in your bunch of worms they make "tracks" for the nearest fish. When you feel them fastened on him, give your line a smart jerk, and your hook will sing—will probably enter the fish. Then the real excitement begins, and continues with—with—unabated fury till the "beast" is either lost or landed. Some

—er—er—evil-disposed people say that for this kind of angling the worms are unnecessary, and that the bare hook, with some lead attached, would do equally well. These people ought to get some lead attached to their centres of gravity, and be thrown into the water.

Fishing with maggots is a most—most—entrancingly pleasant nocturnal pastime. Maggots are reared somewhere about slaughter-houses, as they are especially fond of raw flesh. For fishing purposes, you get them mixed with oatmeal in a coffee tin. In maggot-fishing you use your ordinary fly-cast, and put a maggot on each hook. I once had a nice bit of preserved water in my eye, and as I could not obtain permission to fish it with daylight, I went at night and fished it with maggot. I hooked a fish, and out ran my line. It was most exciting in the darkness. He must have been a three or four pounder! I never saw him, however, for he made straight for some tree branches which dipped in the water at the opposite bank, and I lost both fish and cast-line. Accidents of this kind are incidental to trout fishing, even in the daytime, for, if fishing fly, you are quite as liable to hook the branch of a tree as a trout. It is a most—most—invigorating exercise, however, to climb up a tree and release your hooks—it is the—the—soul of patience and perseverance. And it is the never-ending variety of incidents which occur that lends a charm to the gentle art, which it would not otherwise possess.

Sometime thereafter I again proposed to try the maggots, and after getting rod and tackle in order, lifted down the tin from the shelf upon which it had stood since the night referred to. I took off the lid to see how the animals were behaving, when, thunder and lightning! out flew a swarm of blue-bottle flies, with a "bizz" which made me fancy I had my ear against a telegraph pole in a breeze of wind. Maggots be jiggered! I didn't get a fresh supply.

Many queer things—animate and inanimate—are hooked. I've hooked a rat, a bat, a duck, and an old tin pail—not all together, of course. The queerest fish I ever hooked was at the "pouch," on the Eden. It was one of those days which perpetually occur to unsuccessful anglers, when the wind blew in the wrong direction, and the fish were not taking. After trying various lures without success, I put on a beautiful bait of patent "marmalade," and threw out my line, asking two companions who were close at hand to keep an eye on my rod till I returned from a dwelling a short distance away, and to which I had a message. On coming back I was greeted with the exclamation—

" There's a fish tugging at your line."

Rushing to the bank I seized my rod and drew out—what d'you think? A veritable red herring!

I gazed at it in—in—awe for a moment. It was dead. Possibly it might have died in the time I was absent. But there was no time for it to have got smoked—that was perfectly evident—and under water, too. No—I saw it at once. Those three-cornered, cork-headed putty manufacturers had played me a trick. During my absence they had affixed the herring to my hook, and thrown the line back into the water again. Red herrings be jiggered!

Stone bait, said to be the chrysalis of the May fly; real minnows preserved in salt, and young wasps, are all, in one way or another, very taking, and—and—deadly baits.

It seems to me, on looking back, that about—about seven-sixteenths of the enjoyment—er—er—connected with trout fishing is derived in obtaining your bait. Even digging for worms is exciting, and if you go in for " brandlings" it is doubly so—to the olfactory organs—considering the—the—nature of the soil in which this species of worm delights to ruminate. Then collecting the May fly chrysalides from beneath the stones in the burn is a bit of—er—er—calm, peaceful enjoyment, not by any means exciting, unless the stones are slippery and you fall in a few times—but nevertheless bracing, healthful, and pleasurable. Fishing for minnows with tiny net is an enjoyment of a similar nature.   But to tackle a wasp's nest and rob the young is a feat of daring to look back upon with—with—glorification.   In the sphere of bait collecting, this is certainly the—the—most exciting, for, as a rule, you have to make repeated attacks before you are successful; and if you should happen, after obtaining the nest, to put it inside your vest for preservation, and a few old wasps be lurking in its—its—crevices, the excitement becomes really intense.

The subject is inexhaustible, but time's up.

Said fisherman, " I'm tired of it."
   Said trout, " Don't be so ' huffy ;'
I care not for your brandling worm –
   Let's have a bit of ' stuffy.' "

Said fisherman, " You've cleaned my hook ;
   Confound you for the trouble !"
Said trout, " You ought to feel quite proud
   That you have got a nibble."

WOMAN.

WOMAN is a vast subject to—to—grapple with. I should much prefer to leave her alone, but a sense of duty—er—er—impels me to tackle her. She's a fraud, a con—er—er—yes, a conundrum. Very few can read her. She's a gossiping encyclopædia, a talking dictionary, a screaming nuisance, and a scheming impostor. I've had my own trials with her; have suffered mentally, physically, and—er—er—pecuniarily on account of her, but I've triumphed over her, I've seen through her, I've confounded her plots and her diplomacy. All the world knows that she was formed out of a superfluous rib taken from man's side. I do not suppose this rib caused man any inconvenience while it formed part of his anatomy, but once transformed into a woman, that rib became a—became a—living and moving instrument of torture. In these degenerate days we hear and read a lot of balderdash about woman's mission. It is actually said that she was sent into the world for the purpose of ennobling and refining the male animal—that with her finer feelings, keener susceptibilities, and transcendent what-nots she is destined to transform senseless, brutish, unfeeling man into a docile, tender-hearted being. Humph, a docile, henpecked idiot rather! Don't be led astray with such—such —sophistical rubbish written by ancient "blue-stockings" of the modern school, and æsthetical, crack-brained penny-a-liners. Woman's mission forsooth! Yes, she has a mission, an undoubted mission, and it may be summed up in a sentence— Woman's mission is to nurse man when he is young, that she may torment him when he is old—and this mission she endeavours to fulfil to the letter. By the most sublime strategy she tries to gain a power over man's generous, unsuspecting nature, and her object once attained, she keeps him bound with the most galling and intolerable fetters. Woman's influence forsooth! It's like the influence of the moon upon a lunatic of the cage upon an eagle, like onions to the eyes, hartshorn to the nose, bankruptcy to the pocket. Her influence is over-powering, over-bearing, over-reaching, overwhelming. The male blockhead falls down on his knees and worships her, yea, kisses the ground upon which she treads. Poor infatuated dunderhead ! he is under the spell of the sorceress. Woman be jiggered ! I could squeeze her—I mean I could punch her—in other words, corporally punish her ; but if I did so, I'd be hooted at, called a monster, an old bald-headed—er—er—alligator, and the chances are I would not get off so cheaply. For simply telling one of the sex she was a " she-wolf," I once got a black eye, and a handful of whiskers . torn from my face. Ever since then I have kept close shaved. And suppose you are treated thus by a woman, you dare not lift your hand to her. If you are manly, you must suffer whatever amount of punish-ment she chooses to inflict, or else fly like a coward from her presence. The poor, weak, innocent, tender-hearted creatures ! Oh, yes, *they* can't fight nor scratch nor tear out hair—neither can cats and dogs. *They* can't fly into a passion and scold and say naughty things, the angelic creatures ! Oh, dear, no.

The study of woman is a life-long study. She is always cropping up, and you can't get rid of her. In her time she plays many *rôles*, and her wiles and allurements commence at a very early age—long before the male dolt is out of leading strings. You may see her a timorous, frightened creature when in the company of her intended victim. She screams at the sight of a mouse, and her heart goes pit-a-pat if she sees a cow in the distance, for fear it may be the bull ; and this same tender-hearted, timorous thing will smack the ears and tear the hair of her companion who has offended her, when no male dolt is looking on. This timidity is all a ruse, but it appeals power-fully to the—the—chivalric feelings implanted in the bosom of the male booby, who feels himself called upon to act the part of protector. I remember when—when I was young, of a would-be timid maiden trying to—to—inveigle me. We were in an old abbey, and she had clambered up on some of the broken masonry. "Oh dear, my head reels; how am I to get down?" I heard her call out. I saw through her little game. She expected me to come to her assistance, put my—er—er—arms around her and lift her to the ground, when, in all probability, she would have fainted in my arms, and—and—goodness knows what would have happened. "Come down the way you got up," I said, and you should see how nimbly and swiftly she did come down—and you should hear the volley of invective and high-flown abuse to which she treated me—the timid, innocent creature! Yes, timid as a hyena—innocent as a sleeping crocodile.

Another time you may find her vivacious and loquacious, which is a taking *rôle* with young fellows of a bashful disposition, who rather like a girl with some "spunk" in her, to draw them out a bit. Then you may find her goody-goody, setting her cap at the young minister—or all gush and sentiment, reading novels and writing mysterious love-letters to editors and professional celebrities.

After she gets married she finds scope for her—her—mission in new grooves. Not contented with having ensnared and fettered the poor idiot who is now her husband, she sets about match-making for her unmarried female friends and companions, and teaches them all the—the—the nefarious arts and wiles and spells which she has herself practised. I have often wondered where all the handsome—er—er—good-looking women disappear to after marriage, but have never been able to discover. I have heard it said that when their victims are trapped, they—they—are denuded of their sorceress spell, and are forced to appear before the world in their unpadded and unvarnished reality. It may be true, and serves them right.

In conclusion—I'm done. I might have said more, but I want to live a few years longer; and woman, when roused, is the very—very—incarnation of all that is blue. She's a swindle—a veritable apple of Sodom!

NOTHING.

NOTHING is a most—most—stupendous subject. When we—er—consider that not only this planet of ours, but the whole—er—system of the universe was created out of nothing, we can at once see what a stu—what an immense—er—er—something nothing must be. Yes, nothing is the—the—the—substratum of everything. The world rests upon it—revolves upon it. Take any object you choose—this table, for instance. It has certain—er—er—qualities, such as flatness, smoothness, square-ness, hardness. We know it is made of wood, and wood has its distinguishing qualities. But beyond these, what do we know about this table, or any other object in creation? Nothing—simply nothing. And this vast—er—er—incomprehensible nothing is nothing else than that something which—er—philosophers have named "substratum," because they know nothing about it. The dictionary defines nothing as being 'not any thing'—dictionary be jiggered!—and at the same time informs us it is a *noun*. Now, that famous authority, Lindley Murray, teaches that "a noun is the name of any person, place, or thing." As nothing is neither a person nor a place, it must consequently be a thing, so that the dictionary definition is wrong—decidedly wrong! To tell you exactly what nothing is—is—im—er—would take up more time than I have at my disposal; but if you close your eyes you will see nothing; if you put your hand into an empty pocket you will feel nothing; if you listen when no sounds are audible you will hear nothing; if you put a scentless flower to your nose you will smell nothing; and if you put a glass ball into your mouth you will taste nothing. Now, how in the name of—of—wonder should a thing which is—er—perceptible to all the five senses be described as "not any thing?" It is most—most preposterous!

I discovered at a very early age that nothing was something. I was sitting in school writing my copy-book. The sun shone in through the grimy windows in all the glory of a summer's day, and I began thinking of—er—whin bushes and birds' nests, and for a short time became oblivious of my copy-book. My reverie was rudely interrupted by the—er—tawse being flung at me from the other end of the schoolroom. Glancing in the direction whence it came, my eyes—er—er—encountered those of the teacher glaring at me. It couldn't be meant for me I concluded, and turned my attention to the boy sitting next me.

"Come up here, Tobias Blogg, and bring the tawse with you," bawled Dominie Galloway.

Conscious of my innocence, I stepped boldly up and placed the tawse on his knee.

"Hold out your hand," said the Dominie.

"Please, sir, it wasn't me, sir—I was doing nothing," I explained.

"Yes, I'm aware you were doing nothing, and that's the reason why you deserve to be punished. Hold out your hand, sir."

I got my *pambies*, and thus early learned that doing nothing was a punishable offence.

But what does doing nothing mean? It seems—er—clear to me that if we *do* we must do something, and hence when we're doing nothing we're doing something, and the reason why it's—er—punishable, is because it's doing something we know nothing about. Doing nothing is very—er—laborious employment, and very—er—er—unremunerative. Some persons with more money than brains have attempted to do nothing. But they never thoroughly succeeded. They found the work too hard for them, and for relaxation had to engage in—er—horse-racing, pigeon-shooting, hunting, yachting, or gambling.

The Dictionary plays strange tricks on us. It tells us that

the man who knows nothing is an ignorant man. What absurdity! The man who knows nothing knows the—the—origin and substratum of everything. He knows the hidden qualities of that—that—that boundless something called nothing, and which is the original material out of which the universe was created. This all-pervading nothing is the—er—er—abstraction of everything, and when this world will have passed away like a—like a scroll, nothing will again occupy its place ; and then the man who knows something about nothing will stand upon the pinnacle of everything, and teach those ignoramuses who have spent their time in studying something, and who don't know anything about nothing, that nothing is an—er—er—universal, all-embracing, and all-absorbing something, which holds together anything and everything.

MATRIMONY.

OF all the queer businesses into which poor, stupid men embark, matrimony is the—the—queerest. It is a sleeping partnership, established on the—er—*unlimited* liability principle, the functions of Banker and Board of Directors being vested in the—the—the wife. Its—er—capital consists of unredeemable bonds on the Bank of Love, and it has a sunk fund of freedom, comfort, and all the fond day-dreams and joys of bachelorhood sunk beyond—er—er—recall. Matrimony be jiggered! It is a most ruinous business, for the husband, yielding not only trouble for his pains, but—er—pains and trouble combined for his best endeavours. Stock is taken nightly—by—by—the wife, and the dividends are cent. per cent. of blighted hopes, with large—er—bonuses of fresh cares. When I see a poor imbecile enter into this most—most unprofitable co-partnery, I say to myself, "There's another donkey led tail foremost on board ship." Before he knows what he's about the anchor of—of youthful happiness is weighed—the—er—sweet haven of bachelorhood fades in the distance, and the trapped victim only comes to his senses when tempest-tossed on the—the pillowy—the billowy ocean of wedded misery.

From the outside, matrimony looks somewhat inviting, and thereby the unwary are beguiled. But it's a whited sepulchre! It looks best at a distance, and much better at a greater distance. Shun it if you are wise, for once in, there is no getting out. You can't get in on approbation. Inside it is a perfect—er—er slough of despond—beneath your feet a quaking mire—above your head a shaking—er—er—poker. Don't tell me of happy husbands, for it's all humbug. They wear their sweetest smiles, and look—yes look—pictures of contentment in presence of their wives, because they must, or—or—suffer the tortures of that—er—hymenial rack which awaits them when they retire

I

into the domestic *sanctum sanctorum*. If they do have short intervals of real enjoyment, it is only when they steal an hour to spend with a "chum" at his—er—er—club, or in some other place of—of—relaxation. Keeping "bachelor hall" is an event, too, which all—er—er—right-minded husbands thoroughly enjoy, although they—they—dare not admit it. What a happy week in their otherwise chequered existence, when the wife requires a change of air, and goes on a visit to dear mamma! Old associates are visited and invited, and old associations while away the—the—the—enraptured hours. "Here's a hand, my trusty friend," with its accompanying atmosphere of—er—er—sincerity and good fellowship, is once more in the ascendant. But the wife's return puts an end to it all, and the unhappy, downtrodden husband sinks back into his—er—er—unreal, stage-play existence. Don't din my ears with your joys of matrimony, for it's all bosh! Like the schoolboy who falls into the ditch, and, because people are looking on, rises up whistling when he feels more inclined to weep, is the husband who whistles the tune of wedded bliss. Poor, broken-hearted wretch, he must put the best face he can on his misfortune. Joys of matrimony forsooth! If becoming your wife's message-boy be a joy; if to be converted into a—er—er—warming-pan for her bed be a joy; if to be roused in the dead watches of the night to dandle a baby, squealing with—er—internal pains, be a joy—then—yes —then marry and be joyful.

Children come as the crowning—er—crushing evil of matrimony, and no husband long survives the toils, worries, and expenses of rearing a family. He has to feed, clothe, and educate a lot of brats who, as soon as they can earn a livelihood for themselves, snap their fingers at him, if he asks a penny to be refunded of what he has spent on them. It was all very well for King David to sing—

> "O happy is the man that hath
>   His quiver filled with those,
> They unashamed in the gate
>   Shall speak unto their foes."

But King David was always requiring soldiers to fight his battles for him, and from a military point of view he was fairly "on his eggs." Now-a-days it isn't good enough to rear a family for fighting purposes. Indeed, for any purpose it is a profitless and thankless undertaking. Family be jiggered! The fool who now rears a large family transgresses against the—er—er—common sense of mankind. He is a nuisance to society in general, and to—to—house proprietors in particular. Why do ye not combine, ye noble-minded speculators in stone and lime, and refuse to let your houses to—to—to—malefactors who have the audacity to bring more children into the world than they can take care of? If ye did so, ye would compel those—er—er bloodguilty progenitors of large families to drown, or otherwise dispose of their brats in infancy, and—er—er—sensitive, peace-loving people could enjoy their fireside evenings, instead of being driven half-distracted, as many of them are at present, with the pattering of feet, and the screaming and yelling of fighting demons overhead. Then ye would be able, ye noble and philanthropic band! to augment your princely contributions to the schemes for the conversion of the Jews and the Christian education of heathen children, from the saving effected on repairs to property. Then I, too, and those similarly situated, would have a smaller education tax to pay. Free education be jiggered! Why should I be compelled to pay for the education of other men's—er—er—encumbrances? It's most iniquitous —most—most—heartrending!

It is astonishing what an amount of rubbish is retailed about matrimony, as if it were gospel truth. That ".marriages are made in heaven" you hear people repeating with all the authority of a bible quotation. But if these people read their bibles they will find that the first marriage took place on earth, and that so shall the last, for in heaven there is no marrying. No—er—er—sensible person ever supposed there was. That bone taken from Adam's side and formed into a woman, has been a "bone of contention" to the whole race of mankind, and sure enough, poor man suffers plenty from it in this world without having to be under its influence in the next. What misery and—and—heartburnings would have been spared him if the—er—original way of creating man had been continued, and woman never appeared upon the scene ! Why, there would have been no Fall, no Flood, no henpecked husbands, no—no—nothing to disturb the peace and equanimity of supremely gifted man. Then he would bloom amid his native heather in all his pristine beauty—all day long—er—sunning himself like a—like a dandelion in the warm rays of heaven, and at night reading his paper and sipping his—er—er—gruel, before the bright and glowing fire—free and unmolested.

HEAVEN.

THOSE who have read the preceding story of "Old Blogg" will be aware that he "committed" matrimony in his old age. Thereafter his ideas on various subjects were considerably modified. He admitted that there was one good woman in the world after all, and that possibly there might be a few more. Although, as he said himself, he never had a baby in his arms but once, and that time he let it fall, he made no secret of his regret that he did not marry sooner, and rear up a family of young Bloggs. After his marriage he attended church so regularly that he was chosen for an elder, and at the urgent entreaties of Mrs Blogg he accepted office.

"I've got to speak to the Sabbath School children next Sabbath," he remarked to Mrs B. one evening.

"Eh, Tobias, but that's graund !"

"But I don't know very well what to speak about."

"Ye needna be sair pitten aboot for something tae speak aboot, Tobias. Ye maun gang tae yer bible, ye ken, and speak good words tae the bairns. Ye could speak aboot Daniel in the lion's den, or Jonah, or heeven, or something o' that kind."

"Heaven ? Yes, I consider heaven would be a very appropriate subject."

"See an' say something awfu' nice about it than, Tobias, for I'se warrant there'll be folk takin' notes."

Sunday evening arrived, and Blogg was up to time. Gazing upon his youthful and somewhat fidgety audience, he commenced—

"Well, my dear children, I've come here to speak to you on a very—er—er—important and highly—er—er—entertaining subject. Now, could any of you boys or girls tell me where—where—heaven is ?"

Blogg stood with beaming countenance waiting for an answer, but received none.

"Dear me, can none of you tell me where heaven is?"

"No!" shouted a youngster in the front seat. At the same moment the School Superintendent tugged the tail of Blogg's coat and whispered something in his ear. Turning again to his audience, his face livid with suppressed excitement, he said—

"Yes, my boy, I've been informed that you're right; that none of you know, and that I don't know myself, where heaven is. So be it. One thing I know, that—that—when we get to heaven, and I hope we may be all there soon, we will have no doubt—no doubt—as to the—the—the—geography of that—er —er—important place. Now, boys and girls, what shall I say next?"

"Say 'amen,' mannie, an' sit doon!" broke forth from the promising urchin aforesaid.

And Blogg sat down.

He never addressed Sunday School children again.

MISCELLANEOUS PAPERS.

A SEARCH FOR COMMON SENSE.

Hast thou an object in life, reader? I had none until long after my wisdom teeth were grown—indeed, so long thereafter that I began seriously to wonder if all the fine talk about life objects was not so much " high falutin' " after all. But a time came when I discovered that life's objects were realities, for a time at least, although in the end—but let the end speak for itself.

The Reverend Samuel Wiseman informed his congregation one Sunday forenoon, that a number of new office-bearers required to be elected, and very particularly impressed upon the members the necessity of returning men of good common sense. As I happened to have a vote in their election, I immediately began to consider upon whom I should bestow it—who were the men endowed with this necessary qualification of common sense? It was then it first occurred to me that my own knowledge of common sense was imperfect, and after very carefully revolving the matter in my mind, I was forced to the humiliating conclusion that if I were asked to define common sense I could not do so. In vain I turned up every dictionary I could lay hands on. I read Locke and Berkeley, Hume and Spurgeon, Butler's Analogy, and Dante's Inferno, but instead of receiving enlightenment my ideas became more confused than ever. Although extremely unwilling to display my ignorance by inquiring its meaning of any of my friends, I felt that I must do so, or else die in ignorance of common sense.

My principal reason for fixing upon Mr Buzzard, the green-grocer, as the first individual from whom I should seek enlightenment, was the fact that he regularly supplied the Reverend Samuel Wiseman with cabbages. A minor reason was that he sold hard peas, for which I had a special relish. Having purchased a quantity I commenced to chew them, and in the course of conversation asked Mr Buzzard if he could tell me what common sense was. Thrusting both hands deep into his trouser pockets, he surveyed me from head to foot, and then burst into a fit of laughter, as if it were the best joke he had heard for a long time.

"Odds man, dinna ye ken what common sense is? Ha! ha!"

Looking fixedly upon the floor, I reluctantly admitted I was not quite sure that I did.

"What! yer surely jokin' noo. You're the first that ever I heard sayin' they didna ken what common sense wis."

"But what is it?" I meekly enquired.

"What is it! What d'ye think it was gaein' tae be? Why, ye blockhead, it's juist common sense."

"So I understand, but what *is* common sense? Define it," I said, more boldly.

"Toots man, dinna be speakin' balderdash. I ha'e nane o' yer lang nebbit words tae define it wi', but I ken the meanin' o't weel enough for a' that. The verra sense o' natur' micht teach ye."

The "sense of nature," whatever that was, did not teach me, however, and I came away from Mr Buzzard deeply conscious that I was an ignoramus, or something worse.

The subject remained uppermost in my mind, and I was

losing my appetite and my sleep with pondering over it. Passing one day through the streets, I was attracted by two individuals engaged in animated conversation.

"And do you mean to tell me that common sense is transparent nonsense?" one of them exclaimed, while I stood on tip-toe to hear what was to follow.

"Yes, I do," replied the other; "common sense is simply transparent nonsense—that is, nonsense seen through."

"Good for you, but pray what is nonsense?"

"Why, it's just common sense in an inverse ratio."

"So, then, you hold common sense and nonsense to be the same, but different?"

Before the other could reply, a mad ox, being driven to a neighbouring slaughter-house, rushed between the speakers and rather abruptly terminated their conversation, to my great and everlasting regret. But what I did hear put me upon a new train of thought. Could common sense be related to nonsense after all? Formerly, I had considered the one to be the antipodes of the other. I must find out. Though all the world sneer at me and call me blockhead, I'm determined to find out!

From that moment I felt that I had an object in life, and in furtherance of its attainment attended, that same evening, Dr Greatthought's lecture on "The utility of moonshine for boot polish," to which I listened with rapt attention. It was, no doubt, owing to my natural defectiveness that I was unable to make head or tail of the lecture. My ideas were always very sensitive, and on hearing any new theory propounded were sure to get frightened, and fly away, helter-skelter, to the four corners of my brain. In passing out I chanced to encounter my friend Scrimp, the apothecary, and there and then resolved to have his opinion at all events.

"Well, Mr Scrimp," said I, patting him on the shoulder, "what did you think of it?"

"Not much, to tell the truth. I've heard many a better

lecture from an old wife at the fireside. Why, to say that a man with two pairs of boots is better than a man with only one pair is confounded nonsense. To identify a man with his boots, as if they were part and parcel of his manhood, is simply absurd. I say 'a man's a man for a' that.'"

Had I got a clue, then, towards the attainment of my object? Yes, if I could get Scrimp's opinion sufficiently corroborated, I felt I had found one thing which was *not* common sense, and this would be a beginning.

It seemed lucky that no sooner had I parted from Scrimp than I should meet Rosin, the bootmaker, who had also attended the lecture, and I at once took the opportunity of putting Scrimp's opinion to the test.

"And what did you think of the lecture, Mr Rosin?" I asked.

"Very much—capital lecture—one of the best I have ever listened to."

My countenance suddenly fell.

"Indeed, and what is your opinion of the theory of the man with two pairs of boots?"

"In my opinion it is most sensible. Confidentially, I don't consider a man possesses common sense unless he have two pairs of boots."

"Ah, you don't? Well, Mr Rosin, everybody is not of the same opinion. There's Mr Scrimp, for instance, who says the theory is confounded nonsense."

"Scrimp can have any opinion he likes for me."

"But when you find two men of opposite opinions, how are you to know which is right?"

"By exercising your judgment, of course."

"And is your judgment infallible?"

"Yes, if it be based on common sense."

"Common sense! there's the rub again. I wish you would tell me what *is* common sense."

"Do you mean to say you don't know?"

" I confess I don't."

" Enough, sir," said Rosin, drawing himself up to his highest altitude, and bestowing upon me a look of withering contempt. " Enough, sir ; after such a confession I would be prostituting my intelligence conversing, let alone arguing, with you. Good-night, sir."

With a terribly sarcastic bow he quitted my side, leaving me in utter bewilderment. My ideas took fright as usual, and scampered off to their accustomed hiding-places. All that remained to me was a kind of instinct which enabled me to get home and find my bed.

For days thereafter I moped about in a state of semi-somnambulism, and as my scattered wits gradually collected, a fierce conflict waged within me. There was a voice which said —" Trouble no more about common sense ; thou hast existed hitherto without knowing what it is, and so mayest thou continue to exist. This quality or myth, or whatever it be, called common sense, all men seem to know, and but for thy confessed ignorance, no one would suspect thee of not knowing. Profess, like other men, to know what common sense is, and save thyself a world of trouble."

In opposition, there was another voice which said—

" Not so. If thou knowest not what common sense is, up and find it out. Don't go through the world under false pretences. Up and find it, if in the world it is to be found."

The latter voice prevailed, and I braced up sufficient courage to call upon Professor Oldtory, who was at the time President of " The Society for the Conservation of Common Sense," and reputed to be a man of great erudition. Curiously enough, I discovered the Professor in his kitchen superintending the filling of a Scotch haggis ! After we were alone, he explained that when a boy, he had formed the opinion that he was an adept in this special branch of the culinary art, and added, " A correct opinion once formed should never be changed—this is the first principle of common sense."

I briefly made known to the Professor that it was in reference to that very point I had taken the liberty of calling upon him ; and that I would feel for ever grateful if he could enlighten my darkened understanding by defining common sense.

"Well, my young friend," he replied, pompously though kindly, "this is a subject to which I have devoted many years of my life, and I would say, in a sentence, that common sense is to be firmly convinced of the correctness of your opinions."

I immediately took out my note-book and made an entry— "Common sense—to be firmly convinced of the correctness of your opinions." I read it slowly over, and must say that I thought there was a want of logic or coherency, or that something was wrong about it, but what I could not tell.

"But if an individual have no opinions ?" I blurted out.

"Stupid lad, stupid young man," he replied in tones of compassion. "The individual who has no opinions is devoid of common sense."

I had not another word to say, and thanking him for his information, retired.

My whole soul being now devoted to the attainment of my life's object, I called the following morning upon Dr Bumpus, for the purpose of submitting Professor Oldtory's opinion to his critical judgment.

Dr Bumpus was medical practitioner to the public generally, and physician extraordinary to my aged grandmother, having helped her off in her last illness. I had no personal acquaintance with the Doctor, but the fact above stated, and a distant recollection that he had once written a book or delivered a lecture on "The Practical Side of Nonsense," influenced me in deciding to pay him a visit.

I found him pacing up and down his narrow surgery. He seemed excited. There was a phosphorescent glare in his eyes. I stammered a few words of apology.

"Five shillings !" he shouted, gruffly.

"Beg pardon, Doctor, if I am intruding," I said very meekly.

" I have not called upon you in your professional capacity, but merely to ask a single question—Is it common sense to be firmly convinced of the correctness of your opinions ?"

" Get out, puppy !" he roared, in a voice of thunder. " What business have you to interfere ? Get out of this, or by my skeletons ! I shall kick you into cod-liver oil !"

Thereupon he rushed at me like an infuriated bull, and I narrowly escaped contact with the toe of his boot. In my hurried exit through the street door I collided with an individual who stood on the pavement, to the sad detriment of my front teeth, which struck against his elbow.

" Hope you ain't hurt ?" said he, at the same time steadying me on my legs. " S'pose your business with the Doctor has been similar to mine. Paid me the same compliment ten minutes ago. Furious brute ! Madman !"

" What is the meaning of it all ? I can't understand it," I gasped, in the utmost amazement.

" Can't understand it ? Oh, then, I'll enlighten you. You see I took ill—lay in bed—called in Dr Bumpus—examined me—said I suffered from wind on the brain—mixed up physics —bottles by the dozen—pills—powders—blisters—wet cloths. Well, you see, I swallowed them all—applied them all—got no better—got worse. Not satisfied with Dr Bumpus' treatment, called in Dr Puff—told him my supposed malady. ' Nonsense, nonsense,' said he—' brain healthy—stomach wrong—cobweb on the stomach.' More medicines—different treatment— shower baths—vinegar—salt—potassium—got better—all sound —strong as ever. Well, you see, Dr Bumpus sends me bill— attendance and medicines, £5 5s. Five guineas for nigh killing a man ! Shall I pay it ? No, by the powers, says I—no. Called on Bumpus—told him whole affair—how he was mistaken—said he must cancel bill. Well, you see, Bumpus got angry—swore—stamped with his feet—said he would have his money. I got angry likewise—said he wouldn't—wrong treatment—Dr Puff's opinion. Bumpus got fiercer than ever

—didn't care a d——n for Puff's opinion—would stick to his own opinion against the world! Stick away, said I, and I'll stick to the five guineas. Scuffle ensued—rushed at me like madman—seized me by coat tail—received sharp stroke behind, and found myself quickly in the street. Ha, ha, Bumpus, but I'm not done with you yet."

The cause of the doctor's rage was now quite intelligible. My visit had been rather inopportune, and my question exceedingly so. Turning to my new-found friend I related to him, in return for his communicativeness, the object of my visit to the Doctor, and the difficulties I had encountered in endeavouring to discover what was common sense.

" Ah, you have taken the wrong method," said he. " Common sense ain't to be found so. Look here—travel the whole world —converse with everyone—in their own opinion everyone speaks common sense. Well, you see, when you have done all this, you have still to ascertain from whence comes all the nonsense and humbug and double-distilled bosh. Searching for common sense? Ha, you'll never find it that way."

" In what way is it to be found, then ?" I inquired.

" By first finding nonsense—much simpler thing—plenty of it agoing. Well, you see—nonsense found—invert it—result— common sense. For instance, I stand on my head—nonsense— invert me—set me on my feet—common sense."

I grasped my companion's hand in a paroxysm of joy. The thing seemed clear as sunlight, and the illustration was so beautifully striking. Ha! this was truly a step in advance. I recalled the conversation I had heard in the street some time ago, and now I had got these opinions in a measure corroborated. I almost danced for joy.

" Good-bye, friend," said I, when we parted. " Good-bye, and may heaven bless you for your kindness in putting me on the right road."

Once more I drew forth my note-book, and made the follow-ing entry:—" Find nonsense—invert it—result—common sense."

I was hurrying homeward, my mind full of the subject, when I was roused from my reverie by a sharp cry of—"Look oot, mannie." Looking out, I could only discover a couple of boys gambolling on the pavement in front of me.

"Tak' care o' oor bools, will ye ?"

The warning came too late. I had already kicked one of their marbles aside.

"Ye blin' duffer," was the salutation I received in passing, to which I paid no attention.

"Hey, look at yer hat, mannie," the same precious urchin called after me.

"What's wrong with my hat ?" I asked, turning round and addressing him.

"Lor! dinna ye see that it's roond !" he croaked, with a grin, and instantly decamped.

I hesitated to take off my hat and examine it, yet feared it might have received some damage in my hurried flight from Dr Bumpus. The other boy, observing my hesitation, came running up, exclaiming—

"There's naething wrang wi' yer hat ; it's a' buff."

Buff! An idea struck me.

"Come here, my boy," I said, waving him towards me. "What do you mean by *buff* ?"

"Nonsense."

"And what is nonsense, my boy ?"

"What'll ye gie's if I tell ye ?"

"I'll give you this coin," I said, taking a halfpenny from my pocket.

"Gie's the *maik* first, then."

Could I trust him ? Yes, there was something in his face which bespoke integrity.

"Very well, here is the halfpenny ; now tell me what is nonsense ?"

"Sippin' porridge wi' a stockin' needle !" he promptly replied, and ran off to spend his halfpenny.

Bravo! capital! Sipping porridge with a stocking needle is certainly nonsense. And now to apply the rule. Let me invert it. By Dr Bumpus' skeletons, here's a puzzler! It's not so easily turned from head to heels as my late friend would be, and transformed into common sense. Oh, that I had him here to explain! But let me see. Sipping porridge with a stocking needle is nonsense. Invert it—Sipping a stocking needle with porridge is—common sense? Never! Oh, that I had——

Good gracious! what has happened? I am struck to the ground; the world is reeling around me—spinning quicker than any spinning-jenny. Through the centre of the earth I sink, sink, and likewise revolve with such velocity that I no longer feel—I can only hear. I have become metamorphosed into an immense ear, which, like a blown bladder, is filled with loud rushing noises, as if besieged on every side with fiercest hail-storm—now louder, as of the prancing of ten thousand horses; now louder still, as of the general conflagration and crash of doom, till with a terrible cannon-like boom the bladder bursts, and I am annihilated. No longer do I exist as an entity, nor have I any recollection of a former existence. I have become a part of everything. I am conscious of forms and shadows—strange and fantastic—coils of live ropes uncoiling and coiling in an element of darkness—transparent darkness, in which everything is visible. Ages seem thus to pass away—the ropes ever coiling and uncoiling.

At length a change takes place. I am again conscious of having a separate existence. I have become a head—a huge head, full of eyes and ears, and am sent to roll over the universe. I pass out of darkness into light. I gaze upon sun, moon, and stars, and roll over mountains and valleys, over rivers and seas, and over cities inhabited by men. Like a monster wheel of Juggernaut, I crush men and women to death. My ears are pierced with their dying shrieks, but I have no heart to pity them. And thus for ages more I roll on.

Again a change takes place. I have ceased to roll, and out of my head has grown a body with arms and legs. All still I lie, because unable to rise. The sun by day scorches me, and I shiver with the dews of the night. The din of voices fills the air around me. Goddesses, nymphs, and demons hover near me. I am cold and hot and thirsty. Oh, how thirsty! but no one heeds me or ministers unto me. Desperately I struggle to rise, but my head is too heavy—I cannot raise it. I have got a voice, and call for help, but I remain unheeded. Oft do I call to a beautiful goddess when she passes before my vision. Oft do I call to the black demons which surround me. Oh, that even demons would minister unto me! But no, no!

Once more a change takes place. My head has decreased to its normal size. I can rise, sit, or walk about. I bear the form and impress of a man, but am withal a god—the god of common sense. I reside in a palace, and proclaim to the mortals who surround me my great heaven-ordained mission. Courtiers and statesmen, poets and philosophers, eagerly drink in the words which flow from my lips; but there be some who sneer thereat. "Foolish mortals! self-satisfied idiots!" I say unto them, "Cease your vain jargon and babblement—learn wisdom. Ye think ye have found common sense, and yet sneer at me who am sent by heaven to proclaim it unto you. Your common sense is the refuse of the devil's nonsense—the scrapings of his frying-pan, which his imps even will not eat."

Then I speak to them all in a milder tone, and promulgate my Proverbial Philosophy—

A shovel hat makes a bishop, and money a gentleman.
Stained glass aids devotion, and spectacles a blind horse.
Drink whisky, and pray to be kept from intoxication.
Feed well the stomach, and the mind will feed itself.
Drive folly from the heart of a child with a penny, and give the keys of your cash-box to a robber.
Poverty is worse than profligacy, and a balance at the bank of more account than piety.

K

Fair dealing tendeth to leanness, but a man of understanding waxeth fat.

Cheat the devil if you can, and then go to heaven in his
livery.

Then the devil comes towards me in a rage.

" False devil !" I cry, " I shall fight thee—come on—I shall
fight thee !"

My attendants buckle on my armour—my coat of mail—but
ah, me, it is too heavy. I cannot raise my arms to fight, and
succumb to the blows of the devil. Exhausted, I fall asleep
and dream. I fancy myself back in forgotten ages—again a
mortal searching for common sense. All the events of those
days pass before my vision, until that moment when I fall
through the centre of the earth. A second time I feel myself
falling—beginning to rotate, and in my struggle to regain the
surface I awake.

I am conscious of being a man once again. I feel weak and
faint, as if released from a nightmare. Where I am I know
not. I lie on a bed, from which I am powerless to rise, nor can
I move a limb. I seem to be tied down. Gazing around, I find
I am alone in a narrow room, into which a stream of shaded
light issues through a stanchioned window.

While thus gazing in deep wonder, and vainly trying to recall
recent events, an individual in uniform approaches my bedside
and surveys me.

" Where am I ?" I ask.

" In your state chamber," he replies.

I had then passed into some new phase of existence, I
thought.

" And who are you ?" I further enquired.

" Why, I'm the devil. You tried to fight me last night, and
don't know me to-day."

I saw he was making sport of me.

" Do tell me where I am, and allow me to rise," I said
imploringly.

"He, he; it aint time for a god to rise yet—it wouldn't be common sense, you know."

"Man, if you have any feelings, don't trifle with me," I said, passionately.

The individual to whom I addressed this appeal, started back and gazed upon me in astonishment.

"Have his senses returned?" I heard him mutter. My senses returned! Ah, the truth flashed upon me that instant. I have been insane, and am even now the inmate of a madhouse!

Yes, it was true, reader. In my search after common sense I had landed here. On the morning of my episode with Dr Bumpus, while returning home, I was knocked down by a carriage, one of its wheels passing over my head. For months I lay in a very precarious condition, and when I recovered bodily strength, my mind was found to be affected. For upwards of a year I was confined in a lunatic asylum, until my sudden recovery set me free.

I no longer search for common sense. I have learned what it is to be without it, and value all the more the modicum of it which remains to me. It may be inverted nonsense for aught I know; but I am inclined to think that, after all, the best definition is that of Mr Buzzard, who said it was "juist common sense"—the sense which is common to humanity—that "touch of nature which makes the whole world kin."

PROFESSOR BUMBLETON INTERVIEWED.

I FOUND the Professor seated in an armchair, his left foot upon his right knee, and endeavouring to remove a corn from his little toe, with a formidable-looking razor.

He politely asked me to take a seat, which I did, with a slight presentiment of terror.

"I amuse myself practising a little surgery occasionally," he remarked, smiling grimly.

"Corns are annoying things," I said.

"Not at all, sir; you're decidedly wrong," he replied, energetically. "Nature, which never errs, places corns on our feet for wise and beneficent ends. They often prevent an over-straining of the physical system, by acting as a gentle drag upon our pedestrian proclivities. Then, they're a great source of revenue to cab and omnibus proprietors, in helping to promote the principle of 'the greatest happiness to the greatest number,' by keeping men in employment. They are likewise invaluable to the student of human nature, as there is no better way of ascertaining a man's true disposition, than by treading upon his corns. But, above all, they afford the mind that relaxation which is so necessary to it. Were it not for these corns, sir, I believe that from sheer study my brain would, ere now, be soft as butter-milk."

I smiled faintly, and began to wonder if softening of the brain had not already set in.

"You made use of the remark just now, Professor," I said, "that nature never errs. Now, isn't this a point——"

"It can't be a point," he said, interrupting me. "There are no points nor straight lines in nature."

Meanwhile he had put on his slippers and lit his pipe. As I gazed upon his portly figure, seated back in his cushioned chair, with both feet stuck over the fireplace, I could not help thinking that, after all, professors were not greatly dissimilar to other men, and ventured to reply—

"You misunderstand me, sir. You said nature never errs, and if this be so, how do you account for Siamese twins, Barnum curiosities and monstrosities, giants, dwarfs, and men without legs and arms? In the vegetable kingdom, too, we find various freaks of nature, which lead one to suppose that she does make occasional mistakes."

"No, sir," replied the Professor, "I cannot admit that nature ever makes mistakes. Such instances as you adduce are just what you call them—freaks or frolics perpetrated by nature, when in a frolicsome mood, and simply prove nature to be natural, for you know

"A little nonsense now and then
Is relished by the wisest men."

If you read my work on 'The Philosophy of Visualized and Coruscated Tissues in its relation to the Noetic Nullifidianism of Sentient Structures,' you will find this subject thoroughly reasoned out."

"Why, Professor, I have tried to read that work, but its intricate reasoning goes beyond my powers of comprehension."

"I do not wonder at that," he replied; "there are depths of argument in that work, sir, which I myself am unable to fathom. But such is the taste of the age, you know."

"How the taste of the age?"

"Why, you see, unless you write a book which goes beyond the mental calibre of everybody, nobody will lionize you nor call you a great genius, and, consequently, nobody will buy your book."

"I fear, Professor, that the man who publicly expressed these sentiments would be considered slightly cranky, or, for the time being, under the influence of liquor."

"And suppose I were under the influence of liquor—what then?" he retorted, knitting his brows.

"I should consider it very unbecoming in a Professor," I replied.

"Ah, my dear sir, there's where you display your ignorance."

"How so?"

"Why, the very fact that a man has a relish for intoxicating liquor, proves his mental superiority, not only over the lower creation, but also over his uncivilized fellowmen. When I see a man intoxicated, I feel perfectly sure that I gaze upon a civilised being. Why, the desire for ardent spirits is one of the first results of civilization and missionary enterprise to a savage community. Beer and the Bible go hand-in-hand. If history and statistics prove anything, they prove that religion and mental culture progress in exactly the same ratio as the consumption of spirituous liquor increases. Look at Scotland, for instance—where will you find a country on the face of the earth, possessing more churches and learned institutions, in proportion to its size? Where will you find a people more religious or more intellectual? And, on the other hand, where will you find a country so famed for its whisky distilleries, or a population which consumes the ardent spirit to the same extent? Ignorant people laugh at Darwin and his theory of the Origin of Man; but, to my mind, the fact that monkeys will drink grog, is most convincing of the soundness of Darwin's theory. I have observed that monkeys can chew tobacco, too; and the only other animal that I know of, having a similar propensity, is the ass; from which fact I am inclined to conclude that there is a distant relationship between the donkey, the monkey, and the man."

"Your ideas are perfectly novel to me, Professor," I said; "in fact, they are so wonderful——"

"No, sir, there is nothing wonderful to the man of science. It is only the ignorant who see wonderful things. And, after a time, things cease to be wonderful even to them. I might instance two modern inventions—the telephone and the phonograph. Even lucifer matches were considered wonderful

when they were invented, and the time was when an eclipse of
the sun or moon was regarded with awe.   Indeed, if we could
go back far enough, I have no doubt we would find men so
steeped in ignorance, that the very rising of the sun filled them
with wonder!   No, sir, there is nothing wonderful to the man
of science in this enlightened age.   I may inform you that I
hope shortly, to astonish the world with some new inventions,
which will, no doubt, be considered wonderful for a time."

"And what are they, pray, if it be your will to inform me?"

"Well, I am meantime writing two treatises to prepare the
world for the revolutions, both physical and moral, which my
inventions are calculated to produce.   One treatise is entitled
"Inverted Pedestrianism," and the other, "The Philosophy of
Optical Delusions."   The first will demonstrate the practicability
of human beings walking up the walls and across the ceilings of
rooms, as flies do.   This is accomplished by the application of
suction valves to the soles of the feet, and by the transference
of the brains to the region of the stomach—the latter a peculiar
and exceedingly delicate operation, of which I flatter myself to
be the inventor.   Its objects are manifold—First, to bring the
centre of gravity of the human body nearer the point of contact
with the material it treads upon ; second, to give more room for
the brain to expand, as the cranium often proves of too limited
capacity for its proper expansion ;   and third, to allow the
cavity formerly occupied by the brain to be utilized for the
proper development of the ocular nerves ; and then, the ocular
delusions which presently exist will be entirely dispelled.
What do you think of this?"

"Certainly most extraordinary theories, Professor," I said,
but added, "I don't see what benefit is to be derived from
inverted pedestrianism."

"Ah, you don't?" he said, sarcastically.   "I suppose you're
one of those who can't see what benefit is to be derived from the
discovery of the North Pole nor the Sources of the Nile.   You can
see no benefit in Capital Punishment, nor the Conversion of the

Jews; in the Capture of King Coffee's Umbrella, nor the Relief of Emin Pasha. You're one of those——"

"Stay, stay, Professor, I'm sorry for interrupting you; my remark was doubtless stupid. Pray proceed with your interesting statements. What about your other treatise on 'The Philosophy of Optical Delusions?'"

"Ah, yes, in that book I demonstrate to a certainty that opaqueness is simply an idea, and that it is quite as possible to see through stone walls as through glass walls—in fact, that opaqueness and darkness are both optical delusions. My invention consists of a most intricate piece of mechanism, which I must decline to describe until it is patented. This, after the removal of the brains to the region of the stomach, is introduced into the cavity left in the cranium, and by being brought in contact with the ocular nerves, a most surprising result takes place. Stone walls, and brick and wood partitions, become transparent, and we are enabled to see the inside of any house we look at, and everything that takes place therein."

"You don't mean it, Professor! that we can see who say their prayers before going to bed and who don't? and—and—oh, dear me, such a state of things would be fearful—it would be quite intolerable."

"Yes, to the wicked and hypocritical, whose deeds won't bear the light. But once they become aware that everything they do may be seen by others, they will soon amend their ways. This invention, sir, will occasion the greatest revolution in our social and moral existence that ever burst upon the world."

I thought so too. At the same time, I inwardly shuddered at the bare idea of such a discovery, and trusted the invention would never be perfected. I did not express myself thus, however, but simply said—

"Astonishing!"

"Yes, sir, these two works will be unique in their character; will be profusely illustrated with engravings and diagrams, and will prove valuable additions to the other sublime scientific treatises, which the great minds of the age are so lavishly bestowing upon the world."

" You must have a very fertile brain, Professor," I remarked.

" Yes, sir, it is astonishing what a number of new ideas are hatched here," he said, placing his hand upon his stomach. " Last night, an idea struck me, which, I have not the least doubt will, after a little thinking out, prove to be an invaluable invention to sportsmen and all who use the gun. The principle of the invention is to feed grouse, partridges, hares, rabbits, and other birds and beasts of sport with loadstone powder, which in the course of a short time will impregnate their blood and render them highly magnetic. Then by using steel shot, the animals are sure to be killed, without the trouble of taking an aim, as their magnetism will attract the steel, even round a corner."

" Such an invention may be all very good for sportsmen," I remarked, "but poachers would take advantage of it, and it occurs to me that the game would very soon be exterminated."

" Possibly," said the Professor, " but a bit of money could be made of the invention before that time comes."

I felt shocked at such mercenary ideas, but not wishing to give offence, started on a fresh topic.

" You are aware, Professor, that at this moment the whole civilised world eagerly demands the solution of certain problems, and I would impress upon you the necessity of laying the result of your indefatigable researches and the products of your comprehensive mind at the feet of society. For instance, I feel assured you can supply some invaluable information on that vexing question—the age of the world."

" Ugh," he said, " I have solved that problem. The world is almost fourteen million four hundred thousand years old."

" So you don't believe in the six thousand years theory?"

" Not at all, sir. This world existed over fourteen million years ago, and at that time was no larger than a lump of coal."

"A lump of coal! And how large might that be?"

"You have seen a lump of coal, I suppose?"

"Very often."

"Then, why ask silly questions?" he said, with a scowl.

"Proceed, Professor," said I, meekly; "I am not accustomed to such learned disquisitions. Where did the lump of coal come from?"

"From the sun, of course—thrown out by some internal convulsion, or blown off by a breeze of wind. At all events, it was hurled into space, and flew at an immense velocity until arrested by the repulsion of the moon. Being thus suddenly brought to a stand, it, as a matter of course, commenced to spin round, and by virtue of the centrifugal and centripetal forces which all revolving bodies possess, it created its own atmosphere and became a miniature world."

"And how did it arrive at its present size?"

"By natural growth. Our world is increasing year by year in size. As near as I can calculate, it grows at the rate of three feet in diameter every year. You can easily see that the immense quantity of decayed vegetation, and the dead bodies of men and beasts, which annually mix with the soil of the earth, must of necessity increase its size."

"Well, Professor," I said, "since you have enlightened me on this point, there only remains another that I am meantime anxious to obtain your opinion regarding, namely, the origin of life."

"Ha! that has been a puzzling question for a long time, but I have now fully solved it. I have discovered that the sun is the source of all life—animal and vegetable. You have but to take a dead dog or other animal, and expose the carcase to the rays of the sun, and in the space of a few days it will become a moving mass of living organisms—of maggots. And these maggots, sir, can be developed into other organisms by a system of feeding and breeding, with which I am presently experimenting. I could let you see maggots which I have got to grow more than an inch long, and by the aid of the microscope I can distinguish legs beginning to develop on them."

"Most astonishing!" I exclaimed. "I won't wait, however, to inspect the maggots to-day, but will be glad of an opportunity of, doing so some future time. One question more, Professor, and I will leave you to your studies. From whence did the sun receive its life-giving power?"

"The sun," replied the Professor, "is a vast subject, and I really have no time to enter upon it at present. When you come back to see the maggots in process of development, I will be glad to enlighten you. Good day."

I thanked Professor Bumbleton profusely for granting me such a lengthened interview, and he politely bowed me to the door.

Some weeks thereafter the Professor was developing maggots in a way he did not calculate upon, but it won't pay to explain everything in one volume.

ESSAY ON MILK.

By JOHNNIE BOUNTREE.

Milk is a liquid, and sometimes in summer the heat of the sun freezes it into a solid. Some animals and fishes don't have milk, but I think the whale has. It is the she sex that has milk. The he sex, both of people, beasts, birds, fishes, and all other insects, don't have milk—leastways, I've never heard of it.

The first milk we know about is mother's milk. Babies are great lovers of it. They prefer it to buttered toast, or even mince pie. When I was a baby I got fat on it, but I don't remember now how it tasted.

The right milk is cow's milk. It is consumed and drunken by every kind of people, as well as infants and young children. It was originally intended for calves, but now they kill the calves to make veal. Milk may be had cold, warm, or sour. It is made warm by pouring warm water amongst it. I have heard it said that sour milk is intended for bachelors, who have got no women for their wives. Butter-milk is for making butter with, but I don't know what kind of cows give this milk. Another lad told Pete my brother, and Pete told me, that it was the bull, but I don't think this is true.

People who are unwell drink goat's milk and mare's milk. I have also heard of turkey's milk and pigeon's milk, but have never seen any of it. I've heard Pa speak about the milk of human kindness, which he said was very scarce to be got.

Cream is produced from milk. The law of gravitation makes it rise to the top, as it is thickest. It is then skimmed off with a broken saucer or a table spoon. Cream is cold, and of a white colour, but a good deal yellower than milk.

The druggists sell cold cream, but nobody should buy it from them, as it is a spurious imitation.

RAVINGS.

Saw ye the man? One moment he wavered upon the giddy height—the next disappeared into the abyss—the seething, boiling abyss of fiery-tongued torments. Ambition! where is thy height? Lost amid the vapoury clouds of the never-to-be explored. Ambition! where is thy depth? Lost in the bottomless chaos of wrecked energy. And thy breadth? Broad as the universe. Thine arms would grasp the heavens—yea, would encircle hell itself. Mortal! try not to scale the slippery steep. Thy breath will fail thee, for there's no atmosphere up there. Goad him not on, O popular applause! Soft breathings of adoration! goad him not on. Mocking demons! goad him not on. There is honour. He has reached it, but unsatiated, higher he mounts. There sits the bauble reputation. It bursts while he grasps it. There is gold, too. He makes a clutch at it, but, ah! it is too heavy. Shining nuggets fall upon him, and bear him down, down to the abyss. He has found gold, and dies rich. Chuckle not, scoffing demons! He has left the gold which crushed him down, to build a church. Why sneer, ye scoffing demons, and say it is only because he could not take it with him? He dies rich! Did ye hear it? And what then? A funeral—an oration—a panegyric—a newspaper notice, and the world moves on as before. The sun rises and sets—stars shine and cease to shine, and an atom is not missed from the boundless immensity. Men die and men are born, and the crowd is ever the same. O, the strange, many-visaged crowd! the noisy-silent, slow-hurrying, happy-sorrowful crowd! the thoughtful-unthinking crowd! The voice of mirth mingles with the wail of sorrow. Splendour and plenty rub shoulders with rags and poverty. Beauty and distortion go side by side. And what is beauty? Does it fade? So says the world; but beauty—*beauty!* cannot fade.　It mounts to heaven, and lives beyond the wreck of worlds!　I see a being the world calls beautiful.　Avoid her, my son, as thou wouldst a viper in thy path.　Oh, beautiful decrepitude—daughter of shame! return to thy father's house.　If thou hast a mother, she is praying for thee.　If thou hast not, return all the same.　Breast the swift-flowing current, if thou art able.　If not, then glide down with it.　Niagara's brink is near, and then? the world sees thee no more.

I hear the sound of revelry, the laugh-croak of voluptuousness. The stream flows on—swift and deep, and muddy—this Stygian stream.　What is that?　A cry of rage—fierce imprecations—horrid owl-screechings.　Fiend! dost thou lift thy hand against high heaven to smite the wife of thy bosom!　She calls thee devil, and dost thou spit in her face?　Mystery of mysteries! One flesh!　Love and cherish!　Laugh, demons; wag your tails, for your handiwork reflects you credit.　O, pollution—wormwood—hell-fire—red-hot ashes!

I have heard men speak of happiness; and there is a thing called Constancy.　Tell me not thou hast found it, my son. Behold, a green-eyed monster is already in thy path—the sworn enemy of Constancy.　Thou keepest it within thy heart of hearts; thou hast locked the door upon it, and buried the key; thou sayest, "I shall never let it depart."　Delusion!　Like smoke, it finds an outlet—like water, it evaporates, and is not. O, changeling! thy heart of hearts is full of emptiness.

NANCY THISTLE.

THE subject of this sketch was born amid the bleak wilds of Caithness-shire where, previous to the introduction of the railway, the aborigines existed in a state of semi-barbarism. The male population roamed about in kilt and bare legs—many of them bare-headed and bare-footed; while the females clothed themselves in coarse homespun, known as "scourings," the upper portion of their bodies being covered with a "short goon" of printed calico, and their heads with a handkerchief of the "snuffy" pattern, tied round the ears. When a consignment of leather boots was first sent them by the good people of the south, who felt for them in their half-clothed state of savagedom, many of them appeared not to know the use of boots. The writer has seen them—male and female—trudging bare-footed along their rough foot-tracks, their boots dangling from their necks, as if intended for ornamentation.

In this inhospitable, treeless region, John and Mary Thistle reared up a large family of sons and daughters. Talking of trees, I remember, on my first visit to *Ultima Thule*, asking one of the natives why there were no trees growing around their homesteads or roadsides, and receiving for reply, in the peculiar vernacular of the district—"'Ee trees wis a' ayten up wi' 'ee sheep last winter." John Thistle's family consisted of seven boys and eight girls. Missionaries had already introduced the Bible into this remote region, but being barely half civilised, the people, in their ignorance, believed that the divine command to multiply and replenish the earth was specially addressed to them, and they acted up to it to the best of their ability. They did not once think of the horrible sin of bringing children into the world to become possible paupers, but had a superstitious belief, which they expressed in the proverb—"'Ee Lord never sent a bairn bit fat he sent a bwite an' a brot wi't."

John Thistle had a croft, consisting of a few acres of moor-
land, and cultivated patches here and there, in which he grew
as much corn and potatoes as fed his family, horse, and pig; and
by grazing a stirk or two in the summer months and selling the
pig, he managed to pay his rent.

Nancy was the eldest of the family, and from her early
infancy she had to assist her mother in her multifarious household duties. It is needless to say that John Thistle's children
were not clothed in scarlet nor sumptuously fed. They were
neither petted nor pampered, and yet they throve. Another
superstition which prevailed among the natives of this region
was, that health or sickness were matters entirely beyond their
control. "If he lives he lives, an' if he dees he dees—it's the
Lord's will," was their ignorant conclusion in cases of sickness.
They had no knowledge of sanitary and hygienic laws, and never
heard of the germs and microbes of disease, in regard to which
we are all so enlightened.

The diet of this family consisted of oatmeal brose for
breakfast; potatoes and salt herring, followed with bere scones
and sowans, for dinner; and oatmeal porridge for supper. By
way of variety, they sometimes had the porridge in the morning
and the brose at night.

It was quite a treat to see them at feeding time, and, in fact,
it was nearly always feeding time, for the children were so
numerous that they had to be fed in relays. The porridge was
cooked in a large pot, and when sufficiently cool, as many of the
youngsters as could get around it took spoonful about until
all were satisfied. There were no piles of dirty dishes to wash
when they were done, nothing but a few horn spoons. When
the diet happened to be brose, the lid of the "girnal" containing
the oatmeal was opened and a cavity formed in the meal, into
which boiling water was poured, and then stirred about until the
requisite quantity of meal was saturated. Then the horn spoons
were again in requisition, and it was spoon about until every
stomach was filled.

The house in which the family was reared would be more fitly described as a mud hut. No stones were used in its construction, except a few which formed the doorway, and the two or three holes in the wall which did duty for windows. The roof was of thatch, and the floor of clay. The erection was divided into three compartments, the central being the kitchen where the peat fire burned on the centre of the floor, the smoke finding egress as best it could through a hole in the roof. Here one half of the family slept, and the other half in the "ben" or end compartment. The compartment at the other end was occupied by the horse, pig, and other live stock which required shelter.

Amid such surroundings Nancy Thistle lived and bloomed until she was fourteen years of age. About this time some home missionaries penetrated into the barbarous region, and taking compassion on this family of young savages, prevailed upon John and Mary Thistle to allow Nancy and a younger brother to be sent to an institution in the south, where they would have the benefit of a good education. Nancy displayed a wonderful aptitude for learning, and in three or four years thereafter, she obtained an appointment in the Post Office. By steady perseverance and attention to her duties, she soon rose to fill an important position in the Telegraph department. It was, no doubt, during those years that she encountered the "Fellows" portrayed in her sketches.

Nancy was a strapping, rather good-looking damsel, with the flush of perfect health on her cheek. She was vivacious, straightforward, and outspoken to a fault. Some people who only read her sketches looked on her as being a "blue stocking" or some faded flirt, who took pleasure in vomiting her spleen on her former sweethearts. But to those who knew her, she was far different from this. She sometimes did not feel quite at home amid the conventionalities of refined society, and always retained a tinge of what might be called uncouthness, both in her movements and expressions. But she was warm-

L

hearted, clear-headed, and the very soul of truthfulness and sincerity, qualities which did more than atone for the slight shortcomings we have referred to. It is indeed wonderful that she turned out so well as she did, considering her youthful upbringing, and the fact that she had savage blood in her veins.

It was the forenoon of one of our January holidays, and snowing heavily. I had occasion to call upon a lady friend, and being on familiar terms with the occupants of the house, finding the door ajar, I stepped in without ringing. Advancing to the door of my friend's room, I found it likewise partially open, while she and Nancy Thistle stood looking out at the window, engaged in animated conversation. I did not intend to be an eavesdropper, yet hesitated to disturb them.

"Now, isn't it lovely?" said Nancy. "I wish we were in the country, where people wouldn't see us; I'd drag you out and make you stand beneath the snowflakes till you would be covered with a coat of purest white, and look like an angel."

"Ugh, you make me shiver. It would be a cold garment for an angel."

"I shouldn't feel in the least cold. I wonder what people would think were I to go and stand on the middle of the street just now? I've a great inclination to go."

"Why, they would think you were mad, Nancy."

"Yes, I daresay the spectacle would astonish your shivering, muffled-up tea drinkers, who are continually toasting their starved feet at the fire. Just look how they go rushing along with umbrellas over their heads. What horrid desecration!"

"What do you mean, Nancy?"

"Why, God giving them an opportunity of being clothed in the nearest earthly approach to heaven's garb, and they shielding off the silvery snowflakes from their unworthy carcases with abominable umbrellas. If this isn't desecration, I don't know what is. It's as bad as shielding off God's sunshine."

"What a girl you are, Nancy. But look—there comes a

gentleman without an umbrella. I suppose you'll have a special regard for him ?"

"I have indeed. Bravo ! thou lord of creation. How noble he looks with his beard

> ' White with other snows than those of age.'

I am certain he enjoys a treat, he walks so leisurely, no doubt thinking of angels' kisses as the soft flakes fall on his lips."

"Oh, you absurd girl ! He may be the greatest scoundrel in the world for all you know."

"Impossible ! If he hadn't a warm heart within him he'd be hurrying along like the others."

Being desirous of seeing the gentleman who was attracting their attention, I made my presence known by stepping up to the window, and judge of my surprise when on looking out I recognised my old friend and classmate, Joe B——, just returned from America. I rapped on the window, and he having recognised me, I beckoned on him to come inside. Meantime the girls had rushed away from the window in a flutter of excitement, and I was called rude and impertinent, and all that sort of thing.

But when I introduced Joe as an old and esteemed friend, and he having quite a captivating manner with the ladies, I was speedily forgiven for my forwardness, and we all passed a pleasant afternoon together.

The outcome of it was—and I still get credit for bringing it about—that an intimacy sprang up between Nancy Thistle and Joe which ended in their marriage, and she still declares that her husband is the best " fellow " she ever knew.

IV.

FELLOWS I HAVE KNOWN.

By NANCY THISTLE.

THE FELLOW WHOM HIS SISTERS SPOILED.

MOTHERS' pets generally become mothers' plagues. A petted child is a spoiled child, because trained up in the way that it should not go. It is a great pity that some mothers—ay, and fathers too—are so foolish and short-sighted as to evince a partiality towards some particular member of their family. Such indulgence is almost certain to bear bitter fruits; for that individual must be possessed of an extraordinary amount of sagacity and common sense who, getting his own will when a child, does not take it when a man. As a rule, the family pet is a boy. I suppose girls are not considered worth making pets of, and so much the better for them. This system of petting and pampering the boys accounts in a great measure for the self-willed, conceited, idle, dissolute, good-for-nothing fellows who are so frequently to be met with. What a different result a judicious use of the cane would have effected! I'm a believer in original sin, and in the rod as the most effectual means of driving folly out of the heart of a child. So was King Solomon. People talk much now-a-days about moral suasion, but, in my humble opinion, it is altogether a puny, feeble thing compared to a cat-o'-nine tails. I have no doubt some of my readers will shake their heads, and consider me a very cruel person. Perhaps I am, but I cannot help it. I confess it would afford me gratification to stand by and see a good many fellows flogged. I think it would do them an immense amount of good.

George Proudfellow was spoiled by his sisters. His mother commenced the operation, but it was fairly completed by them. He was the youngest of the family and the only son, and of course Master George became the lion of the fireside. "Girls," his mother would say to Jane and Mary, " see that you be kind to George ; you mustn't strike him back although he strikes you, but just let him have his own way, for he's a boy, you know. Poor fellow, he'll be a man yet. Who knows but he'll be a Member of Parliament, or even Prime Minister ; and you can never be this, for you're only girls, you know." And because Master George was a boy he got liberty to do as he pleased. His sisters were taught to regard him very much in the light of a god. If they complained to Ma that some privilege denied to them was granted to him, Ma's invariable answer was, " Oh, but he's a boy, you know."

So Master George's every whim was indulged, and when his mother died he was a capricious, selfish, little despot of eight years. The care of him then devolved upon his sisters, who continued to bring him up after the manner Ma had taught them. They could not think of sending him to school, because he would there mix with bad boys, and might get contaminated. George, in their eyes, was such a superior boy, that they fancied a school would be the means of blunting his fine susceptibilities and ruining him for life ; they must educate him at home, they reasoned. And so they set about educating him. But Master George did not much care for study ; he had a decided preference for barley-sugar. After repeated refusals on his part to learn lessons, Jane and Mary held a consultation together, and came to the conclusion that he would learn as he grew older; that it was very wrong to force boys to do things against their wills; that, as no amount of education could confer genius, and, being confident that George was a born genius, it did not much matter whether they educated him or not. And so they left his education pretty much to his natural genius. Unfortunately, he did not possess any, and grew up a full-fledged numskull.

I became acquainted with his sisters, and had heard a great deal about George long before I saw him. George said this, and George said the other thing; George approved of this, and disliked that. The name of George was so frequently dinned in my ear that my curiosity became excited to see this wonderful specimen of masculine humanity. I remember, about the commencement of our acquaintanceship, asking—

" Who is George ?"

" Our brother. Don't you know him ?" asked Jane.

" No. What does he do ?"

" Well, nothing as yet. Unfortunately, he cannot find scope for his talents here."

" What does he incline to be ?"

" He has never decided. Ma, before she died, said he ought to be a statesman; but I suppose he would require to go to London to be that ?"

" Yes, I fancy he would," I replied, forcing back a smile; " but I think he should aspire to something less ambitious in the first place."

" Oh, but he has talents, you know, and all talented people are ambitious," replied Jane, somewhat testily; and the subject was allowed to drop.

At length my curiosity to see this embryo statesman was gratified. I called one evening, and commenced talking to Mary, when she raised her hand and said—

" Whist !"

" Why, what's the matter ?" I inquired.

" George is ill."

" What's wrong with him ?"

" He's got a boil on his toe."

" Is that all ?" I exclaimed, lightly.

" You have no idea how painful it is, or you wouldn't say that. Jane and I have been attending him the whole evening."

" Is he in bed ?"

" Oh, no ; he is sitting before the parlour fire. You will see him if you step in."

I did step in, and I think the most ludicrous spectacle that ever I witnessed was George Proudfellow that evening. He was enveloped in a dressing-gown and red nightcap, and was propped up in an arm-chair, with a number of pillows and cushions beneath and on every side of him. His foot was wrapped up in pieces of flannel and handkerchiefs till it exceeded the size of his head, and rested upon another chair in front of the fire. But what amused me most was his woe-begone expression. He groaned, and sighed, and contorted his face as if he were suffering the most excruciating pain.

" George, dear, shall I bring you another pillow to put under your foot ?" Jane asked him when I entered, to which he replied with a grunt of acquiescence.

" George, dear, this is Miss Thistle," said Mary, introducing me.

" Ugh ! Don't bother me," he growled, burying his head among the pillows which surrounded him.

My first impressions of George were anything but pre-possessing. " This, then, is a sample of our future statesman," I mentally ejaculated.

" Poor fellow," whispered Mary in my ear, " he is somewhat impulsive, and the pain of his foot puts him out of temper."

" George, dear, shall I make beef-tea for you ?" she afterwards asked.

" Beef trash !   No !"

" What would you like, then—wine-negus ?"

" Yes, and make it strong."

Meantime Jane returned with another pillow, which she placed beneath dear George's foot ; and while doing so, dear George uttered some unparliamentary language for being disturbed. When Mary inquired if dear George thought he would be able to reach his bedroom unaided, I considered it time for me to depart, lest I should be asked to assist in carrying him there. So bidding them good-night, I walked home, both amused and disgusted at what I had witnessed.

Sometime thereafter I paid another visit, and invited the girls to a cookie-shine at our house.

"But, George—" said Jane.

" Yes, George—" echoed Mary.

" You know we are to have no gentlemen, therefore I cannot invite George," I put in.

"Yes, we understand," said Jane, " but George——"

" What about him ?"

" We couldn't both leave the house ; George might weary."

'' Weary ! what for ?"

" You know he doesn't approve of our going out, because then he has to stay in ; it seems to put him about so, and he is so sensitive and impulsive."

At this moment dear George entered the room, and I had the honour of a reintroduction, and I must admit he was somewhat more polite than on the former occasion.

" I have been asking your sisters to come over to our house one night next week," I remarked.

"And I suppose they'll expect me to sit in the house here all night," he growled.

"If it wouldn't trouble you too much, George, dear," said Jane.

" Yes, it would trouble me. How d'you think a fellow can spend a whole night in the house alone ?"

" A fellow could read an interesting book a whole night and not feel in the least wearied," I ventured to remark.

" Books be hanged !" he retorted.

" Dear George—" said Mary.

" George, dear, you are too impulsive," said Jane.

" You both shut up, now ! D'you think I'm to be bothered for your cookie-shines ? You shan't go, so that's an end to it."

And, after thus delivering himself, dear George stalked out of the room with the air of a conqueror.

" He is so impulsive," said Mary.

" So sensitive," said Jane.

" It's my opinion he's a great ass," I said, emphatically.

The two girls stared at me in bewilderment.

" I repeat it—your brother is a great ass, and you are yourselves greatly to blame for his being so. You indulge his every caprice, and make yourselves his slaves—in short, you have spoiled him."

" Miss Thistle, we are not to be insulted in our own house," said Jane, haughtily.

" I am sorry you should consider yourselves insulted ; I only speak the truth, and I fear you shall one day find that it is so, to your bitter regret," I replied, as I took my leave.

Is it not strange that people should be so touchy for having the truth spoken to them ? Neither Jane nor Mary ever recognised me again, although very soon thereafter they must have realised the weight of my parting words. Dear George found scope for his talents in a way they did not anticipate. I beg pardon for having said he was devoid of genius. He displayed a remarkable genius for billiards, beer, and horse-racing, and one morning his sisters awoke to find that their dear brother George had appropriated all their savings and decamped.

This is the last I have heard of the fellow whom his sisters spoiled, nor do I desire to hear more, for I fancy it would not be to his credit if I did. Such fellows display a heartlessness of the blackest type. It is one of the anomalies of human nature that the well-beloved child, on whom a mother has lavished all the tenderness of her heart; whom she has loved "not wisely but too well," should in the end, and as the very result of that too fond affection, turn round and despise her, trample on her love, and send her broken-hearted to the grave. The punishment of the mother is severe, but severer far must be that of the heartless wretch who has been the cause of it. I can think of no punishment in this world which can fully expiate his crimes.

THE FELLOW WHO HAD A MANIA FOR KISSING THE GIRLS.

KISSING is a strange custom, when one thinks of it. Fancy a fellow pressing his mouth to yours, opening his lips with a smack, and then feeling quite enraptured about it. Poor dunderhead! he is pleased with little. Man is a peculiar animal: he is a creature of signs and symbols, and may be made to believe almost anything. Even a kiss, under certain circumstances, becomes to him a most momentous matter.

I have often wondered why the mouth has been selected as the medium for imparting and receiving kisses, and an idea has occurred to me which those interested in the philosophy of the thing may have the benefit of, viz., that the custom must have been introduced by a flat-nosed race. Otherwise, I should think that the honour would have been conferred on the most prominent facial organ, and that instead of pressing mouth to mouth, the operation would more naturally be performed by a rubbing together of noses. The very fact that a large development of the nasal organ in many individuals renders kissing exceedingly inconvenient, goes a long way to attest that the inventor of the custom did not anticipate its being handed down to, and practised by, a Roman-nosed race. If he did he was a cynic, and doubtless enjoyed a grim satisfaction in contemplating the nasal collisions which often occur before the operation can be satisfactorily performed.

But, laying hypothesis aside, kissing is a good old-fashioned custom, although, like all such, liable to be abused. What's in a kiss? Nothing—and yet how much! In its legitimate use, it is the outward sign of that most heavenly of earthly passions —love. In its too common use, it is the sign of insipidity and wishy-washiness. A kiss is a mystical thing, and its worth depends entirely upon its why and its when. If it be the sign of true love, it shuns the gaze of the curious, and is a foretaste of heaven. If the passion it ought to signify be awanting, it courts publicity, and is a foretaste of unmitigated humbug.

I have been at several Christmas and New Year parties, where kissing formed a chief feature, but one in particular is vivid in my recollection. Ugh! the amount of kissing which we poor girls had to endure was something terrific. It makes me feel squeamish when I think of it yet.

Simon Spooneyman, one of the fellows there, seemed to have a mania for kissing the girls. None of the others were particularly backward in this respect, but he was ringleader. He was an uncouth-looking monster, with fierce eyes, coarse brown beard, and a moustache, the hairs of which stuck out for all the world like hogs' bristles. Ever since that evening he has been known as the Double-horned Rhinoceros, such being the animal he wanted to see when the curtain was drawn aside, and he gazed upon his own face in the mirror.

As soon as Simon entered the room, he, without waiting to be introduced, and with the most unblushing effrontery, took hold of each girl in succession and kissed her. The other fellows, seized with the contagion, immediately followed suit. It was no use getting into a passion, so we had to endure it all like martyrs. Simon's kiss was somewhat similar to having a hedgehog pressed hard against your mouth. I should almost have preferred to kiss a real rhinoceros. My experiences of this round of kissing were somewhat dreadful. One fellow seized me and pressed back my head in such a rough manner that I imagined my neck was broken. Another came, and the sensation was like having one's face buried in a hearth-brush. The next made me think my mouth was brought into contact with the bunghole of a whisky cask. The next almost poisoned me with gusts of tobacco and other obnoxious odours. And so on, until about a dozen fellows had the satisfaction of kissing me. I didn't know whether my head was off or on, and felt as if I could have taken a drink of ditch water to put the bad taste out of my mouth when it was over. I would have those fellows who drink spirituous liquors and smoke and chew tobacco prohibited from kissing, under the penalty of having their heads shaved and feathers stuck on. To be crumpled up in the arms of these brutes, and then to be half-suffocated with poisonous fumes, is an infliction which we poor victims are expected to bear with smiling faces. Such is the custom of modern society. But modern society is often a bore, and kissing parties are social treadmills.

This first round of kissing was what Simon called "breaking the ice," and but the introduction to the evening's entertainment, which was a continuation of the same thing almost without intermission. Of course there was the game of forfeits, and when a girl was told to kiss the four corners of the room the Rhinoceros was sure to be in one of them, and in two when he could manage it. He went at it like a day's work, and perspired with his exertions. And what unheard-of ways of kissing he had !

Except standing on one's head, I do not think there was a position in which it was possible to kiss that Simon did not suggest, and some of us unfortunates were compelled to undergo the ordeal. There was the rabbit's kiss, that thread-nibbling, slow-torture performance—the kiss through the back of a chair, the inventor of which would need to be chary of his head if I had him in my power—the kiss sitting back to back, a neck twisting over the shoulder volley—the upside-down and the broadside-on kiss—the kiss below the table, and the kiss over the edge of the table, beside a score of others in sundry uncomfortable and break-neck positions.

Simon called me up to do some sort of kiss with him, and as I did not want to be disagreeable, I consented. Two chairs were placed opposite each other in the centre of the floor, with their backs uppermost, on one of which he mounted on his knees, requesting me to do the same on the other. No sooner had I done so than it toppled over, and I came bump against the Rhinoceros, and received a most unmerciful mouth-scrubbing before I could get out of his clutches. I was roused at the fellow, and determined to pay him back. The opportunity for revenge offered sooner than I expected.

He was going to show the company what he called the Kilmarnock kiss, and again chose me for his victim. Putting up his left foot, he asked me to take hold of it in my hand, and then wanted to get my left foot in his hand. But I was one too many for him this time. I gave his foot a smart push upward and tripped him up, so that, instead of kissing me, the back of his head kissed the floor.

Simon ought to be grateful to me for adding one more to his category of kisses. I have christened it the Rhinoceros kiss, and a very effective one it is when properly performed.

As I said before, kissing is a good old-fashioned custom, and I don't like to see it converted into a treacle-and-water spoon-about business. It is not true that one man, or woman either, is as good as another. Indiscriminate kissing is silly, meaningless, and mischievous. I don't object to being kissed, if it be in a proper manner and at a proper time; but I do object to girls being brought together in order that a lot of fellows whom they never saw before, and possibly may never see again, may have the enjoyment of practising upon them. Good gracious! we are not stucco figures devoid of feeling, although it would be a blessing for us if we were, at those times when we have to undergo such rough handling. Besides, I consider a kiss as something too sacred for burlesque, and the fellow who has a mania for kissing the girls as a social nuisance. I would have him confined for six months in a pig-stye, and made to kiss the sow regularly before meals, which, I think, would have the effect of curing him of his nonsensical penchant. There, I hope I have done good service to my sisters everywhere by this outspoken protest against a custom which is, to many of them, well-nigh intolerable.

THE FELLOW WHO WAS ALWAYS IN A HURRY.

In this age of fast trains and fast ships, fast horses and fast men, it is not surprising that we should often meet with the fellow who is always in a hurry. He is generally recognisable by his unkempt appearance—looking as if he had no time to wash himself, and as if he had slept with his clothes on for the past six weeks. He is always running hither and thither like a madman, coming bump against you when rounding a corner, and bolting past in too great a hurry to offer an apology. These fellows make one nervous, and, if they become much more numerous, will certainly drive the whole world into hysterics. I do not like a lazy fellow by any means. Method and punctuality, and going about his business without fussiness, betokens a fellow who knows what he is doing, and who can do it ; but driving about at the rate of 150 revolutions per minute, and 60 miles per hour, betokens a fellow whose mental machinery is completely disorganised. He goes like a clock without its pendulum, and gets run out without accomplishing anything.

Frank Fussiman was continually in a hurry. He never gave himself time to grow, and when he had reached the age of thirty stood five feet two in his stockings. It is not to be supposed that he could find time to shave his beard or cut his hair, which, notwithstanding the pressure of business with which he was constantly weighed down, grew into a most luxuriant crop. Each particular hair was allowed to germinate at its own sweet will till he looked like—well, they say comparisons are odious, but every time I set eyes on Frank I could not help recalling to my mind a certain little box, on opening the lid of which up jumped a wooden-headed, hairy-faced effigy of a man, which used to terrify me greatly when a child. I detest swellish fellows, but Frank went to the opposite extreme. He was utterly careless of his personal appearance, and looked, for all the world, as if his clothes had been tossed upon him with a hayfork.

Frank went to several trades, but he never could find time to learn any of them. At length his energetic habits brought him under the notice of the Society for the Promotion of Industry, and he was appointed its agent. One of the branches of the Society's work was an emigration scheme for assisting the industrious to go abroad, and which was extensively advertised in the newspapers. A friend intending to go to America asked me to obtain some information from the Society. I accordingly wrote a letter to Mr Frank, and, as I received no answer, determined to call upon him.

The "Chambers" of the Society, which sounded so fine in the advertisement, I found to be a single small dingy apartment, containing a writing table and a few chairs, these, as well as the floor of the place, being littered with letters, prospectuses, and all kinds of written and printed matter. The sole occupant of the "Chambers" when I entered was a small ragged urchin, who was amusing himself shooting an elastic band from the end of a ruler, at the flies upon the window.

"Master ain't in just now," he said, making the elastic fly towards a cat in the corner of the room.

"When do you expect him?"

"Don't know; he is very busy to-day."

"You don't seem to have much to do, at all events," I remarked.

"No, master always bein' so busy, never has no time to give me work."

"Do you think I should wait for a little?"

"Don't know; perhaps when he comes he mayn't have no time to speak to you."

At this moment, however, Mr Fussiman's footsteps sounded on the stair, up which he rushed as if the "Chambers" were on fire, and he wanted to save his cash-box.

He bolted past me, puffing and blowing and wiping the

perspiration from his face, which bore a striking resemblance to a boiled lobster.

"Boy, where is my pen?" he asked, seating himself before the writing table.

"In your ear."

"So it is," said he, putting up his hand.

"Confound it !—it's broken. Give me yours—quick."

"Haint got none."

"Got no pen ! What have you done with it ?"

"Gave it to you yesterday when you lost your other one."

"You idle young vagabond, why didn't you tell me before now ? Away and get some pens at once—there's a penny. Now, look sharp, or I'll warm your ears for you."

The boy went off like a shot, and Frank immediately seized a large heap of papers, which he commenced furiously to fumble over, searching for some one amongst them. When about half through, he seemed suddenly to remember that I was standing at the door, and tossing down the papers, advanced towards me.

"You must excuse me," he said, "for not offering you a seat sooner ; but really business weighs so heavily on my mind, and I have so many things to attend to, that I sometimes forget altogether that people are waiting. Pray, come and take a seat. Confound those papers !—how they do accumulate, and I can never find time to file them past," he added, hurling a number of loose letters from off the chair he offered me, on to the floor.

Once more he commenced fumbling over the heap of papers on the table, and had again got about half through them, when the boy returned with the pens.

"I hope you will excuse me for a few minutes till I finish a letter I have to write for the post," he said, addressing me, and once more laying aside the papers he had been searching among.

"There's not a drop of ink in this bottle, boy. How's this ?" he exclaimed angrily, after dipping his pen into an ink bottle.

"You spilt it yourself when you were in a hurry going out in the morning," replied the boy.

M

"Confound it! And why didn't you tell me before? Away and get me some ink at once, you young rascal."

Again the boy disappeared, and again Frank commenced to turn over the same bundle of papers, this time putting off his coat to the operation. When the boy returned with the ink he tossed the papers aside for the third time, without being successful in finding the paper he wanted. Then he commenced furiously to write a letter. Line after line was scribbled off in the most fearful and wonderful manner, and he was writing on the last page, when all of a sudden he stamped his foot, sprang up, looking as if he could have swallowed somebody alive, and tore the letter he had just been writing into pieces. Then he paced round the room three or four times like a demented person, after which he looked at his watch, and addressing me, said—

"I trust you can make it convenient to call again at five. I have a most important appointment in a quarter of an hour, and have yet to search for a letter among all these papers, so that I am in too great a hurry to attend to your business just now."

"I shall not be in any hurry coming back, I can assure you, Mr Fussiman," I said, as I took my departure, leaving him for the fourth time sweating over that heap of papers, to look for a particular letter among which, was like looking for a needle in a haystack.

These fellows who are always in a hurry, would turn the world upside down, if there were no steady-going, cautious people to preserve its equilibrium. They put everything out of its place, and find a place for nothing. They try to accomplish three or four things at the same time, and in the end accomplish nothing. And yet the din and the fuss they make leads the uninitiated to fancy that they, and they alone, are doing the world's work. Although good at throwing up dust, they can't throw any in my eyes. The world is bad enough already, but if its work were left entirely in their hands, disorder, confusion, chaos, would be the inevitable result.

THE FELLOW WHO DIDN'T KNOW HOW MANY
SWEETHEARTS HE HAD.

SOME girls cannot see through a fellow, because they never try. A confiding, unsuspecting nature is to be admired—in view of an approaching Millennium—but under the present dispensation we must keep our weather-eyes open, my sisters, if we would save ourselves from heartburnings and shame. Who says that we are deficient in discriminating power? I most emphatically deny that we are, and will wager my head that any number of girls, provided they be told to look, can see as far through a mountain as an equal number of fellows can—ay, and farther, too. The mischief of it is that we are so seldom told to look—that we are systematically taught not to look. The artificial manner in which many girls are brought up, and the rice-and-sago education which is doled out to them, go far to stultify the higher faculties of their mind, and to render them the undiscriminating creatures many of them seem to be. And who says that the notion of man's mental superiority is exploded? All humbug! Girls from their infancy, by signs and symbols, and whispers and mute beckonings, are taught their inferiority to, and dependence upon the other sex. If we show symptoms of possessing minds and wills of our own, we are called "Blue Stockings." If we have the hardihood to break through those prison walls of etiquette with which custom has hemmed us in, the act is characterised as rude and unwomanly. The short and long of it is, we are taught to believe that our highest object in life is to get married. What bosh! As if a husband were such a mighty godsend to a girl. Oh, ye gods and water-kelpies! save us from hysterics! Why, I've seen some husbands—said to be models, too—but, upon my word, I wouldn't have a score of them.

It strikes me I've lost the thread of my subject, or, rather, I have not found it yet.   I intended to speak of the fellow who didn't know how many sweethearts he had.   And now, when I think of it, my object in penning these introductory remarks was to point out some of the reasons why girls are so often carried away with the loud talk and Brummagem glitter of dashing young fellows who display as much "gab" as they do starch, and possess as much true manliness as brains.   It is a trait of human nature to judge others by ourselves.   Hence the innocent heart fails to discover villany beneath the treacherous smile of the deceiver; and some girls never being taught to exercise their powers of discrimination, are deceived with the spurious metal, because it is brilliant to the eye and has the loudest ring.

Adolphus Bunks was what some people vulgarly term a "heart smasher."   He was proud of the title, too; and, greatest pity of all, he deserved it.   He had, indeed, broken one poor girl's heart, after first breaking her character.   Ay, and he delighted to tell this to his comrades, as if it were a grand joke—the heartless ruffian!

Adolphus was a fellow whose *fac-simile* you may often see in the front box of the theatre or opera.   He wears a coat of the latest design, and displays a large quantity of linen and jewellery.   His cuffs reach to his knuckles, and he has a kid glove on the one hand, and half-a-dozen rings on the other.   He is rather a good-looking fellow, except when he makes himself ugly by placing a quizzing-glass to his eye, and putting his face out of joint to keep it fixed there.   When you come near him he stinks of eau-de-cologne, and when you don't come near him, he takes stock of you through his eye-glass.   In the company of girls he is polite and affable, and can turn off any amount of small talk.   In the company of fellows he is coarse and vulgar, and can turn off any amount of profanity.   Occasionally he says some witty things to the girls, which are borrowed, however, from the comic papers, but of course girls don't know, as they are not supposed to peruse such literature.

I never had a high opinion of Adolphus. He was too much of the swell for me. There was a falseness about his voice which I disliked, and his laugh grated painfully on my ear.

I was returning from a visit to a friend, and having to wait some time for a train, went into the railway refreshment room to have a cup of coffee. In the apartment adjoining mine, and divided off by a thin wooden partition, I heard two fellows in conversation, and judge of my surprise when I recognised the voice of Adolphus Bunks. And, oh! what disgusting language they used. They talked about us girls as if we were so many inferior creatures, to be petted and spurned at their lordly pleasures. And what shocking names they called us, too.

"There is Miss Soapsuds," said Adolphus—"not a bad girl in her way, but too pious for me. She wanted me to church with her last Sunday, but you know I had an appointment with the tallow-faced damsel in the park, which I preferred to keep."

"Do you ever see the laughing hyena now?" the other fellow asked.

"No; I've thrown her completely overboard. She was a hearty brick of a girl, too, but with all her mirth I've got tired of her. By-the-bye, I've got an introduction lately to a regular stunner, and I think she's inclined to be spooney. What would you say to see me marry and settle down one of these days?"

"Why, I should think the world was coming to an end. But who is this new charmer?"

"Her name is Miss Rosa Rumby."

"What! the coalmaster's daughter?"

"The same. I've christened her 'Coal-black Rose.'"

"By Jove! you're doing it heavy. You're a rare hand among the girls, Adolphus."

"I guess you're right. The fact is, old boy, I don't know how many sweethearts I have. It costs me a good deal of trouble to keep them all sweet, too, for one gets so terribly jealous when she hears I've been to some place with another. I generally manage to make it all right with soft-sawder, however. Use plenty of soft-sawder on the girls, and you'll never fail."

This is not a verbatim report, for their conversation was mingled with coarse laughter, and sundry unmentionable interjections, but which I suppose are quite the thing when such fellows meet.

When the train came up I encountered Adolphus and his companion on the platform. The former lifted his hat and greeted me with his most winning smile.

"Don't speak to me, base-hearted villain!" I hissed; and then, to allay the bewilderment which was depicted on his countenance, added, "Your conversation in the refreshment-room is something to be proud of, fellow."

I had no time to say more, but stepped into a carriage, leaving the two staring at each other as if both their noses had been bled. So disconcerted were they that they allowed the train to go off without them. It wouldn't have grieved me had they been transformed into pillars of saltpetre, and stood on that platform for ever, as monuments of a woman's righteous indignation!

Such fellows are a disgrace to civilisation, and ought to be tied by the heels to broomsticks, and ridden by witches to the back regions of the moon. But, as we have little chance of getting so happily rid of them, our only practicable course is to starve them out. Shun their society, despise them, and hold them up to public contempt. Surely girls are become very cheap, if such moral alligators can boast that they don't know how many sweethearts they have. It puts me greatly out of conceit in my sex to think that girls can be so willingly blind. I'm sure it is not difficult to see through these fellows, if they would only look. And, oh! my sisters! if you once saw them as they are, you would spit in their faces, sooner than receive them with smiles into your society or your homes.

THE FELLOW WHO COULD NEVER MAKE
UP HIS MIND.

THIS specimen of the masculine animal is by no means rare. You may often encounter him, and easily knock him down, if you feel so inclined, for he can never make up his mind to fight. He happens to be endowed with a few instincts, which enable him to eat his dinner and go to bed, but it would not be a great calamity to society, were he to be unable to make up his mind to eat for a week or two, and evaporate into thin air.

One fellow in particular is recalled to my recollection. They called him Bob Snoddy. I called him " Snotty Bob," because he could never make up his mind to take out his pocket hand-kerchief when his nose required wiping. I have been told that, when quite a baby, Bob displayed this wonderful indecision to an alarming extent. On one occasion his mother brought him a penny whistle and an apple, but he could not make up his mind whether to blow the whistle or eat the apple first, and as he could not do both at once, he went into convulsions and cried for two days. " It's a whipping you have need of, boy," his mother would sometimes remark when he exhibited similar symptoms, and she was doubtless right ; but then there was no one to give him what he so much needed, as his poor mother, who suffered from maternal affection, could not make up her mind to do it.

Bob was grown up before I knew anything about him. He was a tall, lank fellow, with big hands and feet. He could never make up his mind what to do with his hands—whether to cross them in front or at his back, allow them to dangle at his sides, or shove them into his trousers pockets—in all of which, and sundry other positions, he kept continually placing them. He seemed to regard them as very disagreeable appendages. When you spoke to him he could not make up his mind whether to look at your face or your feet, but perpetually shifted his glance up and down your body. And such eyes! The one was green and the other blue. I could not help thinking he had some hand in the making of them himself, and was unable to decide as to the colour. The few straggling hairs, too, which grew upon his cheeks impressed you with the idea that he had not made up his mind whether or not to grow whiskers. And the very coat he wore was of the same undecided character. You could not say whether it was intended for a sack or a shooting coat, owing no doubt to Bob's inability to make up his mind and inform the tailor which he wanted.

Bob was very obedient. To do as they are told is the chief natural endowment which such fellows possess. His mother told him to go and be a carpenter, and he went. One day he received instructions to saw a log of wood in two, but not being able to make up his mind which half to saw off, he stood with his hands in his pockets. The master told him to go home, and he went. For a long time thereafter he waited for something to turn up; but nothing did turn up save the point of his nose. It was not defiantly cocked in the air by any means, but made rather an irresolute curve heavenwards, as if its possessor had not made up his mind in what direction it should grow.

Fancy this booby going a-courting! That ever he was in love I don't believe, because he could not make up his mind to fall in love; but it is a fact that he proposed to Maria Myrtle— I had it from her own lips. His mother or somebody else must have told him to do it, for he never would of his own accord, I am certain.

"I want to know if you would marry me, Maria?" he said to her one day, with considerable sheepishness.

"Well, I don't know, Bob; I would require some time to consider, at least," she replied.

"Oh, yes, yes; certainly, by all means take time—take time,

Maria—for—for—in fact—that is to say, Maria, I have not exactly made up my own mind about getting married yet, but I thought I would just like to know—that is—if you would be agreeable when I do make up my mind ?"

"Bob Snoddy, if you have not made up your mind, I have. I can never marry you—so go home to those who sent you here, and bother me no more," said Maria, in a considerable passion.

He obeyed in profound silence, and never made up his mind to appear in her presence again.

This inherent quality of obedience which he possessed in such unlimited measure proved a blessing to him in the long run, for thereby he got married to a widow of property. This widow (whose first husband went out of his mind) wanted a second husband whom she could mould to her will, and certainly she found one in Bob, for he was plastic enough. She saw him but once—told him to marry her, and he obeyed. A short time thereafter he accompanied Mrs S. on a shopping expedition, and actually made up his mind that she required a new bonnet, so wonderful is the influence of woman. But, then, he was no longer Bob Snoddy; he had merged his own individuality into Mrs Snoddy, and acted entirely under her directions. On one occasion, when called upon to act for himself by giving his vote in an election contest, he could not make up his mind which candidate to vote for, and being solicited by the friends of each, voted for both, and had to make up his mind to pay a fine for so doing.

But a day came when Mrs S. died. Thereafter Bob could not make up his mind to live, and showed symptoms of decline. Being told by his friends to go a sea voyage, he went. The ship was wrecked, and as he could not make up his mind to go down into the boat and be saved, he went down with the ship and was lost.

I guess there are more Bob Snoddys in the world, and I wonder that people will have the audacity to bring such good-

for-nothing dolts into it.   But the impudence of some people
is beyond comprehension.   It is a mystery to me how such
fellows manage to get through life at all.   It must be on the
principle that light bodies reach the surface, and hence they
float about, being drifted hither and thither by every wind that
blows.   They are made the footballs of society, and are kept
spinning along, until some hard kick knocks the wind out of
them, and they go under.

They don't do any harm, I have heard people say.   No, by
any effort of theirs they are as incapable of doing harm as of
doing good.   But they clog the wheels of progress ; they are
always in somebody's way, and human nature is seldom so
hard-hearted as to run them down.   But if the race were to
become numerous, what would come of the world ?   That's the
way in which I look at the matter.

To get married is the best thing for themselves they can
possibly do ; but just fancy a fellow requiring a woman to
guide him, and to make up his mind for him.   Pshaw ! he riles
me.   *I* could have no patience with such big babies, but would
send them to suckle crocodiles.   Give me a man who can
make up his mind to do something—I don't care whether it be
good or bad.   If he can *do* at all, I am not afraid but the good
can be made to predominate.

THE BUTTERY-TONGUED FELLOW.

MANY fellows have a large supply of butter in their com-
position; they are self-acting churns, ever producing the article
in unlimited quantity. No wonder that they are soft-headed and
buttermilk-hearted, and little else than walking and speaking
automatons. Time was when the wheels of society ran smoothly
without the application of grease, but in these days butter has
become the universal lubricator; and it seems as if society
cannot move a step without it. The world is fast becoming
converted into a buttershop, so thriving is the trade. Speak
your mind, and you have scores of enemies; lay on plenty of
butter, and you slide through life peacefully and pleasantly.
Butter, butter, nothing like butter for success in life! "You
will butter me and I will butter you, and we will all be buttered
and basted together; we will walk knee-deep in butter, we will
rear monuments of butter in honour of each other," is the
language of Butterdom, acted or spoken. Rear away your
monuments, then, if you will. Pile kit upon kit and roll upon
roll, till you have filled the world with your butter *in
memoriams*, and what then? I fancy the butter will one day
melt, come rushing down about you like lava streams, and you
will be swallowed up and drowned in melted butter. Ugh,
what a death!

But hoping so terrible a fate may yet be averted, let me now
introduce to the reader Mr Samuel Spinks, the buttery-tongued
fellow.

"Glad—unspeakably glad to see you. Indeed, it affords me
the most exquisite pleasure to make the acquaintance of one so
transcendently charming, and so angelic in form and feature,"
would be Sam's greeting, if you are one of my sex, and well
dressed.

Should you not happen to be well dressed, the greeting would be much less grandiloquent. Dress goes a long way with these fellows. If they should meet you in a working garb they are certain to turn aside their heads and pretend not to see you, they have such convenient eyesight!

It was not difficult to observe that Sam Spinks dealt in butter —the first look you got of him convinced you of this. Upon the whole, he was rather a smart fellow, although not nearly so smart as he fancied he was. From first to last he was buttery. His face was white and greasy-looking, and his hair was plastered over with grease of some kind. Then when he spoke, his words seemed to issue from a tube lined with butter; they were not by any means silvery or musical, nor yet hoarse and grating, but for all the world resembled the frothy, flabby sound produced by churning. His movements likewise were quick, and what some people might call graceful. His arms moved as if he had a roll of butter under each armpit to lubricate the joints, and he walked with a step as light and noiseless as if he were treading on butter.

I have encountered Sam at several private parties, and have been as often amused as indignant at the unblushing effrontery of the fellow.

"O, Miss So-and-So," he would say, to whoever chanced to sit near him, "you do indeed look charming to-night."

"Don't I always look so?"

"Yes, but to-night you excel yourself. Of course I am not always with you, and pleasant company is a wonderful cosmetic. You are indeed a perfect Hebe or a Venus, and with me for Adonis the picture is complete."

"I fear we would not long agree."

"Oh, dear, don't say so. Not agree with me! I who have such an unspeakable admiration for the feminine graces and virtues. I who never feel happy except in the society of ladies; they are such dear, kind, lovely, angelic beings. What would life be without them? A miserable, bleak desert. They are the chain which binds me to earth. Were there no ladies, I would go and commit suicide."

It would not be a great loss to the world, nor yet to the ladies, I have thought to myself, if he did; but there is small danger of such fellows taking so rash a step.

Once Sam tried to butter me.

" I admire you more than any other lady of my acquaintance, Miss Thistle," he said.

" Indeed! For what reasons, might I ask?"

" Well, in the first place, you are always so charmingly neat, so elegantly handsome, and so intensely becoming. Then, you have such an air of sweetness—such exquisite sweetness—as makes a fellow fancy himself in paradise when he comes into your presence——"

" Stop, stop! I don't like toast buttered on both sides," I said, interrupting him.

" No, upon my word, I would be the last fellow on earth to flatter a lady. I assure you I but speak the sentiments of my heart."

" Did you say your heart, sir? I was not aware till now that you possessed such a thing."

" Oh, Miss Thistle, you are becoming sarcastic."

" I will be still more so if you try any further buttering of me. Once for all, Mr Spinks, let me inform you it won't suit. And I would give you a bit of advice. Cease from buttering the girls, for they know it, and only laugh at you. Be a man, and not a ridiculous ape."

I would not like to repeat what Sam said I was, as he turned towards me his oily face reddened up with anger; but it gave me a glimpse into the true character of the fellow, and showed me what a perfidious hypocrite he was. I had made myself another enemy through speaking my mind, but what mattered it, so long as I had still a friend or two on whom I could depend? Friendship with such fellows I do not desire.

Why are girls specially singled out for being buttered? It

must be with shame confessed that some girls rather like it—ay, and some fellows too.   Flattery goes a great way, and there be few but of whom it can be said, that to them—

> " Praise from the rivall'd lips of toothless, bald
> Decrepitude, is oft too welcome."

But, after all, I cannot admit that girls are most susceptible to butter.   They are not such poor, simple, blind things as many fellows take them for.   No, greasy Sam, they can detect when you lay it on too thick, and have a good, jolly laugh at your expense when you are gone.

Fellows of Sam's type are terribly numerous now-a-days. You encounter them everywhere—at kirk and at market—smiling and bowing and hatting and flunkeying, enough to turn one's stomach, and to put one fairly out of conceit in mankind generally.   I am really alarmed for the future of the world, for it is impossible that society can long hold together, with so much hypocrisy, and sham concern, and sham compliments, and sham everything in its midst.   Talk about the theatre !   Why, every time I go into company I gaze upon a stage play.   Nearly everybody is acting, and everybody seems to know it, and thinks it is all right.   It is the fashion, and we can't get on without it, they say.   Oh, ye shades of monkeydom ! return to us with your realities.

THE FELLOW WHO WAS ALWAYS LATE.

Notwithstanding that we live in an age of patent levers and time-guns, the fellow who is always late may still be met with; indeed, the only time you cannot meet him is when you have an appointment with him.

There are various types of this individual. There is that exceedingly provoking fellow who is sadly deficient in the mensuration of time and space; his five minutes mean half-an-hour, and when he says a mile you may rest satisfied it is three. This is he who keeps his friend standing twenty minutes at the corner of the street, and then comes leisurely up with a complacent smile and says, "You here yet: I had no idea you would have waited." He never considers himself at fault for being late, and when remonstrated with, is always ready with a long-winded excuse. He met a very particular friend whom he had not seen for a long time, and from whom he could not drag himself away; while, if the truth were known, said friend wished from the bottom of his heart that he would move on and let him home to supper. This fellow is crotchety and quixotic. He has always got a bee in his bonnet, and goes buzzing about with all the seeming aimlessness of a blue-bottle. He should never be out of leading-strings, for if he have an object before him, he turns aside to inspect every trifle which comes in his way, and misses his object in the end. He will be hurrying to keep an appointment, already five minutes late, when a dog with a spot on its nose attracts his attention, and he spends five minutes more in questioning its owner concerning the peculiarity. He makes appointments which he never intends to keep—indeed, it would be impossible for him to do so, since he often promises to be in two or three places at the same time. He is an everlasting nuisance, and, worst of all, he does not know it.

Then there is that much-to-be-pitied fellow who, in spite of himself, is always late. Do what he will, he cannot overtake time. He thinks he must be the victim of some adverse fate ever dragging him behind. His watch will persist in going slow, and he wishes to goodness he could carry a sun-dial in his pocket. His intentions are earnest, and he makes bold efforts to be up to time, but to no purpose. Old Father Time plays cantrips with him—gives him his coat-tail to hold on by, and then bolts off with a grin, leaving his coat behind him. You may see this fellow rushing towards the railway station after the train has started; and when he finds he is too late, he showers upon himself a torrent of uncomplimentary epithets. When he does get on the train, you will be sure to find him in the guard's van; he is always too late to secure a seat in a carriage. His professions of regret at being late are profuse. He is extremely sorry for having kept you waiting. He pulls out his watch and says—"Confound it, slow again," and calls himself the most unfortunate beggar in existence.

Then there is the awkward, backward, slow, and easy fellow, who does not like to be first. This is he who, when you accompany him to church or theatre, says to you at the door, "Go you in first; I'll follow." His destiny is to follow, never to lead. He cannot even keep alongside of you when out walking, but invariably lags a pace or two behind. When invited to a party, he has a lively horror of being the first arrival, and to prevent such a contingency, makes himself ten minutes late. His great fault is not that he cannot make up his mind to a thing, but that, after he has made up his mind, he is too late in acting. He fully makes up his mind to ask a favour of my Lord Tomnoddy, but while he waits for the favourable moment his Lordship disappears. He makes up his mind to dance with the belle of the ball-room, and is just considering what he shall say to her, when somebody else steps in and leads her to the floor. He is lazy and off-putting—never striking his iron while it is hot. He waits for a more favourable opportunity which never comes. He takes the current when it does not serve, and so loses his venture.

Bill Tardyshanks was a fellow of the latter type. He was two years old before he was weaned, and took a long time to grow—so long that some people remarked he would be too late to reach manhood. He was late in being sent to school, was regularly whipped for being late while there, and discovered when too late that he had not availed himself of his educational opportunities. On leaving school he was apprenticed to a watchmaker, but, being a bad time-keeper, his master wound up his engagement and told him to go. Thereafter he entered several situations, all of which he lost by not being up to time. He made a good policeman, as he never appeared till the row was over; but on one occasion, being too late in eyeing the Inspector, the latter eyed him, and he got discharged. At length he was fortunate in securing a permanent appointment in the Post Office as sorter of the "too late" letters. Bill was always too late in speaking as well as in acting. In the conversational circle he allowed the opportunity for bringing in his "happy thought" to pass, and when he did give utterance to it, it came like a pun in the middle of a sermon—decidedly out of place.

Being late in everything, he was, of course, too late in thinking of getting married. Once he fell in love, but, as he did not like to be the first to pop the question, he waited until another did so. When he at length braced up his courage for the trying ordeal, he had the mortification of learning that he was too late. He was never up to time in the matrimonial market thereafter, but died a bachelor.

Bill had no rich uncle who cut him off with a shilling for being five minutes behind time, as I have read of some cruel uncles doing; but he had a poor cousin who cut off with five pounds he had lent him, because he was too late in calling for payment. He vowed he would never lend again, but it was too late, for he never had any more to lend. He fell into bad

N

health, and the doctor when called said it was too late. So he shuffled off this mortal coil, and it is but charitable to hope that for once he was up to time.

It would take volumes to write the evils of procrastination, and I fear they would do little good after they were written. It is about as easy to make an elephant fly as to make these sluggish, off-putting, too-late fellows come up to time. Their disorder is chronic and constitutional. From the very commencement of their existence they are "too late to mend." The little girl who wrote in her copy-book, "Procrastination is the mother of necessity," did not commit such a blunder as her teacher supposed. The fellow who is always late is always necessitous, unless born with a silver spoon in his mouth. Time and the world move on apace, but he is always behind both. He cannot put on a spurt and make up to them. He lacks nerve and sinew power. The least exertion puts him out of breath, and so he drifts farther and farther behind, till at last he gets smashed up among the breakers. You can't drive these fellows before you—if you attempt it you will run them down. Sometimes kind Christians throw out a rope and give them a pull, but I confess the act requires the exercise of much self-denial. To paddle one's own canoe is about as much as one can manage in these times. But I suppose it requires all sorts of people to make a world, and I have just been thinking that, if there were no such fellows as those in it, persons of benevolent and good-natured dispositions would have no opportunity of exercising these qualities.

THE FELLOW WHO WAS NEVER IN THE WRONG.

THERE be some fellows who fancy they are paragons of perfection. In their own estimation they are the lights of the world and the regulators of society. You may make a porpoise climb up a tree as soon as convince them of wrong-doing, because they don't know the difference between right and wrong. They have got into their heads certain hazy, india-rubber, aurora borealis kind of ideas which they call principles, and which they profess to follow. And so they do, but in the same way in which a kitten follows its own tail. They do not stick to principles—*their* principles stick to them. Into whatever by-paths or crooked ways they enter they can always look round and see their principles in the rear, and hence they believe they are never in the wrong.

These fellows seem to carry their brains in the wrong place. Instead of being equally distributed over their craniums, they have them crammed away into the back regions, whereby their bumps of self-esteem are bulged out to an inordinate size.

Paragons of perfection, forsooth! Paragons of presumption and affectation. Oh, for a horse-whip and the law on my side! At all events, I can have a slap at you with my tongue. Our sex gets credit for having long tongues ; I wish mine were a yard long when I have to deal with these self-righteous block-heads—what a castigation they should get!

Jeremiah Justman was a fellow of this sort. He had an immensely big head, and wore his hat on the back at an angle of forty-five degrees, so that if you chanced to be walking behind him you could see the entire crown. He couldn't wear it straight up, because it had no support at the front, and would fall over his eyes. When Jeremiah walked through the streets he swung his arms to and fro as far as they would swing, and invariably directed his eyes heavenward, as if he were counting the chimney-pots on the house-tops. When talking to you he would put his hands into his vest pockets, and, standing in a most imposing position, cock his pug nose in the air and sniff you all over in a most disagreeable manner. Little Molly Moss said to me once she thought Jeremiah was such a good, pious fellow that he smelt sin with everybody he spoke to. Poor, little, unsuspecting Molly.

Molly's brother had the misfortune to be an apprentice in the office where Jeremiah was head clerk, and one day the young lad came home sobbing bitterly, because he had been dismissed and didn't know why. His father was dead, and his mother pleaded with me, knowing I had a slight acquaintance with Jeremiah, to go and see him regarding the lad's dismissal. I accordingly made it my business to call on Jeremiah one evening at his lodgings.

As soon as he became aware who was his visitor, he drew a face upon him as long as a stocking, and, drawing a sigh to match, asked me to step into his room.

I at once made known the purport of my visit, and hoped he would inform me for what reason he had discharged the young lad.

"Very serious reasons, Miss Thistle—very weighty reasons, I assure you," he answered, with an air of profound sorrow.

"I trust he has not been dishonest?" I asked, tremblingly.

"Well, no—not in the sense in which the world understands the term," he replied, in his most consequential tone, and then continued—"You know, Miss Thistle, since ever I ascended to my present position I have considered it my bounden duty to improve and strengthen the moral and spiritual condition of the lads placed by Providence under my care; and the more effectually to perform this duty, I provide myself with duplicate keys to their drawers. Lads, as a rule, go astray unless prevented. The Evil One puts novels and other unholy books in their hands, which they read, and become thereby corrupted. Now, if my lads knew that I kept keys of their drawers my benevolent designs would be frustrated, because they would not secrete therein any iniquitous thing; but as they don't know, I am often instrumental in nipping the machinations of Satan in the bud. It pains me very much to tell you what I discovered in young Moss's drawer. Oh, dear, dear, to find a youth like him so depraved. Terrible to relate, he had in his possession a pack of playing cards! The devil's own books! Poor lad, I long feared he was on the high road to Satan."

"And was it for this you sent him away?" I asked, almost choking with rage and disgust at the meanness and duplicity of the fellow.

"Oh, certainly; I could 'not think of retaining a gambler near me—it would be entirely against my principles."

"A gambler! How dare you say so, sir?" I exclaimed, passionately. "How dare you pronounce such a libel upon the character of the lad? I consider it was a dastardly action on your part, in the first place, to pry so thief-like into his drawer, and most ungenerous and unjust of you to dismiss him with a slur upon his fair fame, for having in his possession a pack of cards—very harmless things, certainly."

"Miss Thistle," said he, considerably nettled, "you're but a woman, and I won't argue with you; but I may tell you this. When my father died his last words to me were—'Now, Jeremiah, stick to your principles, and look above yourself.' To my principles I have always stuck, and do always intend to stick. I have a lively abhorrence of evil, and, when in my power, believe it to be my duty to punish the wrong-doer. As to looking above myself, I have endeavoured to fulfil my father's dying command to the best of my ability." (I thought so too, and if the chimney-pots had eyes they would be of the same opinion.) "What my father intended to convey by that expression was that I should look above myself in the sense of not allowing any private considerations to come between me and the performance of duty.   It is often painful to perform a duty ; but principles—principles before everything."

"Jeremiah Justman," I replied, deliberately, "you're a blockhead, and your principles are a pack of rubbish.   The lad has been guilty of no offence ; but, admitting that he was, do you think you took the proper course with him ?   Is it by sending a youth out into the cold world with a blot upon his character that you intend to reclaim him ?   Self-righteous idiot ! you and others like you have been the ruin of thousands."

"Insinuating woman !" he shouted, fiercely, "do you think sin is to go unpunished ?"

"Then you believe you have done right in dismissing the lad ?"

"Most undoubtedly."

"Would you answer me one question, sir—Have you ever been in the wrong yourself ?"

He stared at me for a moment as if taken by surprise, and then answered—

"There is an old saying that self-praise is no honour.   I am not in the habit of sounding my own trumpet ; but, since you have asked, I may just tell you that, to the best of my recollection and belief, I have never been in the wrong.   This arises from sticking to one's principles."

"Out upon you, lump of blind hypocrisy !" I said, rising to my feet; "you and your principles are alike despicable to all right-minded persons.   As for the lad, thank God he has friends, and will in no way suffer for your act of perverted justice.   I leave you with a single remark from an old book which you would do well to study.   It is this—'Let him that thinketh he standeth take heed lest he fall.' "

He regarded me with a look of owlish sanctimoniousness, but made no reply, while I indignantly withdrew from his presence.

I have no sympathy for such fellows, but would stand by to see them flogged.   Yet I fear flogging would do them little good : the only effectual cure would be to collect them all together and ship them off to some desolate island, where they would soon eat one another up, like the cats of Kilkenny. These austere, fiddle-faced, mock-pious quidnuncs are the scourges of society, rendering existence miserable to all who come within their petty influence. How I do pity the unfortunate wives of such fellows! For the sake of a peaceable life they must pander to the vanity of their lords and masters, and pretend to look up to them as patterns of excellence. *I* couldn't do this. No, upon my word, I would marry a Hottentot sooner than the fellow who believed he was never in the wrong.

THE FELLOW WHO WAS NEVER IN A PASSION.

I MAY say, at the outset, that I don't like those bottle-fed, milk-and-water, dead-and-alive fellows who never get angry. There is not much human nature in them. Being of impoverished blood and slow pulse, their hearts do not throb in unison with the great sympathetic heart of humanity. There is too much of the grubworm and too little of the wasp about them. Now, I don't approve of being waspish, but I consider there are some good points about this much-reviled insect, and should infiuitely prefer one of them in my fernery to a grubworm. If you seize a wasp it will sting you, as you deserve. Not so the grubworm. It has not the fortitude to do anything but wriggle. Who ever heard of a fight between two worms? They have not sufficient blood in them to get in a passion and fight. Yet they can, in the most subtle manner, without once getting angry, eat away the life of the fairest flower.

I was introduced to Samuel Blubbery at a soiree, which finished up with a dance. He asked me to dance with him, but there was something in the fellow's manner which I didn't like, and I declined.

He did not press, but walked away towards another lady. Later in the evening I was annoyed to see him come and seat himself beside me. He began a conversation by telling me that while a former dance was going on, a gentleman had snatched the lady who was his partner from his side, and left him standing alone.

" And I suppose you are very angry ?" I remarked.

" Angry ! oh dear, no. I never get angry—I was never in a passion in my life," he said, with a look of injured innocence.

" I don't think that is anything to boast of," said I ; " yet I

THE FELLOW WHO WAS NEVER IN A PASSION.

don't believe you.   Would you not be angry if someone were to strike you ?"

" No, indeed.   If struck on the one cheek, I would turn the other.   I always practise this divine law of meekness and love. I have love in my heart for everybody.   For you, Miss Thistle, there is love here," he said, pointing to his bosom.

" I'm sorry I can't return the compliment," I replied, rising and leaving the fellow, who solaced himself with an idiotic smile of self-complacency.

My astonishment was as unbounded as my sorrow, when sometime thereafter my old companion, Bessie Dot, told me, in a great secret, that she was getting married, and that the object of her affection was Samuel Blubbery.

I did my best to dissuade her from the alliance, but to no purpose.   Bessie wanted a husband, and a husband she would have.

" You seem to be prejudiced against him, Nancy," she said to me, " but that is because you don't know him ; and, indeed, I cannot say that I know him thoroughly myself—there are depths in his nature which I cannot fathom.   But I am not afraid to trust my happiness to him.   I believe he is all right at heart, and then he is a man who was never in a passion in his life."

Poor Bessie, she mistook shallows for depths, shadows for substance, dross for gold, and married the man who was never in a passion in his life.

I only saw her once after she was married.   Did I say once ? I saw her twice, but the second time—ah, poor Bessie !

It would be about six months after her marriage when I saw her the first time, and her picture rises before me now, with her wan, anxious face, and eyes glaring with unearthly brightness. What a change those wretched six months had wrought upon Bessie !   All her former buoyancy was gone ; her silvery laugh, which echoed through the old house in the olden times, was for ever hushed, and a settled melancholy overspread her features.

"You are not happy, Bessie?" said I, putting my arms around her, as in the days of yore.

"I am not, Nancy; and yet I can scarcely tell why. Although my husband has not turned out what I expected, I cannot say that he has used me harshly, or bestowed on me a single angry word."

"But I fear he does not treat you as he ought, Bessie?"

"Oh, Nancy!" said she, in a voice of anguish, "I wish he would get angry with me sometimes. I wish he would get into a towering passion and curse and swear and strike me, for then I could strike back, and my bursting heart would get some relief. But no, he never gets angry—never finds fault with me for anything—never says I do right or wrong. He neglects me. He sees me wasting away day by day, but it gives him no concern. He has no love for me; indeed, I think he has not got a heart at all. Oh, Nancy, what can I do?"

What could she do? Ah, poor child, I saw she could do nothing but droop and die. To expect any change in him was to expect sunshine from a cannon ball. He was incapable of loving, for his blood never rose above freezing point, and he was never in a passion in his life.

The next time I saw Bessie she was in her coffin. How placid she looked then! She seemed to be happy in the release which death had afforded her.

"You are her murderer!" I said to Samuel Blubbery, my blood boiling with anger.

"Don't get excited, Miss Thistle; you will afterwards be sorry for letting your temper get the better of you," he replied, with a sickly, clownish smile.

I felt as if I could have torn the fellow into fragments, if I had him in my power.

"You're a cold-blooded villain!" I hissed. "You professed to love her, when you knew yourself incapable of loving. Your heart is a dry sponge, and your vile insensibility has killed her."

He listened to me without once changing colour, the same sickly smile playing upon his dogged countenance.

"I am not a man that can be put in a passion," he replied; "I know how to curb my temper, and would merely remark that you will be sorry afterwards for what you have now said."

Bestowing upon him my most contemptuous frown, I came away, and never saw him nor heard of him again, but I trust he has by this time received his deserts.

You fellows who pride yourselves that you never get in a passion are blockheads. You are worse than blockheads—you are inhuman, and I detest you. I don't like swearing; it is very unpolite when ladies are present. But ten hundred times superior is the fellow who blows off his steam in a volley of round oaths to the fellow who never gets in a passion. The former has got warm blood in his veins, and can love—he is something which you can understand—in fact, he is a human being.

POEMS.

THE DEMON OF THE LAW: A DREAM.

INTRODUCTION.

SHE meant it to frighten me ;
Grandmother said—
"If you climb up the Law
You may fall on your head.
Then the humphy old man
Who lives in the cave,
Will take you and chain you,
And make you his slave.
The horrid old man of the Law—
With his mouth all awry,
And a patch on his eye—
The wicked old man of the Law.
In his cavern he sits,
And he coughs and he spits
The venom from out of his stomach ;

On reptiles he feeds—
On adders, and lizards, and centipedes—
On hideous rats
And monstrous bats—
On worms with feet, and toads with tails,
And horrible blue two-headed snails.
And when it is night he leaves his cave,
And goes to the spot where the hemlock grows ;
He plucks a bunch, and back he goes
To eat his fill in his cavern dark,
Right under the Law, where never a spark
Of light ever gleamed.
Then he crawls on all fours
To his whinstone bed ;
Where he screeches and groans,
And gutters and snores,
In his nightmared sleep.
This wretched old man on reptiles fed—
This fiendish old man in his den so deep."

THE DREAM.

It made me dream.   Methought I stood
Within the shadow of the Law,
And there a hideous monster saw—
High priest of an ungodly brood.
All crippled and deformed was he ;
His face, on which brutality
And vice indelibly was writ,
Of cuts and scars the traces bore—
With blotch and bruise and festering sore.
There in his den I saw him sit,
While from his mouth vile venom flowed.
Attendant imps around him stood,

And caught the poison which he spued
In brazen vessel—each his load—
Which each conveyed away and poured
In casks within the cavern stored.
And when he ceased, in's loathsome den,
'Mid putrid odours, rank and vile,
He gloated o'er the ponderous pile
Of barrels he had filled again.
" Ha, ha !" he said, with fiendish leer,
" My mortal foes can't touch me here.
The Law above my head is strong—
And from this cave shall issue forth,
To land of South and land of North,
My potion, which doth crime prolong,
Despite the howling, bigot throng
That clamours for my banishment."

The scene was changed.   Methought I gazed
On Noah with his flowing beard,
Who on a judgment-seat appeared.
In front of him there stood, abased,
A score of old-world men in chains,
Brought to receive the sentence due,
And for their crime to know the pains.
" Alas !" said Noah, " proved, 'tis true
Ye've tampered with the wine again.
This hideous vice we must blot out,
For now it seems beyond a doubt
The fearful evil spreads amain,
And soon the race will victims fall
Unless we execute you all."
Hereon the black cap he assumed :
" Base culprits," said he,. " you are doomed
By sharp electric shock to die,
From Japheth's high-pressed battery.

This pleasant, quick, and painless death
In mercy grant we all, save one—
That wretched, miserable man,
Who first abused the gen'rous wine,
And by nefarious, subtle art
Did qualities to it impart
Which baneful are, and do combine
To madden brain and sadden heart.
No mercy can we grant to him;
But life of torture 'tis we deem
His fitting punishment.   Him take
And legs and arms and backbone break;
Then crush him in an iron cage.
Lest he should die, to drink him give
Of Life's Elixir, that he live
At least the quarter of an age.
In thirst and hunger let him pine,
And in that iron cage remain
Until we're pleased to ease his pain
By shock electric through his spine."
This sentence uttered, saw I then
The culprits led away to doom;
While quick dispersed th' assembled men,
Their daily labours to resume;
And Noah to the Ark him hied,
A building near the river-side.

My vivid dream was changed again.
I saw the Ark with sails unfurled—
Sole remnant of a deluged world—
Afloat upon the raging main;
And from a yard-arm hung the cage
Which firm enclosed the mangled man—
A hideous object, weird and wan,
Drenched with the spray from angry sea,

And with the rain from heaven which fell ;
Who laughed aloud with fiendish glee,
As demons laugh 'mid pains of hell.
The waters then were drying up,
And 'bove them mountain peaks appeared ;
While straight away for Ararat
The noble ship was deftly steered.
She struck the mountain rather hard—
Her timbers creaked—down fell the yard
From which the hideous creature swung,
And in the surging deep was flung.
" Quick, launch the dingy !" Noah roared ;
But ne'er a boat was found on board—
It had been left behind by Shem.
" Hard port her helm, and ease her stem !"
Yelled Noah, in a voice of thunder—
" Some one will pay for this gross blunder."

Changed was the scene.   Methought I stood
Down at the bottom of the sea
'Mid Neptune's nimble, sportive brood,
Where there were sounds of revelry.
The den'zens of the vasty deep
High carnival appeared to keep.
Quite plump and fat they all had grown,
For meat, of late, they had to eat,
Which was, till then, to them unknown.
No longer cannibals were they,
Nor fed upon their progeny.
Cod and haddock played together ;
Whale and herring loved each other ;
Shark smiled sweetly on John Dory,
While " Monk" viewed whiting *con amore*.
An object strange they now had found,
Which in surprise they crowded round—

A thing which moved and was alive—
'Twas not a fish, yet seemed to thrive
E'en at the bottom of the sea,
Which filled them with perplexity;
It was the maimed and hideous man
Which they so curiously did scan.
A shark essayed to munch the cage,
But quickly, in a towering rage,
He swam away, with bleeding gums
And eye-teeth broken into crumbs.
But, hush! the waters are disturbed;
King Neptune from the vasty deep,
Awakened from his ten days' sleep
Appears, to know the reason why
Those sounds of mirth and revelry.
With one sweep of his mighty tail
The motley crowd he quick dispersed,
And none remained, save one large whale,
With whom His Majesty conversed.
The cagéd man he viewed in wonder,
Then quickly burst his bars asunder,
And with him straight to his coral keep
He sped, full speed, through the vasty deep.

In hall, lit up with diamonds bright,
Where pearls and rubies shed their light,
With walls and floor of coral rare,
And dome of shells, most wond'rous fair,
He entered, and the creature laid
Upon a couch by swordfish made,
Of whales' jawbones and seahorse hide,
And stuffed with mermaids' hair inside.
At once a bell he loudly rung,
And soon a door was open flung.
A sea nymph came upon the scene,

o

Most gorgeous to behold—
Her long hair glistening with the sheen
Of diamonds, pearls, and gold.
She'd oft climbed up the sides of ships
And listened to the speech
Which chanced to fall from sailors' lips ;
And one old " salt" did teach
To her the language of the earth,
One night she met him in his berth.
And as King Neptune did command,
She kindly took the creature's hand,
And, though her *Gaelic* was not pure,
She interviewed in accents bland,
With winning smile, which did allure
And touch his fossilizéd heart.
He told his tale with right goodwill—
Of Noah and the recent Flood,
Which drowned earth's creatures, and did fill
The fishes' maws with flesh and blood.
His own sad tale he also told—
His crime and punishment inflicted,
Which made King Neptune's blood run cold,
And he the sea nymph interdicted
From further questioning, till he
Had time for thought and reverie.

The scene was changed.   In dungeon deep
Beneath King Neptune's coral keep
I saw the three assembled then—
It was the Demon Sphinx's den.
From out the floor there issued smoke,
As words of incantation spoke
King Neptune, and with outstretched hand
Waved solemnly a mystic wand.
Soon rent the floor, and from below

The Demon Sphinx, with eyes aglow,
And outstretched wings, and fearful claws
Extending from his monstrous paws,
Arose, and angrily inquired
Of Neptune what he now desired.
" Most august Sphinx," King Neptune said,
" A mortal from the earth o'erhead
I bring, with hate to men so strong
That life he wisheth to prolong,
And while earth lasts a Demon be,
Then thine to all eternity.
His *forte* is the liquor spell ;
To make men drink he loveth well."
The Sphinx then fixed his fiery stare
Upon the creature crouching there,
And said—" My son, a vengeance vast
I'll put into thy power to wield.
Safe back to earth I will thee send,
And grant thee life while time doth last,
But thou must keep thy hate concealed,
And great goodwill to men pretend.
When worked by guile, revenge speeds best,
And sure its course as heaven's behest.
With stomach of capacity
Unbounded will I thee provide,
So that with great rapacity
The vine's fruit and the staff of bread,
With others of earth's fruits beside,
Thou may'st consume, and in their stead
A liquid spirit give mankind,
E'en from their rottenness distilled,
Possessing spell man's sense to blind,
And o'er his appetite to wield
A magic power, a mystic charm,
So that he will delight to drink

The potion which is filled with harm,
And in his inmost heart will think
Thou art to him a steadfast friend—
E'en ask a blessing to attend
The drinking of this spirit fell
Which soon will make the earth a hell—
Then say now art thou well content,
And on this vengeful mission bent ?"
" I'll willingly a Demon be
From now to all eternity,"
The creature said, with glaring eyes,
As struggling hard he tried to rise.
With one sharp claw his own breast then
The Sphinx did deeply pierce, and when
Outflowed the blood, the nymph it caught
Into a pearly shell, and brought
An adder's tongue to staunch the wound,
And then to sing her voice attuned.
She placed the shell at the creature's feet,
And sang with the voice of a syren sweet :—

> Drink it again,
> Oh, never refrain ;
> It drives away pain
> For a time, for a time ;
> Then it bites and burns,
> And stings by turns.
> It breeds crime, breeds crime.
> Stir it up well,
> The poison shell ;
> Its fragrance is sweet,
> But 'tis fell, 'tis fell.
> Drink it all up,
> Take a good sup ;
> 'Tis sweet to the lip,
> But it sendeth to hell.

When ceased the song, the sea nymph took

The blood-filled shell, and with a look
Of crafty sweetness, it presented
Unto the creature, nor resented
He the nauseous, sickening draught.
" Wrath to mankind I drink," he said,
As in his hands the shell he caught,
And contents quaffed with upturned head.
As soon's the draught had passed his lips,
He raised himself upon his hips,
Outstretched his arms, and to and fro
His body swayed, and 'gan to glow
His pallid cheek.   A fiendish glare
Lit up his eyes.   " Hurrah !" he cried,
" I'm growing strong—this new blood rare
New life imparts."   To rise he tried,
And hobbled o'er the stony floor,
His body straightening more and more.
" Ha, ha !" he shouted, " I'm a King !
I'll soon be monarch of the world,
And with ' goodwill' on flag unfurled
I'll strife and brawls and horrors bring.
Upon the sons of men my power
I'll wield, and cruel vengeance shower ;
And I will have abundant time—
Ha, ha ! time matters not to me—
To wander throughout every clime,
And foster every vice and crime
With drug of magic potency."
" Then go, thou Demon of my making ;
Thou fiend, thou ghoul, thy undertaking
Befits thee well," the Sphinx exclaimed ;
" Thy passions never be untamed,
Thy thirst for vengeance never slack,
And dupes and drunkards never lack."
The Sphinx his broad wings flapped, and then

Dense smoke and ashes filled the den.
I saw no more, but rushing noise
Of many waters filled my ears,
And sang a rasping, croaking voice,
Which woke in me foreboding fears.
In melancholy monotone
Was sung the song of the o'erthrown :—

Undone, undone, undone.
Would, would I could shun
The gaze of the sun.
Would, would I could hide,
And for ever abide
'Neath the flowing tide.
Think ? 'Tis maddening to think—
I kill thought with drink,
And I stand on the brink
Of the fearful abyss.
No chance of hit or miss,
For 'tis come to this—
Let it kill, let it kill,
I *must* have my fill,
'Tis the least of the ill.
I cannot refrain,
It soddens my brain,
And deadens my pain.
On the road to hell ?
Very well, very well,
I'll answer the bell
When it rings, when it rings.
Afraid to die ? Not I ;
Father Death can try
When he stings, when he stings.

In dream I back to earth again
Was brought. In fertile plain,
Through which a stream translucid flowed,
Its banks with vines profusely clad,
And with ripe fruit their branches bowed,
Stood Noah's tent.

In bed he lay,
And writhed in feverish agony.
He had been sick and vomiting,
And ague, most enervating,
Succeeded had, which left him weak—
Above his breath he could not speak.
His brain on fire—head like to split—
So parched his tongue he could not spit
Beyond his beard.   Bloodshot his eyes,
His knees so shook he could not rise.
With palpitation troubled, too—
Nought could he eat, and nought could do
But welter on his reeking bed,
And o'er the pillow toss his head.
But, worst of all, his mind was racked,
Arising from the dismal fact
That he had lost his memory.
He was not sure how long he lay,
If since last night or night before.
He might have lain a week or more
For aught he knew.   Quite hard he tried
The sequence of events to grasp,
But this his memory defied.
His mind was like a ravelled hank,
All mixed and tangled in a maze.
What dreams were, what realities
He knew not.   "Even now," he sighed,
"I may be dreaming," and he tried
To make himself believe he was.
But in a moment he had cause
In anguish to exclaim—"Ah, me,
'Tis real after all—there's he—
The man who with decoction vile
My sober senses did beguile."
It was indeed the Demon wretch

Who in the tent appeared.
His bony hand he did outstretch
Towards Noah, as he said—" I feared
Thou would'st feel somewhat bad to-day,
For thou an overdose did'st take
Of my Elixir, nor would'st stay,
Though ill I told thee 'twould thee make.
Like all good things, it must be used
In moderation, not abused.
To cure thine ills I've brought a charm,
A toothful, just to pick thee up.
'Twill do much good, not any harm,
If used aright.   A little sup
Will drive thy headache quite away,
And fast restore thy memory."
The fiend then from his pocket drew
A flask with " Cognac" on the label,
And placing it upon the table,
To wondering Noah bade adieu.
" Mayhap I do misjudge this man,"
Mused Noah, as his eyes did scan
The flask upon the table laid.
" 'Twas rather good of him to come
And proffer thus his friendly aid.
I'll have a little drop.   By gum !
The draught indeed is very good,
Used moderately, as it should.
New life to me it doth impart—
Quenched is the throbbing of my head,
And eased the aching of my heart."
Then Noah from the bed arose,
And deftly buttoned on his clothes.
" But still," said he, " I do feel dry ;
An insufficient quantity
I've taken, and a small drop more

May do much good, and can't do harm.
That's better.   Yes, I glow all o'er—
It acts upon me like a charm—
Much better could not wish to feel,
Save that my head doth somewhat reel,
And things seem double to mine eyes.
A worm, too, on my stomach gnaws—
Yea, gnaws all round to get his fill—
I'll have a drop this worm to kill.
Good, good, he's poisoned now, I think—
By Jove, but this is splendid drink !
It makes a man feel glorious quite,
And fills him with supreme delight.
I'll have another drop, to bring
My memory back—the very thing !
I'm feeling drowsy, and must wake
The slumbering functions of my brain.
A small 'sensation' more I'll take
To wake me up, and sure—hic—maintain
That questionless—hic—sobriety
Which marks all good society."
Soon fast asleep in couch he lay
Upon his breast, and heavily
He breathed.
		Then saw I in the tent
A being as from heaven sent.
He seemed an angel, clothed was he
In glistening raiment—majesty
And pity mixed, his face expressed,
As prostrate Noah he addressed :—

" Ah, Noah, thou hast been unwise, and looked
With jaundiced eyes upon this Demon's crime,
When he a man was, and the wine abused.
Thy soul was filled with passion vengeful then,

And thou the attribute of mercy, which
Thou hadst at thy command, didst then withhold.
'Vengeance is mine,' saith God—man's vengeance oft
Dethrones his judgment, and becomes a lash
For his own back, as thine dost lash thee now,
And will thy progeny while time doth last.
The Demon leaves thee, chuckling as he goes,
Elated with the victory he has won
O'er thee, the Father of mankind, whose voice
Rose eloquent in bygone days against
The sin and vices of the old world men.
O'er thee, who walked with God, and in His eyes
Found grace—on earth the only upright one!
Thee who of righteousness a preacher wast!
But now thy fair escutcheon thou hast soiled,
And canker-worm on thy ripe fruit hath seized.
Alas! how are the mighty fallen! man,
Weak man, is but a pigmy at the best;
Temptation comes, and lays him on his breast."

My dream was changed.   Babel voices
Rang around me, and strange noises,
As of conquerors and conquered
In pursuit and retreat I heard;
And shrieks, yells, and imprecations,
As of a world gone mad—
While onward rolled the life of nations.
The song of angels, " Peace and goodwill
To men" was wafted from the sky.
Then shouts of rage the air did fill—
" Away with Him—Him crucify!"
Then heard I loud huzzahs and clang
Of arms.   I saw Crusaders bold,
Whose shouts enthusiastic rang
As forth they marched to ills untold.

And as Time's loom her shuttles plied,
'Mid din of battles fiercely mad,
And fields of carnage blood-red dyed ;
'Mid happy voices leal and glad,
And sound of hammers, as were reared
Men's monuments of energy,
And mind's rich trophies fast appeared ;
'Mid din of fertile industry,
Where steam—tamed monster—by its power
Machinery kept moving quick,
Producing much each busy hour,
I came to modern days again.
Again I gazed upon the Law,
And there an aged seer saw—
A man of venerable mien—
Who spoke in accents clear and keen :—

Almost four thousand years have flown,
   And since that far-off time
The Demon well his power hath shewn
   In every land and clime.
All classes—warriors, princes, kings—
   To him have bent the knee,
And prized above all other things,
   His drug of potency.
That magic drug which first enthrals
   And sorrow kills and cares,
Inspires the heart with fellowship,
   But in the end ensnares.
Makes valorous and voluble,
   Unto the weak gives strength,
Hilarious makes and pleasureful,
   But torture comes at length.
His spell has gone through all the earth,
   And votaries everywhere

Bow low at his unholy shrine.
　　Yes, he takes pains to snare
The best and noblest of mankind,
　　The gen'rous and the good.
The cultured ones of intellect
　　To see in anguish brood
Upon the fate he's brought them to,
　　And what they might have been,
Gives solace to his searéd heart.
　　He gloats with visage keen
To see the guileless-hearted ones
　　His poison mixture quaff,
And see them sit where ribald songs
　　Resound 'mid ribald laugh.
Ah, cruel Demon, well he knows
　　The secret of his spell,
As 'twere the seeds of heaven he sows,
　　But reaps the fruits of hell.
He likes to wait, for he can wait—
　　Years are to him but days—
To see his victim's fearful fate,
　　And he delights to gaze
Upon the raving maniac's face,
　　And on the murderer's blow ;
Delights to hear the mother's curse,
　　And children's wail of woe.
In shame, and cruelty, and crime,
　　His arm he doth make bare ;
He chuckles when the husband strikes
　　Her whom to love he sware.
It makes his Demon's heart rejoice
　　To see the life-blood run
Of brother shed by brother's hand,
　　And father's shed by son.

'Tis slow, but sure, this poison sway—
  O'er sense and soul it steals,
And eats its victim's heart away,
  Till in the grave he reels—
A frightful wreck, a haggard wretch,
  An outcast from his kin,
Who pleased are when the cold earth hides
  His sorrow, shame, and sin.

Oh, horrid Demon of the Law,
Mine eyes the future pierced and saw
A myriad band from near and far,
Who've sworn 'gainst thee eternal war,
Thy stronghold of the Law attack,
With victor shout they forced thee back,
And made thee crouch within thy den.
An earthquake shook the Law, and then
Its ponderous weight upon thee fell,
And crushed thee in a narrow cell.
Then shout triumphant rang—' All hail,
For evermore let love prevail !'
The mystery of iniquity,
'Neath which, since far antiquity
All kindreds of the nations groaned,
At last was wrecked—at last dethroned ;
And venom vile no more went forth
To land of South nor land of North.
Men sang, each face with pleasure flush'd,
' The Demon of the Law is crushed ;
The sway of alcohol has ceased ;
Vice and crime are now decreased ;
Strife and brawlings now are ended ;
Lives and morals are amended,
And the good and true defended !' "

MY BIRTHPLACE.

That place my heart forget can ne'er,
Life's rosy dawn so bright and fair,
So full of dreams and sweet repose—
Blest hours, which only childhood knows—
There have I passed, then wonder not
That I should still revere this spot.
Still vividly before mine eyes
The scenes of long ago arise;
And oft in midnight slumber deep,
When present cares are lost in sleep,
I dream I am again a child,
And rambling 'mid those scenes so wild—
The rocky cliffs and grassy braes,
'Mong which I've climbed in early days—
When full of glowing health and zest :
Now searching for the linnet's nest,
Now gathering ferns and wild rock flowers,
Or sheltering from the falling showers
Beneath some overhanging peak,
Or in the cavern near the creek.
Spellbinding was the mighty sea—
Each wave a hidden mystery.
The tide-mark was enchanted ground—
What countless trophies here were found !
Belched out from old Atlantic's jaws,
When lashed in foaming agonies.
Distinctly each familiar place,
Each rock and cave and pool I trace,
Where oft the summer's eve I've spent,
On catching " sillocks" all intent,

Or wading in the briny sea,
With trousers drawn up 'bove the knee ;
Now retreating, now advancing,
As the crested waves kept dancing ;
Or, happy 'mong a youthful band,
Who've built a fortress in the sand,
With busy hands we'd prop each side
Against the fast-approaching tide.
Afar our ringing shouts would sound
As each succeeding wave swept round
With slow but steady onward pace,
Till of our tower was left no trace.
The seaside was our favourite haunt—
Where we'd full scope to romp and rant
When school was over ; here we came
To play at many a merry game—
At " French and English " or at " catty,"
Or, best of all, the roaring " knotty."
And when we wearied for a seat,
We'd some smooth boulder take, and eat
Our heart's content of salt sea-weed,
On which the nymphs and mermaids feed.
(At least our grandmas said they do,
So then, of course, it must be true.)
Of *tangles, dulse,* and *henware,*
We'd eat our fill with gusto rare ;
No fear had we of indigestion,
Their wholesomeness we ne'er did question.

   .   .   .   .   .   .

Amid such scenes as these passed by
My youth.   Upon my memory
In golden letters they are writ,
And ne'er can be effaced from it.

DESPONDENCY.

WHEREFORE this moaning,
And winds so piteously sighing?
My soul it disturbs,
And shadows around me are flying.
Tell me, things of air,
Do ye wail for the year that is dying?
And will ye disappear
With his funeral bier?

Fantasy's children!
Your vigils unwelcome still keeping.
Why, when I sow'd love
Should I nought but anguish be reaping?
Go, go with the year,
Nor vex me, nor force me to weeping:
The dead past I disown,
With its hopes, which have flown.

But come, thou New Year,
With other joys and wings of healing;
To thy diadem
I'll bow, and at thy footstool kneeling
Kiss thy youthful hand.
Methinks a calm is o'er me stealing,
Though in the dark I grope,
Still hoping against hope.

SONNETS.

I.

THE baby sleeps—how tranquil her repose;
No fitful starts disturb her pillowed rest,
For yet unruffled is that tiny breast
By worldly cares, nor sin nor sorrow knows.
The baby smiles—how lovely now that face;
I wonder what celestial sights appear
Before her sleep-wrapt eyes? are angels near
To prompt the smiles which her young features grace?
Sweet one, I know not what thy dream may be,
Yet can I wish less pleasant thoughts may ne'er
Disturb thy breast, nor cloud thy brow so fair,
Throughout thy voyage on life's stormy sea.
Alas! the wish is vain; if thou are spared,
Life's cares and crosses must by thee be shared.

II.

WHY do they weep? Ah, is the baby dead,
The little, tiny thing we held so dear?
Lies she now cold, and is her spirit fled?
Ah, yes—the prating voice no more we'll hear;
'Tis hushed—for ever hushed—and sad are we,
And weep as passes out the sombre bier.
A father's pride, a mother's joy was she;
They mourning go, and oh, the house is drear.
Yet weep not for her—she has been borne away
On angel pinions to the choir above—
That choir of babes who stand in white array
Around the throne, and sing their Saviour's love.
That we may join her there, oh, let us pray,
And with our voices swell the never-dying lay.

P

WISHING FOR THE MOON.

At twilight, near the window, father sat
With Johnnie on his knee, in fond chit-chat;
He was his first-born child, a ruddy boy
Of tender years, that doting father's joy.
And as the chattering tongue wagg'd furious
In childish tattle, and with questions curious—
Great posers oft for Dad—the moon on high
Burst from her cloud, and caught the youngster's eye.
" Oh, Daddy, vat vound, shiney sing me see
Above ze houses—say, Dad, vat it be ?"
" It is the moon, my child, and up, up high
Above the clouds, where God reigns, in the sky."
" Oh, Daddy, bling it down, me vants to see
Ze bonny, shiney moon; div, div it me.
Tomollow me vould 'ike vis it to play,
And loll it on ze darden-valk all day."
" My child, this moon is not for thee a toy ;
I cannot bring it down, you foolish boy."
And hereupon the child began to weep,
Nor would be soothed till he was wrapped in sleep.
Yes, foolish boy, and yet we all must own
In wishing for the moon thou'rt not alone.
See yonder stalwart man, how hard he toils
For Fame, whose boldest efforts all she foils,
And soars beyond his grasp—he, too, will soon
Find that he has been wishing for the moon.
And this poor, careworn waif, upon whose face
Stern sorrow has imprinted deep her trace,
Who sighs for happiness—ah, well, I ween
'Tis like the moon, far in the distance seen,

But not to be attained. Vain all his sighs—
The thing he seeks dwells only in the skies.
And thou love-stricken youth, whose thoughts abide
In dreamland, with fair Jenny as thy bride ;
While she, hard-hearted maid, on thee ne'er thinks,
But from another's smile love's nectar drinks.
Ah ! blinded youth, thy cherished, wished-for boon
Is from thy reach far-distant as the moon.
The mewling child, the full-fledged bearded man,
All eagerly their airy castles scan ;
Before our eyes fond phantoms ever keep,
And for the moon despairingly we weep.

JOE WOOD.

Joe Wood, he was a carpenter,
    A straight-edged man of rules ;
A cold once seized upon his chest,
    And a thief upon his tools.

He called his wife in through the panes,
    And tho' much pained, he kissed her ;
She placed a blister to his chest,
    And for her pains he blessed her.

Next day he found his pain removed,
    His tool-chest likewise gone ;
" 'Tis plain I cannot plane," he 'plained,
    " For planes I now have none."

To quench his grief and drink relief,
   He drank a pint of gin ;
His wife she thought a screw was loose,
   When he came hammering in.

" You're on the beer !" she quick exclaimed ;
   " Not so," said Mr Wood,
" But being in so great a strait,
   I've got a little screwed.

" You know I have no compass now,
   Tho' compassed round with care ;
My square is also stolen away,
   And hence I'm off the square.

" I ne'er again shall see my saw,
   Nor mend your chairs and stools ;
Oh, may the thief be braced to bits
   Who chiselled all my tools.

"I am indeed a hard-ruled man,
   If I ain't ruined, *axe* me ;
To think I cannot cramp a frame,
   Cramps all my frame and racks me.

" And now I sit upon the bench,
   And on my panels gaze ;
No rays of hope within me rise,
   Another pint to raise.

" To dream of being a gentleman
   I henceforth must forbear ;
For if I cannot drive a nail,
   I cannot drive a pair."

CASTLES IN THE AIR.

MANHOOD's a goal, and every child
   To reach it, O how fain ;
How long they think the time ere they
   A score of years attain !

What airy castles youth doth build :
   What fancies strange and wild
It pictures of that time when it
   No more shall be a child !

The little rosy-cheekéd boy,
   Just left the nurse's knee ;
E'en he will lisp about the time
   When he a man shall be ;

And in his childish prattle light
   Some grand exploits will plan,
Which only wait th' accomplishment
   When he becomes a man.

The schoolboy, with his sulky brow,
   Forced 'gainst his will to school ;
How hard he thinks his lot ; poor thing,
   His heart of grief is full.

He, too, looks forward to this time,
   And in the distance sees
Himself a man ; quite rich, of course,
   And living on in ease.

Soon, soon, my boy, the goal is reached,
   And you a man have grown ;

You're surely happy now, with all
    Your early sorrows flown?

Ah, no; 'tis very different, friend,
    From youthful fancy's picture fair;
You little knew the load of cares
    You longed to have, and now must bear.

WITHERED FLOWERS.

A BUNCH of withered flowers
    The pathway strewn upon,
Lying crumpled up and jaded,
Their lovely hues all faded—
    Their perfumes sweet all gone;
Bespattered in the miry street,
And trampled 'neath remorseless feet.

Just a bunch of withered flowers
    Tossed all in a heap;
Because they could not stay
The progress of decay,
    Nor their beauty keep,
They were cast forth from some fair room
Once scented with their sweet perfume.

Poor withered flowers! ah, me!
    What do they bespeak?
Let Youth and Love draw near,
And Beauty shed a tear,
    Let Meditation seek
Meet musing for her lonely hours,
And sing the dirge of withered flowers.

Youth ! thou bright-eyed youth,
  Laughing to the breeze
Which tints thy cheeks so rosy red,
And floats thy ringlets round thy head—
  Such golden ringlets these !
But soon, too soon, thy bloom is shed,
And thou'rt cut down and witheréd.

Love ! thou tender thing,
  Most sensitive of flowers,
Blooming fragrant for a while,
Drinking bliss from angel's smile,
  Ensconced in fairy bowers ;
But soon the angel flits away,
And thy soft petals close for aye.

Beauty ! ah, thou fragrant rose,
  Admired of every eye ;
Transparent as the rainbow bright,
Glittering in the soft sunlight—
  A gem of purity ;
But, ah, thou meet'st thy doom, fair flower,
When thou hast bloomed thy little hour.

Friendship ! stalwart, stately flower,
  Though strong thou seem'st to stand,
Smiling to the sun above,
Nurtured with the dews of love,
  Thy name is writ in sand ;
Adversity comes prancing by,
And cuts thee down to fade and die.

Hope ! thou water lily fair,
  Buoyant, full of pride,

Floating on the waters clear,
Riding 'bove the waves of fear,
   All fearless of the tide
Which soon shall rise and whelm thee o'er,
And dash thee, stranded, on the shore.

Slowly chant the mournful dirge
   When Love trips o'er the plain ;
As withered flowers defile the air,
So withered hope turns cankered care,
   And life is sad and vain ;
'Tis far away beyond the tomb
That aramanthine flowers do bloom.

A KISS.

A KISS—what is it ?   A mystical thing ;
An ideal love-bird with quiv'ring wing,
Which sits on our lips, ever ready to fly
To somebody's lips when temptingly nigh.
Soft tresses flowing down over your arm,
And breath on your cheek so gentle, so warm ;
Lips so inviting, so dexterously parted,
Which seem to say "Taste us, and don't be faint-hearted ;"
Locked to your bosom a warm, heaving breast,
To your quivering lips two honeyed lips pressed,
And then o'er each heart-string a quick throb of pleasure—
Fortissimo swelling, 'tis bliss beyond measure !
Thrilling deep down to the heart's inmost core,
A smack and a blush, and love's first kiss is o'er.

THE DYING YEAR.

HARK! 'tis the midnight hour : the chiming bell
In measured peals resounds the knell
   Of the dying year;
While from the motley, clam'rous crowd
There bursts, in accents shrill and loud,
   A ringing cheer.
'Tis thus men bid their last farewell
   To the dying year.

But ah, departed shade, it is not meet
That I, with voice of joy should greet
   Thy ended sway;
To me thy reign hath all been bright,
Nor dimmed with shadows of the night—
   A lengthened ray
Of sunshine : oft thy hurrying feet
   I fain would stay.

Visions of the past, and many a tender tie,
Doth knit thee to my memory;
   And gone thou art
Like some sweet dream too soon dispell'd,
Or friend of youth in fondness held,
   From whom we part
No more to meet, with sad good-bye,
   And aching heart.

HOPE ON.

Oh, tell me not, in doleful strains,
   That life is vain and void of cheer,
Though now some disappointment pains,
From grief the heart no solace gains,
   Look up and dry each tear:
      Hope on.

What though wealth be thee denied?
   Not for lack of gold repine;
Wealth ebbs and flows like Pentland tide—
To-day it is thy neighbour's pride—
   To-morrow 't may be thine:
      Hope on.

What though mankind at thee sneer,
   And thy best motives misconstrue?
Have patience—give not place to fear—
Time will prove thy motives clear,
   If to thy soul thou'rt true:
      Hope on.

What though trusted friends forsake thee?
   Friendship's oft a broken reed;
To earnest, upright work betake thee,
So thou other friends wilt make thee—
   Truer, nobler, friends indeed:
      Hope on.

What though from thy breast be torn
   Love's fond hopes concentred there?

Dejected be not nor forlorn,
Truer hearts are not unborn,
  Nor other forms as fair:
      Hope on.

What though Death's cold hand be laid
  On the one thou lovest well?
The dearest here must wane and fade;
Oh, grieve not, but ask heaven for aid—
  There let thy best hopes dwell:
      Hope on.

Say not that real joys are few—
  That brighter days can ne'er return;
With virtue's balm thy youth renew,
And tell mankind it is not true
  That man was made to mourn:
      Hope on.

In love survey this world so fair,
  No heaven-sent blessing proudly spurn,
Of every good thing guard thy share,
The bad eschew with special care,
  So may'st thou never mourn:
      Hope on.

A NICHT WI' THE BAIRNS.

Gae tae yer beds, ye howlin' brats,
For, sure, a pack o' hungry cats
A worritin' ten thousan' rats
     Wad' mak' less noise.
Ye've deaved the drumstrings o' my lugs,
Deranged the hoose, and waked the bugs,
     Wi' yer daft ploys.

I wish yer Mammie wad come hame,
For she's a siccar, sober dame,
An' kens the wye tae curb an' tame
     Yer mad career;
Guidsakes! ye wadna mak' sic tussle,
Nor fitba' play wi' her new bustle,
     Gin she were here.

Gaukie Bell, the lang-leg'd simman,
Though but a bairn, she looks a woman;
Her tricks the nicht consist in gummin'
     Biled tatie-peelin's
An' auld post-stamps on Lizzie's nose,
Which soon results in cuffs and blows,
     For Lizz has feelin's.

There's Mem, the leddy o' the hoose,
Sits on her chair an' craws fu' croose;
She's mair for ornament than use,
     Miss Mary Prim,
She reads her book and plays her tune,
An sometimes girns at Jock the loon,
     An' rooses him.

Big-heided Jock, he's nae that saft,
Though aften he spiers questions daft;
His skull's sae thick that hammer shaft
  It scarce impresses.
An' whan in mischief he's afoot,
Or tak's the sulks, then mammie's boot
  His back caresses.

The neist in turn comes dainty Lizz,
The bissim's like a bottle o' fizz,
But always has an eye to bis',
  An' does her wark.
She'll licht the fire, put on the kettle,
An' ha'e the room a' in guid fettle
  E'en in her sark.

An' Pete, the roarin', rantin' loon,
Wha climbs an' swings, an' cracks his croon;
He'll either wear a lawyer's goon
  Or sodger's coat;
For he can lee wi' serious air,
An' fecht till a' his banes are sair,
  Nor care a groat.

The neist, wee chatterin', lispin' Jenny,
Aye teasing Dad tae gie'r a penny.
The critter's ane amang the many
  That's unco gude
When saired wi' a' she wants, but when
She's crossed or checked, ye'll find her then
  In different mood.

Last o' a' comes toddlin' Dolly,
Snappish as an auld grey polly;
Just coonter her, and then, by golly!
  Look oot for squalls.

She's mistress o' the hoose, I tell ye,
An' when she's roosed wi' sticks she'd fell ye,
      Or spoons or dalls.

Now Doll is playin' wi' the clock,
An' Jen a cheena bowl has broke;
Pete has stealt a sweet frae Jock,
      The girnin' sinner :
He turns on Pete like fiery bull,
But in his guts frae Peter's skull
      Receives a pinner.

I tak' the clock frae Doll by force ;
She shies at me a widden horse,
An' oot o' spite or else remorse
      She wats the flure,
An' dances in it wi' her feet,
Endeavourin' tae skirl an' greet
      Wi' a' her power.

Big Bell she's playin' pranks on Lizz,
An' puttin' her intae a fizz ;
I lift a dishcloot an' lat whizz
      At Bella's lug :
She dooks, an' I knock oot the gas,
While mantel nic-nacs lie *en masse*
      Upo' the rug.

Expectin' that some peace 'twad bring,
I rise an' fasten up the swing.
I wish I'd never done sic thing,
      For fearfu' row
At aince begins, till I am fain
Tae tak' the blamed thing doon again ;
      I'll dae't I vow.

Pete tumbles ower upo' his croon,
Jock trips on him when he is doon,
An' Doll strikes Jenny wi' a spoon
        Upo' the nose,
Then tak's possession o' the swing,
An' winna budge for anything,
        Till doon she goes

Upo' the hard flure wi' a thump,
She skins her broo and dirls her rump,
An' on her elbow mak's a lump.
        Wi' sudden ire
I seize the swing, its hooks unhing,
An' gi'e the cursèd thing a fling
        Ahint the fire.

Mamma comes in amid the row—
Not in a pleasant mood, I vow—
An' there was silence then, I trow,
        Save sabs and blurtin'.
" Oh, sic a skerrie hoose," says Ma,
" An' yer tae blame !"   " Na, na," says Pa :
        Let's draw the curtain.

JEMIMA.

Jemima was a girl, she was ;
   More tough was she than tender,
And somewhat masculine in mind,
   Though feminine in gender.

I asked Jemima to the play,
   And gained her sweet consent ;
So, sitting still, we moved away—
   For in a cab we went.

Her hand I squeezed, and asked her if
   She thought a kiss amiss,
When lo, she turned her face aside,
   And so I missed a kiss.

" A kiss you'll never miss," said I ;
   " Come, dear, I won't seek two."
" A Miss you'll never kiss," said she,
   " While I'm alone with you."

Chagrined was I at this reply,
   But did the insult pocket—
Likewise my hand, and forth I drew
   A real sham gold locket ;

And bending on my bended knee,
   Did place it in her lap,
Remaining wrapt in rapture till
   My head received a rap.

"Get up, you nasty beast," she said ;
  Such language was not meet,
For although my legs were doubled,
  I had not got four feet.

" False maid !" I cried, " you've broke my heart,
  And severed every tie ;"
My braces, too, with stooping broke,
  Which raised my choler high.

My heartstrings then I cut in twain
  (I'm speaking in a figure) ;
I stopped the cab, and stepped to earth—
  The cabby was a nigger,

Who clamoured for his fair-earned fare
  Like any fair-skinned man ;
" That fair maid there will pay your fare,"
  Said I, as off I ran,

And quickly reached the rocky rocks,
  Where foamed the foamy deep ;
Upon a cliff I standing stood,
  Determining to leap—

To leap and drown my sorrow great,
  And drown myself to boot,
When suddenly it came on rain,
  And home I came on foot.

THE CLOSING YEAR.

THEN fare-thee-well, old year, for it is meet
We part as we have met, good friends and true.
Thou'rt old, and yet to me how young thou seem'st !
'Tis but as yesterday that ringing shouts
Of mirth and folly rent the midnight air
As thou wert ushered in, a king uncrowned,
Save with a diadem of fleecy snow.
But soon thy swaddling clothes were cast aside,
And thy young life did germinate and bud
With happy promise of good things in store
When thou should'st reach thy manhood's glorious prime.
Ah, me ! and now thou'rt old and grey, and pin'st
In second childhood, thou so lately crowned
With summer's rosy splendour, and bedeck'd
With autumn's golden wreaths and laurels bright.
Methinks I hear thy death-throes even now
On the wind's wings borne doleful to my ear—
Now weak and feebly sighing, and anon
Bursting in wild convulsive agony,
Making every limb of Nature shiver
As thou dost struggle in the grip of Death.
Soon, soon the ghost thou shalt yield up, and o'er
Thy funeral bier the naked trees shall mourn
With bended heads and shaking knees, and winds
A mournful requiem wail as thou art borne
To the vault of the Past to lie embalmed.
Thou goest to thy death—and what is death ?
'Tis not annihilation, but a change—
A waking from a fitful, nightmared sleep.
Thou art not dead, O year, though passed away,

In other ages thou shalt live and speak.
We live and dream, but in the sleep of death
We wake to real life.   How strange it seems !
Oh, year of gladness, soon to pass away,
To stay thy hurrying footsteps I am fain.
Yet go.   Though gone I still can call thee mine,
While memory lives, the past is never dead.
It rules the present, yea, it stretches forth
Into the future, and with clasp most sure
Doth link the two eternities.   God's book
Is writ in part by man : its leaves are years.
Man traces day by day on its broad page
The record of his doings, and, alas !
How oft it is a blotted, dark-stained page
Which record bears of his depravity.
Think of it, man, the power is thine to-day
To colour bright or dark the aspect of
The past : the present only is thine own—
The past is God's, and irrevocable.

RETROSPECTION.

How sweet in life to cast
A retrospective glance ;
What fond remembrances we find
Fast flooding in upon the mind,
Of scenes and sports which once
        We loved to share,
        Enjoyments rare,
Now numbered with the fleeting things that were.

Blest childhood's happy dawn,
Of all our days the best,
When round a father's knee we play'd,
Or on his loving bosom laid
Our little heads to rest;
　　　　When first we heard,
　　　　With brightening eyes,
About a happy land beyond the skies.

Our school and playmates near;
The schoolmaster so kind,
To whom we lisped our A B C,
And thought that none so wise as he
In all the world could find.
　　　　How rapidly,
　　　　Before mind's eye,
These youthful scenes in bright succession fly.

But now those days have passed
Like dreams with morning light;
And scenes more stern our minds engage.
Yet though around us storms may rage,
Still onward let us fight,
　　　　And play our part
　　　　With steadfast heart,
Till from life's stage we shall at last depart.

THE BAIRNIES AN' ME.

THE bairnies are sleepin', d'ye hear hoo they're snorin'?
    Noo, Dan, if ye wauken them angry I'll be;
Haud aff wi' yer capers, an' nae set them roarin'—
    Yer aye playin' pranks on the bairnies an' me.

I'm sure there's nae quateness but whan they're a' sleepin',
    For Jockie an' Kitty can never agree;
But in a wild uproar the hoose they're aye keepin'—
    Sae gang tae yer ain bed an' lat the bairns be.

My Kate is a romp—just a rampagin' jadie—
    She's fu' o' mischief, an' as daft as can be;
She'll skirl an' she'll fecht just like ony wild laddie—
    Sure, Kitty, the man 'ill be blest 'at gets ye!

They aftentimes put me fair intae a passion;
    When new washed the flure they'll bounce in wi' a glee,
Their feet fu' o' gutters, as aye is their fashion—
    Ochone, what a plague are the bairnies tae me!

They draive me yestreen a'most fairly dementit,
    But little cared they for the fricht they gaed me;
They cam' boundin' in wi' their faces a' pentit—
    My heart gaed a loup, an' I thocht I wad dee.

An' although I sud lick them ten times in a day,
    It's just a' the same, an' nae better they'll be;
Lat me dae what I lek, they'll ha'e their ain way—
    But mebbie they'll yet be guid bairnies tae me.

JOCK M'GEE: A TALE.

A'BODY kent big Jock M'Gee ;
A burly son o' toil was he—
By trade a joiner, but he could
Dae any kind o' wark in wood ;
Was baith cartwright and undertaker—
Wheelwright tae, and cabinetmaker ;
Nor wad he stick if he were sought
Tae pent a sign or build a boat.
Nae doot he was a clever chiel',
An' kent tae dae his wark richt weel ;
But still a'e muckle faut had he—
Sometimes he wad get on the spree.
Not aften either—only twice,
Or, at the very outside, thrice
Within the year ; but aince begun,
For months his drucken coorse wad run.
He wadna stop until he found
Himsel' completely run aground—
Then penniless upo' the shore
O' lake Repentance he'd deplore
His miserable lot, and swear
He'd never pree the gill-stoup mair.
But to begin my tale—A'e nicht,
Whan Jock was juist aboot the heicht
O' a'e gran' spree—he'd drinkin' been
In company wi' Joe M'Queen,
Doon intae Luckie Mousie's den.
Their freendship they were pledgin', when
The oor arrived which puts a stop
To drinkin' in a public shop.

Much 'gainst their wills they had to go,
An' daurdna 'gainst the law say " No."
Aince oot intae the open air,
They baith began tae rage and swear
Against Mackenzie's Act ; the law,
The Parliament, an' Queen an' a'
Received their share o' drucken spleen—
They got their reddin'-up, I ween.
Upo' the subject baith had got
Sae eloquent an' madly hot,
That ere they had gane far thegither
Each had forgot aboot the ither ;
An' whan the Steeple Kirk was reached
M'Queen still fumed, an' sware, an' preached
Juist the stane wa's, for he had lost
His freend before the street he crossed.
Jock, whan he found he was alone,
A street pump sat him down upon,
Expectin' soon his chum t' appear.
He.looked aboot him far and near,
An' waited lang, but ne'er cam' Joe,
Till wearied he resolved tae go.
An' staicherin' aince mair tae his feet,
He fand he'd got nae better beet
But mak' for hame.   He reached the door
An' fand it barred : a chill cam' ower
His frame, for now remembered he,
When last nicht he was on the spree,
Betty, his wife, kicked up a row—
Ca'd him a dirty, drucken sow ;
An' at him her twa big fists clenchin'—
Wi' epithets we daurna mention ;
Sware upo' aith by a' that's blue,
That if the neist nicht he was fou
He'd bide ootside, for she wad lock

The outer door at ten o'clock.
Sae, poor man, Jock was in a swither
What tae dae—to knock or whether
He'd bide ootside till mornin' licht;
But then it was a frosty nicht,
An' he wi' claes was nae weel happed,
He screwed up courage, an' he rapped.
A noise he heard, and looked aboon;
There at the window, in nicht-goon,
·Was his gudewife.   In wrath she cried—
"Wha's knockin' there?"   Poor Jock replied—
"It's me—yer husband—ope the door
An' lat me in this a'e nicht more."
"Husband! husband indeed," quo' she;
"It's ye is't—drucken Jock M'Gee?
Get aff, man, far frae oot my sicht,
Ye winna cross this door the nicht."
In no guid mood was Jock, I trow,
But desperation seized him now.
"Gude-bye for ever, then," cried he,
"Nae mair alive ye will me see;
My bluid be on yer guilty heid,
The morn ye'll get me hame stiff deid."
"Then I'll be pleased," said dame M'Gee,
An' weel rid o' a beast like ye;"
An' instantly drew in her heid,
The window closed, an' gaed tae bed.
Jock ne'er looked back; wi' a' his speed
He ran.   Upo' the dreadfu' deed
Resolved was he, an' a' the way
These words he micht be heard to say—
"I will dae it—yes, I'll dae it—
She'll mebbie in the mornin' rue it;
My body dreepin' frae the sea
Will be a gran' revenge for me."

Meantime he reached the wimplin' burn,
An' loupin ower it, took a turn
Straicht for the precipice, whaur he
Proposed to leap.   The roarin' sea
Loud sounded in his ears, but still
His purpose firm remained.   "I will,"
He muttered, as upo' the brink
At last he stood, nor did he shrink.
Wi' a'e bold spring, oot ower he reeled
An' landed in—a tatie field !
A piece of ground which slanted doon
Unto the sea, while high aboon
On either side steep rocks did rise.
Tae ane it wad gi'e nae surprise,
Wha kent the place, tae hear that Jock
Mistook this for anither rock,
An' mair especially, too,
The nicht bein' dark, an' he bein' fou'.
On makin' sic a desperate jump,
He strack the ground wi' fearfu' thump,
Which dang him senseless on the spot.
But shortly he some better got,
An' by-an'-by wis lookin' roond,
An' wonderin' hoo he wisna drooned.
"I see it now," at length he cried—
" I jamp, an' didna ken the tide
Wis back."   Then graspin' tatie shaws
Wi' baith his hands, " Whate'er befa's,
Here will I bide," he said ; " here bide
Until comes in again the tide.
I'll by the *tangles* here haud on,
Until the sea has ower me flown."
Determined full his threat tae keep,
He soon fell ower in drunken sleep.
The news neist mornin' quickly spread,

That Jock M'Gee had been found dead.
This proved, by luck, untrue, although
For many weeks he was laid low
Upo' a bed o' grief an' pain
Before he did his strength regain.
Wi' lyin' oot he got a cold
Which took upo' his banes a hold,
An' he rheum-pains had to bear,
Which vexed him lang and racked him sair.
But, as folks say, there ne'er was yet
An ill win' but blew good wi' it,
Sae unto Jock this awfu' nicht
A blessing proved—he got a fricht
Which spained him frae the drunkard's cup.
He drank nae mair, clean gave it up,
An' lived a douce an' sober man
Till end o' his allotted span.

A DREAM.

Last night I dreamed that I had wings, and flew
With bird-like swiftness through the balmy air.
Beneath a wondering crowd at me did stare
With upturned eyes, till I was lost to view.
Yet up and up through hazy clouds of smoke—
Through snow and ice, I sped my heavenward way
Beyond earth's ceiling, where the eternal day
Unclouded reigns, and, sneezing hard, awoke!
I felt my sides, but ah, no wings were there—
My fancied flight was but a flight of fancy;
The truth then flashed on me, this dream so rare
Was caused by eating bread and cheese with Nancy.

SUNSET.

MAJESTIC is the thunder's voice,
And terrible the tempest's roar,
As billows dash with angry noise
Upon the quaking, spray-clad shore :
But neither storm, nor sea, nor thunder,
Speaks soft sublimity like this ;
With dread they fill, with awe and wonder,
But ne'er with calm, sereneful bliss,
Entrancing, dreamy joy like this.
Slowly sinks the orb of fire,
And in the glassy river dips ;
Samson-like he doth expire,
And mid-day splendour doth eclipse.
Oh, what a sight for mortal eyes—
What silent eloquence is here !
Rich glory shrouds him as he dies,
And bathed in gold, the clouds appear
Like seraphim attending.
Emblem of mortality—
Emblem of victory !
Triumphant in death—heaven-ascending !
'Twas thus the world's Redeemer died,
Stretched on the cross at Calvary ;
" 'Tis finished," the God-man cried,
And burst the fragile bands of clay.
Sublime his life, but like this sun
He died 'mid glory's concentration ;
Then he conquered—then the vict'ry won—
Then the grand—the final consummation.
'Tis thus the Christian dies—

Around his head a halo bright,
The world receding from his sight,
His spirit peers beyond the skies,
It mounts—it flies !

AUTUMN LEAVES.

Poor autumn leaves : summer has fled ;
   Your short-lived hours of life are o'er,
   And now ye fall to rise no more,
But on the ground lie witheréd.

Poor autumn leaves : mark how they fall ;
   Not in thick clusters as they grow
   Upon the parent stem ; ah, no,
But one by one they drop off all.

"Brother mine," each says to me ;
   "Though now thy summer's sun doth shine ;
   When autumn comes, our fate is thine ;
Alone thou must meet death as we."

Poor falling leaves, 'tis true ye say :
   Like ye I am a thing of dust,
   And in the autumn fall I must :
But not like ye, to die for aye.

I have a hope again to bloom
   Beneath a fairer sun than this,
   Where all is happiness and bliss—
That happy land beyond the tomb.

TRUTH.

WHAT is Truth?   This Pilate asked;
And what is Truth, do thinking souls in every age enquire—
        And still, save in small part, remaineth masked
The problem ; none to solve it doth aspire—
We cannot rede the riddle, try it till we tire.

        Too vast is Truth for mortal ken ;
        'Tis boundless as the infinitude of God ;
And he who furthest soars but gains a fragment, when
        Beneath that fragment's load
His spirit bursts its clay encircling bands,
And in the fathomless, invisible Inane he lands.

·   'Tis true that we do live and move—
That we have hands and feet, and have to use them too.
Our headaches, toothaches, and our heartaches prove
Existence real ; and that we have stomachs it is true.
        And money is a world-wide truth—
        The want of it especially so—
        An ever-present and depressing woe ;
        We feel this even in our youth,
But in maturer years, and other mouths to feed full,
Then money—money is the one thing needful.

These lower truths do all men know in part,
And some contented are no more to know.
        The wayward human heart,
When pampered with the good things here below,
Oft goes to sleep, oblivious of time's onward flow—
        Perchance rebellious grows,
And 'gainst the truth with cursing and malignity o'erflows.

But, ah, resplendent heaven-born Truth !
        Unchanging thou dost e'er remain.
        Though man forsooth—
        Ignoble man doth deign
To shroud thee with thick crust of superstition vile ;
E'en tries to pound thee in the mortar of hypocrisies,
        And with the compound doth his soul beguile ;
        A time comes when thou dost arise,

And, shaking off the cobwebs and the dust of ages,
        Dost to the denizens of earth proclaim
In " still small voice" of heaven-instructed sages,
Or rolling thunder from the cannon's mouth, the same
        Eternal fact that Truth alone is true,
And cannot be o'erthrown, whatever man may do.

        " I am the Truth," the Master said ;
" Blasphemer," vaunting hypocrites replied—
Religious fable-mongers, who Truth's glorious fountain-head
In their sad spectre-play did spurn and cast aside.
        Thus self-deceiving souls and blinded eyes
In darkness grovel, revelling in unrealities.
        Truth's lustrous glare
Expose would their hypocrisies—its light they cannot bear.

        Amid the bustling energy
        Or slumbering lethargy
Of every age doth Truth immaculate remain,
        And of every age the history,
Good or bad, depends upon the truth or no-truth which it doth
    maintain ;
        Whether with seeing eye it glean
Some threads of Truth from out the tangled skein

Of falsehood among which it hid doth lie,
      Or in its folly or its blindness
      The Truth doth fail to recognise,
And weave around itself a web of fatuous lies.

      Sometimes 'tis superstitious Faith,
And sometimes Reason, that doth sway the age,
      And oft Hypocrisy with baneful scathe
Becomes its queen, and leaves its serpent's trail on history's page.
      Oft Hate and Terror hold the reins
'Mid shrieks of passion and 'mid streams of blood,
      And oft Somnambulism gains
Ascendency, and of fair promise nips the bud.

      Most to be pitied is that unbelieving age
Which insincerely trusts in insincerity, and only dreams that it
    believes,
      Which of Religion hath a superficial show,
      But all is death and rottenness below.
      Then Truth retires, and men engage
In apish ceremonial, each thinking that his neighbour he deceives.

      On learning Truth dependeth not,
      Nor civilisation in its highest grade ;
E'en from the middle ages, dark as they are thought,
Come gleams of Truth. Old Hermit Peter preaching his Crusade,
      And 'neath the banner of the Cross
Marshalling armed men to march to Palestine—
Who looked not at its worldly profit or its loss,
But at their Master's honour—was a truth divine
To them, and still to us doth with a hazy splendour shine.

      Eternal Truth ! like wingéd dart
      From heaven it flies, to pierce the heart,
      And there to shed a radiant light.

With sophistry most plausible it is not so,
Though driven home with arguments beyond our confutation
    quite,
The inherent majesty of Truth and its irradiating glow
       It lacks.   That Thesis *may* be true ;
We can't confute it, yet we have no firm conviction.
This other comes with power " distilling as the dew ;"
We feel that it *is* true beyond all contradiction—
       And that is Sophistry—but this is Truth.